Only the e...
Athena A...
Oracle—a covert intelligence
organization so secret that not even its
members know who else belongs.
Now it's up to three top agents to
bring down the enemies who threaten
all they've sworn to protect....

Kim Valenti:
An NSA cryptologist by day, this analytical genius
and expert code breaker is the key to stopping
a deadly bomb.
COUNTDOWN by Ruth Wind—April 2005

Diana Lockworth:
With only twenty-four hours until the president's
inauguration, can this army intelligence captain
thwart an attempt to assassinate him?
TARGET by Cindy Dees—May 2005

Selena Jones:
Used to ensuring international peace,
the FBI legal attaché had her biggest assignment
yet—outsmarting a rebel leader to
save hostages abroad.
CHECKMATE by Doranna Durgin—June 2005

ATHENA FORCE: Chosen for their talents.
Trained to be the best. Expected to change the world.

Dear Reader,

June marks the end of the first full year of Silhouette Bombshell, and we're proud to tell you our lineup is strong, suspenseful and hotter than ever! As the summer takes hold, grab your gear and some Bombshell books and head out for some R & R. Let us entertain you!

Meet Captain Katherine Kane. When she uncovers a weapons cache and a dangerous criminal thought to be behind bars, this intrepid heroine gets the help she needs from an unlikely source, in beloved military-thriller author Vicki Hinze's riveting new novel in the WAR GAMES miniseries, *Double Vision*.

Don't miss the incredible finale to our popular ATHENA FORCE continuity series. A legal attaché is trapped when insurgents take over a foreign capitol building—and she'll go head to head with the canny rebel leader to rescue hostages, stop the rebel troops and avert disaster, in *Checkmate* by Doranna Durgin.

Silhouette Intimate Moments author Maggie Price brings her exciting miniseries LINE OF DUTY to Bombshell with *Trigger Effect*, in which a forensic statement analyst brings criminals down by their words alone—much to the dismay of one know-it-all homicide detective.

And you'll love author Peggy Nicholson's feisty heroine, Raine Ashaway, in *An Angel in Stone*, the first in THE BONE HUNTERS miniseries. Raine's after a priceless opal dinosaur fossil—and to get it, she'll have to outwit and outrun not just her sexy competition but a cunning killer!

Enjoy all four fabulous reads and when you're done, please send your comments to my attention, c/o Silhouette Books, 233 Broadway, Ste. 1001, New York, NY 10279.

Best wishes

Natashya Wilson

Natashya Wilson
Associate Senior Editor, Silhouette Bombshell

Please address questions and book requests to:
Silhouette Reader Service
U.S.: 3010 Walden Ave., P.O. Box 1325, Buffalo, NY 14269
Canadian: P.O. Box 609, Fort Erie, Ont. L2A 5X3

DORANNA DURGIN
CHECKMATE

Published by Silhouette Books

America's Publisher of Contemporary Romance

Special thanks and acknowledgment are given
to Doranna Durgin for her contribution
to the ATHENA FORCE series.

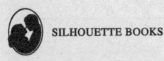

SILHOUETTE BOOKS

ISBN 0-373-51360-7

CHECKMATE

Copyright © 2005 by Harlequin Books S.A.

www.SilhouetteBombshell.com

Printed in U.S.A.

Books by Doranna Durgin

Silhouette Bombshell

Exception to the Rule #11
Checkmate #45

Silhouette Books

Femme Fatale
"Shaken and Stirred"

Smokescreen
"Chameleon"

DORANNA DURGIN

spent her childhood filling notebooks first with stories and art, and then with novels. After obtaining a degree in wildlife illustration and environmental education, she spent many years deep in the Appalachian Mountains. When she emerged, it was as a writer who found herself irrevocably tied to the natural world and its creatures— and with a new touchstone to the rugged spirit that helped settle the area and which she instills in her characters.

Doranna's first published fantasy novel received the 1995 Compton Crook/Stephen Tall Award for the best first book in the fantasy, science fiction and horror genres. She now has fifteen novels of eclectic genres on the shelves and more on the way. Most recently she's leaped gleefully into the world of action-romance. When she's not writing, Doranna builds Web pages, wanders around outside with a camera and works with horses and dogs. There's a Lipizzan in her backyard, a mountain looming outside her office window, a pack of agility dogs romping in the house and a laptop sitting on her desk—and that's just the way she likes it. You can find a complete list of titles at www.doranna.net along with scoops about new projects, lots of silly photos and a line to her SFF Net newsgroup.

Thanks to William Sanders and Robert Brown
for wicked cool gun trivia, and to Judith Byorick
for finding the inadvertently silly bits and to
Evanescence for providing Selena with a theme album.
And big thanks to Catherine Mann, for making sure
I got the Predator details down right!

Dedicated to survivors everywhere.

Chapter 1

Berzhaan.

What a mess. Political unrest from within, political pressures from without, a country seething with unreleased social tension and unspoken dangers.

It was exactly what Selena Shaw Jones needed. *Distraction.*

She stood on the crest of a rubble-strewn hill in Berzhaan and knew herself for a coward. She stood amidst the revered ruins of the Temple of Ashaga and knew she should have been at home, working things out with Cole. She shouldn't have retreated like a wounded child, unable to face the truth. It wasn't a reaction typical of her—of the controlled, perfectionist FBI Legal Attaché who traveled the world to develop counterterrorism programs in other countries and to create teamwork between those countries and the United States. Of a woman with extensive experience and training in dangerous situations, from fraught negotiations to fire-fights.

Emotionally, unexpectedly wounded. And no idea how to deal with it. So Selena had indeed retreated, all the way across the ocean to the brand-new legate office in Berzhaan's capital, Suwan. So brand-new that her support staff had not yet arrived, and she spent most of her time with the U.S. ambassador, strategizing ways to build trust with a wary Berzhaani prime minister—or with the prime minister himself, attending flashy government functions to establish her presence here.

The rest of the time she spent learning the lay of the land—figuratively and literally. It was one reason she'd come to this shrine of ruins. The other…she'd heard this was a peaceful place. A contemplative place. A place where even a distressed Special Agent might sort out her thoughts.

She looked back down the steep hill she'd just ascended, a challenging obstacle course of rocks both large enough to climb over and small enough to turn an ankle. Below, the village of Oguzka looked peaceful, unchanged by its proximity to the shrine. No tourist attractions, no shacks lining the road offering trinkets to rich Europeans and Americans. Just families, going about their lives.

As it should be. One of Selena's jobs was to keep things this way, wherever she went.

The house closest to the foot of the hill boasted a large backyard, unenclosed. A dormant garden covered nearly a third of it. Goats stood idly in a pen at the back, and the stone-walled house boasted a tidy, weed-free exterior. *Peaceful.* A little boy darted around the side of the house, young enough to stumble every third step and also young enough that he didn't care. He played with a string of scrap material, letting it flutter in the wind.

Selena's eyes burned, unexpected and startling, almost as unexpected as the sudden closing of her throat.

He was the reason she'd come.

He was also one of the reasons she'd run.

Family. Children. Plans and hopes and visions of a future with Cole that included cribs and baby mobiles and a thousand pictures of that first crawl, that first step, of a plump little mouth forming those first words...

Selena whirled away, taking a few abrupt steps toward the temple. She carefully wiped her eyes and re-tied her modest and respectful head scarf against the stiff winter breeze. She refocused on surroundings of ancient stone and ancient, eternal flame. Stone walls defined the courtyard, covered with moss and lichen, their once-square edges crumbled into softness. Built against those walls, low, dark religious cells waited for the return of the pilgrims who had once flocked here. Before her, a square shrine stood stolid against the years, precisely fenestrated to reveal the eternal flame within. This, the Temple of Ashaga just outside Berzhaan's capital city of Suwan, held the muted awe of generations. A quiet place; a revered place.

Just what she'd wanted. Needed.

Then...why wasn't it helping?

Because it definitely wasn't helping.

Selena deliberately turned to matters more directly at hand. *Distraction.* Berzhaan had wedged itself between the tumultuous Middle East and acquisitive Russia, swapping between freedom and occupation too many times in the last century. The changes made for a country in turmoil, seething with unrest and jam-packed with diplomatic complications that filled Selena Shaw Jones's hours and let her tumble into bed exhausted, knowing she was doing her best to keep terrorism away from the little boy down below as much as from those children in the States. If only Razidae would let her build the network between their countries that would allow the communication, intelligence gathering and local counterterrorist education that it was her job to establish....

A faint noise caught the edges of her attention. Was that—?

No. She was on edge, that was all. She'd had no way to know when Cole would return, and no intention of waiting him out in their oh-so-empty condo. She'd asked for this overseas assignment to get perspective on her life. And while she'd already earned Ambassador Dante Allori's highly relieved respect with her ability to translate the most delicate political statements and to quietly, politely persist in her efforts to woo reluctant Prime Minister Omar Razidae, she still failed miserably in her own personal goals.

There he'd been. Her husband, kissing a beautiful woman right out in Constitution Park.

Big deal, she'd told herself. He was a CIA field officer—Jason P. JOXLEITER in the CIA's eyes, and his friends got a kick out of calling him Jox. He was a field officer down to the silly all-caps assigned surname, and that meant putting up a front—wherever he was, whomever he was with—to suit his cover.

Except he was supposed to be out of the country. And while he never told her details of an assignment, she always knew his location. Always overseas and never with the CIA's Foreign Services Bureau that worked

U.S. turf, and she always knew just where. Then if something went haywire in the world, she knew whether to worry. It was the one stable thing in their relationship, the one thing she could always count on.

Not this time.

And how many other times had he lied? How many times had he used CIA guile against her?

Another harsh sound scraped up from the small village at the bottom of the hill. Selena turned into the wind to look down upon the picturesque area, frowning at the gusty blast that obscured any additional noises from below. After a moment in which she saw nothing out of place, she turned back to the temple, walking slowly around the shrine. She put her hands up to one of the openings, feeling the mild heat through her finely stitched black leather gloves.

It wasn't enough to warm her. The depth of her feelings frightened her, kept her from thinking clearly.

Ironically, if the sounds she'd heard had actually been gunshots, she would have felt perfectly able to deal with them—the Athena Academy had given her that much, and more: her cache of fluently spoken languages, her self-confidence, the background to excel at Harvard Law School and then as an FBI legate assigned to situations as tricky and demanding as Berzhaan's. The accomplishments to be tapped as an Oracle agent. Selena knew how to handle herself in court, behind a translator's smooth detachment and in the field.

What she couldn't seem to do was stop the way her throat constricted into tight pain at the thought of that moment in the D.C. park.

A sudden report on the wind stopped her short; she looked up from the rock-strewn path to narrow her eyes at the village below. There was no mistaking it this time. *Weapons fire.* Automatic weapons. Behind the house nearest to Selena, the young boy darted out across the rocky, close-cropped land to crawl between the crooked slats of a goat pen a hundred yards behind the house. The four goats there parted to accept him as if used to his presence.

An abrupt burst of activity at the back of the stone-walled house followed—the quick flurry of what looked like a woman trying to exit until rough hands hauled her back in, her shriek of protest clearly audible as it rode the wind up the hill.

Trouble. Not ordinary domestic trouble, no indeed. Kemeni rebels? And if it was, was this a calculated large-scale action, or a handful of overeager rebels causing trouble?

There was no telling. Turmoil gripped this country like a lover. Kemeni rebels—supposedly backed by the U.S., although Selena knew better—increasingly threatened Prime Minister Omar Razidae's government. Russia had become keenly interested in this territory; they, too, were wrongly convinced that the U.S. treated with Razidae with one hand and fed arms and money to the Kemenis with the other. The Q'Rajn terrorists, convinced of the same, wanted the States out of Berzhaan altogether and had taken their fight to U.S. soil to face recent defeat at the hands of two of Selena's Athena Academy classmates.

And then there was everyone else in the world, keeping an eye on Berzhaan's undeveloped oil resources.

All the while, the people of Berzhaan struggled to survive, caught in the middle. And down the hill from Selena, a small boy cowered behind his unconcerned goats, probably not realizing they were truly no cover at all.

Selena did a quick weapons check. Sturdy Beretta Cougar .45 DAO in her pocket holster, several slim knives secreted at ankle, waist and right collarbone— where she could dip into her sweater from the neckline and acquire steel before any threatening agent even thought to consider whether she might be anything more than the sleek, tailored American she appeared to be. Then she headed down the hill, striding firmly in spite of the footing but not drawing attention to herself by running. As she moved, she pulled a hair band from an inner pocket of the coat and reached beneath the silk scarf to gather her long, layered hair at the nape of her neck. She drew her Beretta, holding it down at her side where the folds of the coat obscured it and she could easily keep it hidden if her concerns were for nothing.

She didn't expect to keep it hidden.

As she neared the base of the hill and angled for the stone house, the boy darted out from behind the goats and ran into her path, babbling in his native language so quickly—with a young child's creative use of words—as to challenge even her excellent Berzhaani language skills. She put a finger to her lips and then his, startling the child, and in that moment of silence she said, "Slower, *bibcha*."

His eyes widened with surprise all over again; his gaze darted over her from head to toe, taking in her attire and her head scarf, her appearance—dark blue-green eyes, razor-cut chestnut bangs emerging from the scarf and all-American features—and trying to reconcile it all with her use of his own language. She crouched before him, her gun still lost in the black leather folds of her coat. "Tell me," she said. "Why are you frightened?"

He touched the bright red leather piping on the front edge of the coat, following it briefly with his finger as if to confirm this was indeed something out of his ken—but his round, light tea-colored little face with its pointed chin looked about to crumple.

"There, now," Selena said, fairly brusquely, fighting her natural inclination to soothe him—it would only release those tears, and then she'd learn nothing. "When a brave young man such as yourself runs to greet me, I must listen. What have you to say?"

The boy hovered on the edge of tears for another moment—and indeed, one slipped out to track its way down the baby fat of his cheek. But he pressed his lips together and then said, "Bad men are in the house. Don't go in there! Auntie told me to run and hide, just like we practiced."

"I saw you." Selena couldn't stop herself from wiping away that single tear where it had trickled out partway down his face. "You hid very well. Do you think you can do it again?"

"With Spotty and Eleny?"

She could only assume these were two of the goats. "Farther," she said. "In the temple, where the pilgrims used to sleep when they stayed there."

He shook his head, flinching at the sound of breaking pottery from within the house. "I'm not allowed—"

"This once, you are," she told him.

"Mama said—"

She put her finger to her lips again, and gave him a slow, reassuring smile. "I'll tell her it was my fault."

He returned a solemn, dark-eyed look, lower lip protruding slightly with the effort of his decision. Selena all but held her breath, waiting, knowing he might well be unable to trust her, as much as he'd been willing to warn her. The Beretta felt solid and familiar in her hand, and just as suddenly as if it could not possibly belong there while she spoke to this child.

Abruptly he bit his lip and nodded. "Will you hide, too?"

"Yes." She stood; the wind tugged at her open coat. She wished she could pull off her sweater to give him—he wore only a thin wool jacket over his own baggy, loosely knit sweater—but to do so would reveal her knives and her gun, a revelation likely to break the tenuous connection between them. "But I'm going to hide somewhere else, somewhere I can get help for your people."

This made no sense, of course. But she hoped he would grab for the reassurance without working through the logic. She didn't give him much time to think about it, not as a muted cry reached her from the still-cracked back door. "Go now!" She pointed up the hill. "As fast as you can! Someone will come for you when it is safe."

This time. For this child truly to be safe, Selena would have to accomplish much more than this chance, unexpected interference with one besieged house.

After the briefest hesitation, the boy sprinted away, his barely coordinated limbs putting much effort into the action. So young…

Selena smoothed her scowl away and reached for focus. She was on the job now, albeit in a fashion never formally acknowledged. She eased up to the side of the house, up to the small window with open shutters on the outside and a film of curtains covering the glass from the inside. She winced as something else within the house broke, something wooden and splintering this time, followed by another cry of fear. The window showed her little…a gash of sunlight over the floor where the front door had been left open, a chair overturned against the wall, a bread plate smashed near the entrance to a back room. No one in sight. *Great.* She'd have to slink around and hope another window would reveal how many intruders had—

A stutter of automatic weapons fire sounded from down the street. *More than just this one house at stake.* And from within, a woman screamed, a full-bodied shriek of fear and denial. *No more time. Start with this house, worry about the rest later.* She moved swiftly to the front corner of the house, confirmed that no one waited out front and made it to the doorway itself. A quick peek-retreat revealed the main room of the house to be abandoned. From within the room beyond, a man shouted harsh demands for cooperation and the sharp slap of hand against flesh struck Selena's ears. *Bastard.* Of course he was going to rape her. *Of course.* And in this society where the conservative chador was no longer required by law but still often used by custom, rural women still paid every price for rape above and beyond the violation of the act itself.

Selena did another peek-and-duck, still saw nothing, and eased into the house with silence as her shield, her coat whispering around her in swirling folds of leather. A quick glance through the doorway beyond showed her a tiny bedroom, one man in Kemeni green and tan colors pressing a diminutive woman into the corner while his loosely gripped Abakan Russian assault rifle—*Abakan…strange choice*—pointed at the floor, his avid gaze riveted on the bed. There a second man crouched over a wildly flailing woman, struggling to shove aside the copious material of her modest chador robes. As Selena retreated, taking a deep breath, her gun held two-handed and ready, another resounding slap marked the man's impatience.

Selena surged around the door frame and shot him in the ass.

He cried out in shock and tumbled to the floor. The woman scrambled back against the wall at the head of the bed, frantically rearranging her clothing, and the second man, caught in flat-footed surprise, started to raise his badly positioned Abakan rifle. The woman he'd squashed into the corner let out a deliberate, ear-piercing shriek, her only remaining weapon.

It bought Selena an instant, and an instant was all she needed to drill the man twice, her finger steady on the long pull of the double-action trigger. Once in the knee, once in the right biceps, and then the woman in the corner gave a fierce cry of triumph and leaped for the rifle. Selena caught a glimpse of the look in her eye and instantly targeted the woman even as she shouted a warning—and reassurance. "Leave the rifle—I am your friend!"

The woman hesitated long enough to realize she was in Selena's sights, but as she straightened with the Abakan carefully held by the stock alone, she leaned sideways to spit on the floor. "My *friend*," she said. Unlike the other woman, she did not wear a chador, only a colorful punjabi and matching *hijab* scarf. Her thick, woven shawl lay crumpled on the floor in the corner. "*American.* If you had not been supplying the Kemenis, they would not now be in a position to act—or des-

perate enough to send out men like *this*." She kicked the
man in his bloody knee, eliciting a scream. She didn't
wait for Selena's reply, but went to the woman on the
bed, leaning the rifle against the headboard with a
frightening familiarity.

Selena lowered her gun but didn't holster it, not with
the stutter of gunfire echoing in her memory. These two
pathetic so-called freedom fighters weren't the only
problem this village had. Moving swiftly and not at all
gently, she patted them down for weapons, glad for her
gloves. Rank sweat and bad beer and gun oil stung her
nose. Stepping back from them with a new collection
of knives and two more handguns, she piled the stash
on the foot of the bed. "Do you have rope? Can you tie
them until an army unit arrives?"

The woman looked as though she wanted to spit
again. "What makes you think Razidae's army cares?
What makes you think they will come?" She caressed
the cheek of the other woman, a soothing gesture.

Selena reached into a pocket for the familiar feel of
her cell phone. "Because I'm going to call them."

She'd have preferred to call in American troops, but
she'd already gotten a glimpse of the reception they'd
endure. So she made the call, a short, concise conversation with the American Embassy, informing them of
the situation. "Let Razidae's people know," she told the
embassy warden's assistant. "And keep me out of it—
it's the last thing any of us needs. I'll be gone by the
time they get here."

"They're on alert," the man told her. "They won't
take long."

"Neither will I," Selena assured him.

But she didn't leave immediately. She selected one

of the knives from the bed, the one with the dullest gleam of an edge when she held it up to the light from the room's single small, high window. The one that would hurt the most—and the one her chosen victim, the man still scrabbling around on the floor trying to find a way to clamp both hands to his bleeding buttock at once and not leave himself entirely vulnerable from the front, had been prepared to use on these women.

She crouched before him, the Beretta held in a deceptively casual grip in the hand that rested on her knee, and gave the knife a speculative look before she turned her gaze on the man.

"Woman," he said. *"American.* You are nothing to me. Your people betrayed us."

Kemeni, all right, even if his tan and green clothing hadn't given him away. Kemeni, and convinced that the recently deceased Frank Black had been working with the States when he'd supplied the rebels with arms. Instead, Black had done so at the behest of Jonas White, a man who liked to play whole countries as if they were game pieces, and whose name popped up in connection with far too many successful black market ventures.

"My people were never behind you," Selena told him. "And fortunately for my ego, you're nothing to me, either." *Except a source of information.* "Are you just out to curdle some cheese here, or is there some purpose behind this attack?"

"Our business is not for your ears."

"Shouldn't have shot you in the ass," Selena muttered. "I scrambled your brains." She gave a meaningful heft of the knife, eyeing various parts of his body in the most obvious way. And then she slid her eyes over to the woman who comforted her sister.

The man took note. His expression grew more stubborn.

"Well, maybe you aren't Kemeni after all," she said. "The Kemenis have honor and purpose—of a sort, anyway. But these women have more honor than you."

The man's face darkened; his lips worked. "I spit on your—"

Selena prodded him with the knife in the vicinity of his bloody butt cheek. "Don't," she warned him. Then she held the knife out to the woman in the punjabi. When the woman hesitated, Selena gestured with the knife, affirming her intent.

The woman's fingers wrapped around the hilt to grow white at the knuckles, a grim determination taking over her expression. "No one need know how he died," she said softly. "They need not know it was I."

"Might as well pin it on me," Selena told her. "Although if he answers my questions, perhaps you could settle for scarring him in some way that he would never admit came from a woman's hand."

The woman only smiled.

"You cannot expect me to take this seriously!" the wounded man shouted.

Selena had to give him credit. For a man bleeding badly from his tush, his bleeding partner offering nothing but the sullen silence of someone who hopes not to be noticed, he had courage.

Or perhaps he simply truly didn't understand his situation.

Selena gave him a beatific smile. "I expect you to take it very seriously." She used her gun to tick off points on the fingers of her other hand. "Point—I speak seriously kickin' Berzhaani. Point—I'm very good from this end of a gun. Point—Did you see me sweat when I took you boys down? Now take a moment to think. Think hard. What sort of American woman are you likely to find here in the heart of Berzhaan with all these things in her favor?"

Someone to take seriously, that's who.

He didn't want to think about it. He wanted to hold on to his self-righteous rage and scorn, glaring at her from deep-set eyes just made for the expression.

"Did the Kemenis send you?" she asked.

He didn't answer directly—but he looked away. It was enough.

"I gather they didn't send you to behave like this in particular." She tapped the muzzle of the Beretta thoughtfully against her knee. The motion kept his attention on the weapon—helped him to realize that this was no lady's pistol, but a gun of sturdy heft that fit comfortably in her equally sturdy hands. That she wielded it without a second thought. "But here you are, causing trouble in an otherwise unremarkable location. The shrine is fascinating, but not a political touchstone." And the Kemenis, suddenly bereft of their American benefactor, were desperate. Desperate enough to make a real move on the country's power base? Her eyes narrowed; for the first time she let a glimpse of her anger show through. "But this *is* close enough to Suwan to cause alarm…close enough to draw off troops in response." *And I've just initiated that by calling in.* And now the capital would be more vulnerable to terrorist action.

Again he looked away, trying to hide the subtle retreat with an uncomfortable shift to relieve pressure on his wound.

"You're a sacrifice," Selena said. "Contributing to a larger goal…."

Suwan…the embassy…the capitol. One or all of them, the real targets.

He glared again, and the curl returned to his lip as he opened his mouth to say something crude.

She smacked her pistol against his shin, a casual but precise blow that struck the crucial nerves there, numbing his leg with excruciating pain and with very little effort on her part. He made a wordless noise of surprise and gaped as his eyes watered, mouth quickly pursing for more imprecations.

"Don't," she said sharply. "Just…don't." She exchanged a glance with the woman who now held the knife, saw the uncertainty rising there and straightened. "I'm not sure," she said to the woman, "but it might well be that his humiliation is complete without any extra scarring, especially if he were cast out at your doorstep in a pretty bundle for the National troops. It's entirely up to you, of course. I'm afraid I have to leave now."

The woman in the chador leaned toward the other, murmuring something worried.

"A boy," said the first woman. "Did you see—?"

Selena nodded. "I sent him up to the shrine to hide, with the promise I would take all blame for it. I'm sure he's waiting for you there."

"Thank you," said the woman in the chador, sitting for that moment like a queen on her throne instead of a nearly violated woman on her thoroughly rumpled bed. But she could not hide a quivering twitch of her mouth or the tears of relief welling in her eyes.

Selena thought it was her cue to leave. That and the distant sound of helicopter blades thumping the air. She emerged from the house with caution, the automatic gunfire still clear in her memory—but either no one else had intended to come to this far end of the town, or the arriving troops had caught their attention. She made it to her Russian Moskvich sedan without incident, folding herself into the driver's seat with the Beretta in easy reach. She hoped to swing around the village and make it into Suwan without any trouble—but if trouble came along, she'd be ready for it.

She had to reach the embassy. She had to warn the ambassador…and she had to warn Berzhaan.

The Kemenis were rising.

Chapter 2

Colin Jones slung his duffel through the door of the modest D.C. condo he shared with Selena. Modest by choice and lifestyle as opposed to financial restrictions, even here in this area of off-the-chart living expenses. But...

Maybe that would change soon, if Selena became pregnant as they hoped. Maybe their silk plants and collection of sleek sight hound statuary would make way for the real things. Green, growing things. Warm loyalty and four-legged companionship to round out a home that also held the laughter of a family.

Not that it would be easy. He and Lena had already experienced enough rocky moments to be realistic about what lay ahead and even then she hadn't known half the things he'd kept from her in recent months. Things he wouldn't tell her, things he *couldn't* tell her.

Decisions she'd never understand…some decisions he didn't like to think about. But she hadn't known those things, and she'd recommitted to the marriage, recommitting to each other…and immersing themselves in a few brief weeks of passion-filled nights before duty called and Cole had gone off on a long-term assignment, hoping Selena would soon find a posting nearby.

But as he took his first step into the condo, he knew Lena wasn't here. *Damn.* He'd all but felt her arms around him, her hands sneaking beneath his waistband to tug up his shirt and—

Nothing but frustration at the end of those *thoughts.*

The silence of the apartment surrounded him. The stuffy air, scented with undisturbed spice candles. The faint layer of dust settled over the empty table next to the door where their mail tended to pile up when they were home. A glance into their small living room showed no sign of legal briefs, no sign of Lena's latest fiction favorites. Just the cream and maroon tones of the rug, curtains and furniture—a color scheme that had been a compromise between her desire for cool and clean decor and his own need for bold.

The kitchen…not a crumb on the counter. The bedroom…neatly tidied, not so much as a stray sock or one of those hair scrunchies Lena tended to lose track of—and though Cole was much more casual about such things than she, Lena had never obsessed about tidiness, either. Not when she was relaxed and happy. A glance back at the living room revealed the very same quilt square on the wall as had been there two months earlier.

Left not long after I did, did you? For she had an entire collection, and rather than spread them out over the

austere walls she rotated them on a monthly basis—
while the rest of the walls remained uncluttered, a testament to their struggle to merge their styles. The
casual, assertive operative who approached life in the
fast and loose lane, and the FBI legate with a lawyer's
precise, compartmentalized brain.

Not for the first time, he wished he could see her in
action—in *real* action—to get a glimpse of that side of
her. The side that would expose the ferocity of her will
and her ability to take whatever the situation pitched at
her.

It had to be there. Somewhere. It had to be, or she
wouldn't still be alive.

He tore himself away from his thoughts to realize
he'd left the door open. Cole nudged the duffel aside so
he could close himself in. And with Lena out *there*
somewhere, putting this door between them definitely
left him closed in.

It's not like this has never happened before. Time to
find the note, the one they always left each other. Time
to disabuse the uneasiness growing somewhere in the
pit of his stomach, spreading to become tension between his shoulder blades. Lena's notes always gave
him ease, made his inward tension relax to match his
outward appearance.

He knew the things people said of him; he cultivated
those things. He sowed the seeds for his own reputation as the laid-back charmer who took each mission
on the fly, improvising his way to last-moment success.
Even Lena bought into it, not truly realizing how important she was to him, in how many ways…all the little things, like her notes. They were the one place she
cast aside her lawyer persona for pure silliness—catch-

ing him up on the gossip around their condo, informing him how much their silk plants had grown since he was last home, drawing him stick figure versions of her latest adventures in D.C. living. And of course… the challenge of finding the always-hidden note in the first place.

Except…there it was, right out on the kitchen counter, one corner tucked beneath the gleaming white toaster. A sheet torn carefully from a five-by-eight pad of lined yellow paper, inscribed with a few sentences in her neatest hand.

Cole—had an unexpected call to Berzhaan. Things are pretty tense there. I'll let you know more as I can—check your e-mail.

No stick figure. No silliness. Only a sweeping *S.*
Something's wrong.
But she couldn't possibly know—
Very wrong.

Selena blew past the clean, modern outer ring of Suwan, where the post-Soviet restoration efforts prevailed. Approaching the center of the city, she maneuvered through the now-familiar streets into ancient Berzhaan, an area full of impressive stone architecture, and of old fortress walls that came from nowhere and disappeared into nothingness, no longer anything but pieces of their former glory. The streets turned cobbled, the alleys narrowed, and the thick feel of history hung in the air. Here, some of the oldest buildings had given way to Soviet manpower, leaving in their wake impressive new buildings of state. The capitol building was one such; the American embassy a much smaller version of the same, several blocks away.

She drove the Moskvich around the back of the embassy, returning it to the motor pool with a haste that drew the curiosity of the young Berzhaani who took the keys, and entered the embassy through a back door for which few had the special high-security key card. A glance at her watch confirmed her tardiness for her two o'clock appointment with the ambassador and the prime minister. She kicked her pace into a jog, soundless over the luxuriously thick carpeting, and went straight to the ambassador's office in spite of her appearance, pulling off her head scarf along the way. The details of the embassy—trappings both American and Berzhaani—flashed past in a familiar blur, barely noticed.

Had anything been changed, *that* she would have noticed.

She pulled up short outside the open door of the ambassador's outer office. Bonita Chavez looked up from her desk with disapproval deepening the lines of features that had been generous before middle-age and now seemed entrenched in making themselves even more obvious. She glanced at the classy silver and oak clock on the wall. "You're late."

Stern or not, Bonita didn't worry Selena; along with her duties as the ambassador's civil service admin, she seemed to have taken on mother-hen duties. Beneath her current frown lived worry, not anger, and Selena already harbored affection for her.

"I ran into a little trouble." Selena stepped into the office. "Can I go in?"

"He's waiting for you. You can rest assured he knows

you've arrived." Bonita's gaze raked her up and down, looking for telltales of Selena's "little trouble."

"All one piece," Selena told her, opening her coat wide for quick inspection and, as she'd intended, causing Bonita to bite her far-too-crimson lipstick against a smile. Selena forced herself to walk across a carpet of stunning workmanship—she always had to force herself to walk on the beauty of Sekha-made carpets—and rapped her knuckles against the dark, heavy wood door of the ambassador's inner office before pushing it open.

Ambassador Allori looked up from his computer monitor. "Do I guess correctly that you had something to do with that call that came through the embassy, requesting troops at Oguzka?"

"The Kemenis—"

"Yes, yes." He cut her off, frowned at his monitor and tapped a key in response, and simultaneously swept a stiff sheet of paper off his desk to hold out to her. "You'll find this of interest, I think, though you hardly have time to read it. You don't have time to change, either—I doubt Mr. Razidae will be disposed to notice. But you'll want to wash your face. It's got someone's blood on it. Not yours, I presume."

Bonita! She'd seen it, surely. She'd let Selena go on in without alerting her to clean up, and with an admirable lack of telltale expression at that.

On the other hand, perhaps it was done as a favor. Allori could hardly refute the evidence that her delay had been for significant reasons.

"No, sir." She took the paper, recognizing the letterhead of the embassy warden. "Not the least bit mine."

He gave her a moment to glance at the text, which bore the header Surge in Kemeni Rebel Activity:

> The Department of State advises American citizens in Berzhaan to take prudent steps to ensure their personal safety in the coming days. Remain vigilantly aware of surroundings, avoid crowds and demonstrations….

Selena could not help a soft snort. *Too late. Already been there, done that.*

If Allori heard, he gave no sign of it. No doubt he, too, knew the value of keeping American personnel at an official distance from such…*demonstrations.* "I'm glad you're back," he said, which was as close as he'd get to referring to the Oguzka activity. "Now…we leave in less than fifteen minutes. Can you be back here in ten?"

Selena returned the warden notice to his desk and murmured, "See you in eight, Mr. Ambassador." She turned on her heel, using her long legs to full advantage and mounting the back stairwell in twos and threes rather than waiting for the elevator to the third floor embassy staff housing. Selena's chosen apartment, tucked in a back corner, caught sun through two windows and offered an amazing view of the Caspian Sea. Probably a mistake, given the way it reminded her of Cole's eyes.

Sometimes the lake shone an impossible blue, and sometimes the undercurrents turned it a murkier blue-green, but she didn't take time to check today's color. For that matter, she didn't even take the time to remove her coat. She eyed the bathroom mirror, removing the faint smear of blood to which Allori had referred. She removed her knives, knowing she'd have to face a metal detector at the capitol, and then dumped a few extra clips for her Beretta into her coat pocket. The gun and clips would be left at the capitol building's sign-in desk, but given what she'd already encountered today, she didn't intend to go out on the street unprepared.

As for the rest of it…she brushed a damp washcloth futilely over a smudge of…something…on her khakis, and ran it over her leather and nylon mesh hiking boots to remove the dust of the day. She applied a quick, light coat of foundation and a subtle smudge of kohl around the outer edges of slightly tilted eyes, knowing it would echo the look to which the prime minister was accustomed. She tackled her hair, pulling a brush through the tangles the wind had left beneath the scarf, giving herself a critical stare. *Time for a cut.* If she let it grow too far below her shoulders, the strong, lean bones of her face seemed stronger, leaner…she preferred to keep it short enough to square up her jaw and soften a strong chin with its hint of a cleft.

Three minutes remaining and she counted herself ready to go, except for a quick glance at her automatically downloaded e-mail as she closed her laptop up, her briefcase already to hand.

She wished she hadn't.

E-mail from Cole.

Finally.

She knew she'd stopped breathing. Forced herself to begin again. There was no way to look at the message now. No way to look at it until she was through with work for the day.

The next one down in the list was another matter. *Delphi.*

Delphi was Selena's contact at Oracle, and Oracle…

Oracle was a name Selena never said out loud. The elite intelligence-gathering organization predated

Homeland Security, and now quietly provided backup.
Oracle crossed agency lines to garner intel, a cross-
check system designed to prevent terrorist disasters…
and then they acted on it when no one else could or
would. Selena suspected her invitation to join Oracle's
clandestine efforts was another legacy of her days at the
Athena Academy. The organization, its methods and
goals…it tasted strongly of Athena.

     Alerted by the subject header—*Kemeni*—as much as
the sender, Selena accepted that she'd be late to the ambassador's office and opened the e-mail. Even so, she
had time for no more than a glance.

     A glance was all it took.

Chapter 3

But the e-mail warning hadn't stopped Allori, only delayed them a few more crucial moments while he listened to Selena's concerns. And then he'd issued a few quick orders and they'd headed for the Berzhaan capitol.

Late, late and later.

With one careful finger, Selena rubbed the bridge of her nose, not sure if she should have had lunch or if she actually regretted having breakfast. The scene in the lobby of the Berzhaan capitol building momentarily swam in her vision—but the moment passed and then the situation was all too clear: if they'd arrived on time, they would have gotten here before this busload of excited but respectful college students. Their bright winter coats would have proclaimed them foreigners if the quick whispers in English hadn't; Selena heard all manner of accents, from American to Canadian to British. They clustered around the reception desk, trickling through the weapons detector arch one by one.

She and Ambassador Allori weren't the only displaced arrivals. Off to the side, two smiling Berzhaani women—modern women in neat business suits and modest heels, uncovered by either chador or hijab—watched the procession with patience, while a tall Berzhaani man in a designer casual jacket over silk had a distractedly pleased expression. He was worth a second look, sleek and groomed and all cutting edges, his dark complexion giving him the same smoldering good looks that had earned Omar Sharif a generation and more of worshippers. He caught Selena's gaze and raised an eyebrow; the gesture revealed more than he probably ever imagined. Regardless of his trendy appearance, her directness had surprised him, and to some extent offended him—but he saw nothing wrong with letting his gaze linger on her in return, judging her too-casual dress and her edgy red-piped, black leather coat, appreciating her long legs and the way that same tailored coat revealed her figure.

She gave him the slightest of nods, turned away with an ease that probably also offended him and considered the best way to discreetly cut the line.

She didn't have to. The uniformed man behind the standing height lobby desk glimpsed Selena through the crowd, and then spotted the slightly shorter ambassador. He raised a hand high, gesturing to the familiar guard at the security arch. With practiced ease, the guard created a break in the line and then nodded at the ambassador. Selena followed, automatically sorting through the young people they pushed past, hunting potential threats.

There weren't any, of course. Just a slew of impressed and curious expressions. *Who are they? Why are they getting special treatment?* One bold young man gave her the same appreciative once-over she'd just gotten from the Berzhaani man near the entrance, albeit with none of the finesse. The visual equivalent of *hey, baby.*

Selena smiled at him, a knowing smile, and it startled him into a blush; he hadn't expected to get caught. Blond hair, blue eyes; he could have been Cole a dozen years earlier. *Except Cole wouldn't have been caught.*

Wrong. Cole *had* been caught.

A young woman poked the bold young man's arm in silent vigor, blushing even harder than her friend... and sweetheart? Selena thought she saw a flash of jealousy in those wide-set eyes. She turned away, back to business, leaving the young woman a little space for dignity—and already methodically pulling her briefcase shoulder strap free, stripping herself of her gun and ejecting the clip to hand it over to the guard along with the extra magazines. As an afterthought she pulled the knife from the special inside sheath she'd had sewn into the coat. "Sorry," she said. "I meant to get that one before we left."

She thought she heard a stifled noise from her bold young admirer. *Bit off more than you could chew, eh?* She met the amusement in the guard's eyes as he placed her things in a small lockbox and set them aside for retrieval upon exit, and then performed a quick scan on her black leather satchel briefcase. Within moments they'd passed through the security check, where one of the capitol's nameless gofers met them with a smile and apologized for the delay as if Selena and Allori hadn't been late in the first place. As the young man escorted them toward the prime minister's office, he nodded at a hallway that led in the opposite direction. "We're hosting a casual reception this afternoon. The college students, as you saw. And others to meet them, from the government and some of our own learning institutions."

Selena glanced down the hall in question, finding a bustle of people in dignified dark green jackets such as their escort's, pushing serving carts into position and pouring water into crystal glasses. A brief, loud argument between one of the capitol's gofers and a cook took over the hallway just long enough for a woman in an exotic punjabi trouser-dress to intervene. The events coordinator. Selena had seen her before, though she'd never been in that part of the embassy herself. The chaotic nature of the event troubled her; she wished she knew more about it.

But then, she wasn't here as the ambassador's bodyguard.

Allori himself showed no sign of worry on his face— a round face made even more so by the extra weight he carried. He smiled at their escort. "I recall reading about the reception. Excellent idea."

Their escort nodded. He, too, was of dark complexion, an olive cast as opposed to the rich brown tones of the Berzhaani in the lobby. Small, unimposing and unremarkable, he played his role with quiet perfection— drawing no undue attention, making or taking no easy offense. "If the young people of other countries see how forward-thinking we are…then we will have no need to change their minds when they are older." He stopped beside an open door and gestured them in. "The prime minister begs your pardon, but was unable to avoid tending other matters. He'll be with you as soon as possible."

Selena didn't need a translation. *You were late, and he had to move on to other things.* She nodded her thanks and followed Allori into the room—a lush room, the floor soft with a Sekha carpet over the wall-to-wall beneath, the wood accents of ceiling and trim dark and gleaming. A neat serving cart of wrought iron sat against the wall, offering everything from ice water to the finest leaf tea. Allori set his briefcase on one of the round-bottomed chairs and helped himself to some tea, fixing it in familiar ritual as Selena prowled the edges of the small room. He said, "You must have had an interesting morning. You're as jumpy as I've ever seen you."

She frowned at him. The room was undoubtedly bugged, and he was too experienced to have forgotten it.

He looked up from the steeping tea, the corners of his eyes crinkled slightly. Did she or did she not, he seemed to ask, want the prime minister to have terrorism on his mind—as well as the need to cooperate while countering it?

Selena sighed, closing her eyes in apology. The truth was, she *was* jumpy. And she had good reason. Following Allori's lead, she spoke frankly. "I wish you'd taken my warning a little more seriously."

"A warning with no specific source?" He waved her off.

"It's my job to gather just such warnings," she reminded him, arms crossed even with the briefcase dangling from one hand.

"Yes. Of course it is. And I'll consider it later this afternoon, by which time you should have even more information for me."

"You yourself showed me the warden's notice—"

He dangled the tea egg a few times, then laid it neatly aside. "And I've taken it into account. Bonita's packing her bags as we speak. We'll make do with a skeleton staff for now."

"Ambassador—" Selena rubbed the bridge of her nose again, right above the little bump Cole liked so much. *Don't think about Cole.* Fatigue washed over her in a startling rush, turning her stomach. She closed her mouth on indiscreet words, a reiteration of the warning from Oracle—the alarming intel from the CIA, along with other military and agency listening posts with which an FBI legate such as Selena should have no direct connection. Word that the Kemeni rebels were indeed desperate in the wake of their lost faux U.S. support—that they had to grab power *now,* or concede it forever.

There were reports of skirmishes, of dead Berzhaani citizens and one major bombing. The Kemenis had acted as if jabbed with a cattle prod, from quiescence in the shocked wake of Frank Black's death to powerful intent.

Selena doubted the cheerful college students had so much as a clue of Berzhaan's suddenly increased unrest. She herself knew only through Delphi—and the luck to have been in the wrong place at the wrong time this morning. Off to the shrine to seek peace of mind, and she'd found only violence.

"Selena?" Allori set his teacup in the saucer, brow drawing together. "Are you quite all right?"

And just like that, she wasn't. Just like that, her stomach spasmed beyond even her iron control, and she blurted "Excuse me!" and bolted from the room, briefcase clutched in her hand. She remembered the bathroom as a barely marked door down the hall and only hoped she was right as she slammed it open. *Thank God.* Most of the room was a blur but she honed in on an open stall door, grateful for the lavish, updated fixture—

Better than a hole in the floor. Been there, done that.

And when she leaned back against the marbleized stall wall, marveling at the sudden violence her system had wreaked upon her, the thought flashed unbidden and unexpected through her mind: *we were trying to start a family.*

No. Not here, not *now*. Not with Cole half a world away and an even bigger emotional gap between them. She knew he hid things from her; she'd thought she could live with that. *Maybe not.* Selena clenched down on her thoughts the same way she'd tried to clench down on her stomach and stumbled out to the pristine sink to crank the cold water on full and splash her face and rinse her mouth. She raised her head to find herself in the gilt-edged mirror, deathly pale, deep blue-green eyes bewildered—and then those eyes widened and she dashed back to the toilet.

When she lifted her head again, her trembling hand numbly reaching to flush the toilet, she didn't have the strength to make it to the sink. She reeled a clumsy length of tissue from the dispenser and sat against the marble partition, overwhelmingly grateful for the impeccably clean nature of the capitol. She scrubbed her mouth and chin and then the thought came again: *we were trying to start a family.*

Maybe they had.

Selena, only remotely in touch with the members of her divorce-torn family, had never had any heartwarming chats about pregnancy. Not with friends, not with her sisters-in-law, not with her coworkers. But she'd never gotten the impression that morning sickness—whenever it came—was quite this vigorous. Violent, even.

Maybe she'd just eaten the wrong thing for breakfast. Or maybe she'd finally have to admit to herself that in spite of her cool, collected self-image, once her emotions hit a certain amount of turmoil, her digestive system often did the same.

She had to know. To *know*. First chance, she'd hit the little store that catered to the diplomatic staff and she'd get herself one of those little sticks and she'd pee on it. It didn't matter that her period was a little late; that meant nothing. She was notoriously irregular when she traveled. Not until she had the little stick would she know for sure.

And then what?

She climbed to her feet, heading for the sink on wobbly legs. There she repeated the rinse-and-spit routine, unable to get the acrid taste of her sickness from the back of her throat. When she dared to look at her image again, she found that it reflected what she felt: she looked stronger, less green. This particular storm, whatever the cause, was over.

And then what?

What if she was pregnant in a strife-torn Berzhaan, her estranged husband not even knowing he was estranged? Theoretically he was still deeply undercover in wherever it was that he'd gone, unable to do more than send a sporadic e-mail or two. *Theoretically.*

Except she'd seen him in D.C.

Kissing someone else.

And now he'd sent her e-mail from his home address—and she hadn't even had time to read it. But just looking at it confirmed that the one stable, steady thing they'd had between them in their four years of unspoken secrets and long absences was no longer stable or steady at all. That maybe it never had been.

No, no reason for emotional turmoil, not in the least.

Usually she and Cole managed to maintain steady communication when their jobs separated them. But this particular assignment had been a dark one, dark enough that if something happened to him, she'd learn only that he'd died in an auto accident while traveling. The dark assignments came along now and then, especially with the contract employees like Cole. With a two-year re-up on contract employees, the CIA station chiefs were willing to push them to the edge of burnout. It had damaged Cole and Selena's marriage, in spite of their mutual understanding of the unique stresses in each of their careers. It had damaged Selena's trust in Cole, watching him switch ably from role to role, ducking questions and hiding nightmares until she couldn't help but wonder if their marriage was just one of the many parts he played.

Not that it surprised her. In her world, families didn't stay together. People went their own ways when relationships became difficult, whether beset upon by emotional or logistical problems. She and Cole had overcome all manner of logistical difficulties—long-term assignments in different countries, frequent travel, the occasional international crisis. Recently she'd even thought he'd been lost…and afterward, they'd renewed their commitment to one another. Made up in a big way, celebrating the things they loved about one another, the ineffable chemistry that Selena's ordered mind had never come close to explaining.

Even now she could feel it. Leaning against this sink with her throat burning and legs still weak, she could close her eyes and see the way he looked at her, remember the way he touched her…and yearn for him.

She just didn't know if she could forgive him. *Live* with him.

And then what?

If she was pregnant…she'd have to stay here long enough to stabilize this new legate's office, in spite of the unrest. And then she'd have to go home…she'd have to tell Cole. To decide if she trusted him, or if she'd merely contribute to the long line of broken branches in her family tree.

And if this is any taste of things to come, I'll have to carry around a barf bag wherever I go.

The water still trickled. She scooped another handful into her mouth, held it and spit it out. Her eyes stung, sympathetic to her throat. It wasn't until she coughed, short and sharp, that she stiffened—and realized that the uncomfortable tang wasn't coming from her abused throat, but from the air she breathed.

Tear gas.

Trickling in from the street outside? From somewhere in the building?

Damn. Damn, damn, *damn*.

Selena jammed used tissue into the trash, grabbed her briefcase and took a deep, steadying breath, pulling herself away from the emotional wallops of the what-ifs and dropping back into the calm, cool world of black and white—of this end of the gun versus the other.

Except she didn't have a gun, and she didn't have her knives.

Maybe she wouldn't need them. Listening at the bathroom door revealed only silence, and she peeked out. The smoke hung thickly in the abandoned hallway. Selena ducked back inside, took another deep breath— this one to hold—and eased out into the hallway, running silently to the waiting room she'd left so precipitously only moments before.

Empty. Allori's teacup lay broken on the floor, tea soaking the priceless carpet.

Son of a bitch.

The door leading to the prime minister's office stood slightly ajar, and Selena made for it, her chest starting to ache for air. But breathing meant coughing, and coughing meant being found.

She didn't intend to be found until she understood the situation. If then.

Razidae's office proved to be empty, as well, the luxurious rolling office chair askew at the desk, papers on the floor, the private phone out of its sleek-lined cradle—and the air relatively clear. Selena closed the door, grateful for the old, inefficient heating system, and inhaled as slowly as she could, muffling the single cough she couldn't avoid.

All right, then. The building was full of tear gas, the dignitaries were gone—and Selena had somehow missed it all.

They could have blown the building out from under you while you were throwing up and you wouldn't have noticed.

Unless Allori and Razidae had simply gone to check out the tear gas and any attendant ruckus. In which case they could be caught up in it. Whatever *it* was.

Think, Selena. She pressed the heels of her hands against her eyes and calmed the chaotic mess of her mind. She could call for help from here—Razidae's private line might have an in-use indicator at his secretary's desk, but it wouldn't show up on any of the other phone systems, so she wouldn't give her presence away by picking it up.

But there was no point in calling until she understood the situation. No doubt the authorities were already alerted. If she were near an outside window, she might even hear sirens—but Razidae's office was in the protected interior, the only other exit leading to his secretary's office. No, no point in calling. At least, not yet. But she would take this office as her possible home base, with its private phone line and its private location. Razidae was a prime minister who came prepared. All his resistance to U.S. overtures of assistance with Berzhaan's counterterrorism program hadn't been because of his denial that the problem existed. Rather that after years of having his country pulled this way and that, sovereignty lost, he wanted to maintain Berzhaan's independence in all aspects of administration.

Selena couldn't really blame him. But she wished he'd been a little more receptive. Maybe they'd have prevented this day's events.

You still don't know what's going on.

Well, then, she told herself. Let's find out.

Selena laid her briefcase on the desk, thumbed the token combination lock and flipped the leather flap open. She'd left her laptop behind in favor of her tablet PC, and the briefcase looked a little forlorn...a little empty.

Not much to work with. No Beretta, no extra clip, no knives...

Maybe she wouldn't need them. Maybe by the time she discovered what had happened, it would actually be over.

Nonetheless, she took a quick survey: cell phone, battery iffy; she turned it off and left it behind. A handful of pens, mostly fine point. She tucked several into her back pocket. A new pad of sticky notes. A nail file, also worthy of pocket space. Her Buck pocketknife, three blades of discreet mayhem, yet not big enough to alarm the security guards. It earned a grim smile and a spot in her front pocket. A spare AC unit for her laptop, which garnered a thoughtful look and ended up stuffed into the big side pocket of her leather duster. A small roll of black electrician's tape. A package of cheese crackers—

Selena closed her eyes, aiming willpower at her rebellious stomach. *I don't have time for you,* she told it. Without looking, she set the crinkly package aside, and then surveyed the remaining contents of the briefcase. A legal pad and a folder full of confidential documents. She supposed she could inflict some pretty powerful paper cuts. A few mints and some emergency personal supplies she wasn't likely to need if she was actually pregnant.

No flak vest, no Rambo knife, not even a convenient flare pistol.

Then again, there was no telling what she might find with a good look around the capitol. Almost anything was a weapon if you used it right.

Selena jammed the rejected items back in her briefcase, automatically locking it. She tucked it inside the foot well of Razidae's desk and checked to see that she'd left no sign of her presence—except there were those *crackers....*

She made a dive for the spiffy executive wastebasket beside the desk, hunched over with dry heaves. Mercifully, they didn't last long. And afterward, as she rose on once-again shaky legs and poured herself a glass of the ice water tucked away on a marble-topped stand in the corner, she tried to convince herself that it was over. That she could go out and assess the situation without facing the heaves during an inopportune moment. That it was over, because *over* meant she'd eaten something that didn't suit her and not that she'd added pregnancy to this volatile mix of Cole's infidelity and Berzhaan's turmoil.

She dumped the rest of the water into a lush potted plant that probably didn't need the attention, wiped out the glass and returned it to its spot. She very much hoped that she'd creep out to find an embarrassed guard and an accidentally discharged tear gas gun. Then she could stroll up with her pens and her pocketknife tucked away, as calm and cool as though she hadn't been heaving in Razidae's wastebasket moments before.

A stutter of muted automatic gunfire broke the silence.

So much for that idea. Selena's heart, already pounding from her illness, kicked into a brief stutter of overtime that matched the rhythm of the gunfire. "All right, baby," she said to her potential little passenger, pulling her fine wool scarf from her coat pocket and soaking it in the pitcher. "Get ready to rock and roll."

But as she reached for the doorknob, she hesitated. She could be risking more than her own life if she ran out into the thick of things now. As far as she knew, whoever had pulled the trigger of that rifle didn't even know she existed. She could ride things out here with her lint-filled water and her cheese crackers.

Or she could be found and killed, or the building could indeed blow up around her, or whoever'd fired those shots could succeed in their disruptive goal, and Selena and her theoretical little one could be trapped in a rioting, war-torn Berzhaan. She closed her eyes, her mind suddenly full of images of frightened students and dead capitol workers and a dead Allori. She closed her eyes hard.

It really wasn't any choice at all.

Chapter 4

The smoke settled toward the floor in the long hallway. Selena's eyes watered above the damp scarf, but not so much that she couldn't see. The hallway was all hers. She hoped it stayed that way.

If she did this right, she'd complete her prowling unseen; she'd have an idea where Ambassador Allori had ended up and how Prime Minister Razidae had fared. She'd find the college students and even the arrogant Berzhaani businessman from the lobby.

And she'd find the Kemeni rebels.

Steady there. She didn't know the Kemenis were behind this.

Yes. I do.

On this side of the five-story capitol, the prime minister and his cabinet members generally went about their business, addressing the problems of a nation with a tumultuous past. On the other side, ceremonies and social functions filled a dining-ballroom so grandly exotic it would have suited a Russian czar—and, given the country's past annexation, might have once done just that. The kitchens, the maintenance, even a detention area…all on that side of the building. Somewhere.

With some fervency, Selena wished that just once, she'd had a chance to glimpse a blueprint of the capitol. The CIA probably had one…but they hadn't shared, and though she had a request in with Oracle, Delphi hadn't yet come through. For now, Selena was on her own.

All too literally.

She decided to start with the lobby. Moving carefully through the halls, silently over the carpet on her rubber-soled lightweight hikers…she spent long moments listening before she turned corners, stifling the constant impulse to cough and keeping a firm mental control over her unhappy but quiescent stomach. She found signs of struggle—pictures knocked askew, a coffee cup shattered against the wall, stains splashed across creamy paint…even a smudge or two of blood, a handprint where someone had reached out for support. As an undertone to the tear gas, the equally acrid smell of gunpowder grew stronger.

When she peered around the final corner and into the unfolding delta of the lobby, she winced. The faint haze of remaining tear gas couldn't hide the aftermath of the struggle, wasn't strong enough to cover the visceral smell of blood and death. One guard sprawled before the security arch, his face missing. Selena couldn't see the other, though she heard noises from behind the standing desk where he'd been. Still alive?

Behind the desk…that's where her gun had been stored, in its own lockbox. She took a step around the corner, exposing herself. She might as well be as naked as she felt; she was just as vulnerable. She eyed the semi-automatic pistol in the dead guard's hand. Any thoughts she had of going for the weapon vanished as she saw the slide jutting back. He'd emptied it at someone.

Or maybe just at the bullet-riddled wall on his way down.

She could still grab it. She might find ammo if she could locate the security office. But she'd prefer her own familiar weapon, so she took a few more silent steps toward the counter and the rustling noises behind it, the occasional grunt. Her hand dipped into her pocket, her fingers twisting in the cords for the laptop AC adaptor. *David and Goliath.*

She figured she was stamped as David in this particular scenario.

As she reached for the sleek granite desk edge, fingertips hovering and ready to support her as she leaned over, a man popped up from the other side. His bearded face reflected astonishment; he dropped a handful of booty and scrambled to bring up his rifle, catching the muzzle brake on the inner structure of the desk. Selena jerked her hand from her pocket, whipped the chunky little AC adaptor over her head once to gather momentum and slung it against the man's temple. Down he went, falling with a strangely soft landing.

Selena pushed off against the desk, levering herself up to crouch atop it, ready to follow through—to scrabble over the rifle if she had to. But the man lay awkwardly on top of the dead guard from whom he'd been pilfering, the rifle out of reach.

And David wins again. Selena didn't let regret for the dead guard slow her down. Time to grab a weapon— the Abakan rifle, an obvious if puzzling Kemeni favorite, or the lockbox with her gun, or the guard's gun…she didn't care. But shouted alarm warned her; she looked up in time to see green-and-tan-clad figures rounding the corner out of the hallway opposite her own approach path. She instantly dived for escape back the way she'd come, just barely rolling into the movement as she hit the floor. Gunfire exploded into the silence; wood chips and plaster spit through the air. Selena rolled with purpose until she hit the wall and scrambled to her feet, shouting, *"Grenade!"* as she flung the adaptor in their direction.

They didn't stop to think why she'd warn them; they only reacted to the word, flinching and ducking as the adaptor bounced at their feet. It only took them an instant to realize the black device was not a grenade, not even a unique new American grenade—but by then Selena had thrown herself around the corner and driven out into a long-legged sprint. On her way past a stairwell she slammed the door open hard enough to hit the wall behind it but never hesitated, retracing her steps to make the next turn before they gathered themselves to charge the hallway in her wake. In moments she found the waiting room from whence she'd come, hesitating only long enough to leave the door open just the way she'd found it the first time. She dashed through to the prime minister's office, grabbed her briefcase against the faint possibility that they'd trace her steps this far and headed out to his admin's office. There she quickly rifled the desk drawers, ignoring the keyboard and flat panel screen monitor that had been slung across the room as well as the tea spilled across the desk. She hoped for but didn't expect to find a weapon and found more reasonable treasure instead: a ring of keys.

Enough time spent; the echoes of frustrated shouts came faintly through the waiting room on the other side of Razidae's office. Selena ran out into a hall that ran parallel to the one she'd just left, heading for the set of stairs that logic told her would be opposite those on the other side and taking them two at a time when she found them. All the way to the fourth floor, where the secondary residences filled the space. Guests, dignitaries, distant family members…here they lived. A fumbling game of find-the-key finally netted her entrance, and she eased halfway into the hall, not ready to commit herself yet. She didn't think the Kemenis would be up here just yet—they hadn't had enough time to secure all the public space—but she took nothing for granted. She hesitated, taking her breathing back down, listening and watching.

If anyone hid here, they were—quite wisely—still hiding. Selena let the door close behind her, making sure it latched as silently as possible, and then turned in the direction that would take her back above the ballroom, moving at a more cautious and sedate pace.

She had no doubt there'd be plenty of time for more running later.

Chapter 5

"No," Cole said into the phone, more firmly than he should and less firmly than he wanted. "I just got back. I've got something going on here, and I'm not going anywhere until it's settled." He wrapped the damp towel around his neck, a match to the one tucked around his hips, and barely listened to the persistent voice in his ear. Given the frequency with which Selena checked e-mail, he should have heard from her by now. He should have had an answer to his simple, straightforward question.

What's wrong?

"No," he said again, this time with a sharp shake of his head that his caller would have known to heed had he seen it. "Even if you couldn't do without me on this, you owe me. You'd never have uncovered that budding little problem without me—hell, you'd never even have *known* about it. And who else do you have who can switch-hit with the FBI so easily? So back off, Sarge."

The man wasn't a sergeant. But in an organization where rank was rarely assigned, the nickname served its purpose.

"Yeah, okay." Cole pulled the towel away from his neck, idly rubbing it across his still-damp chest, and glanced into the living room where he'd left the television on. Special news flash, generic sort of logo that meant whatever had happened was either too new or too unimportant to have its own catchy headline name. "I'll be in touch at this number. It goes where I go, right? But don't be surprised if I answer from Berzhaan."

That got a little snort of disbelief, a warning to watch his ass if he even looked at that part of the world, and an abrupt sign-off that left Cole looking at his phone in bemusement. Berzhaan wasn't vacationland, but the FBI wouldn't have sent Selena into a war zone.

Especially not now. Not when he had a marriage to fix—and needed the chance to do it.

Except he looked up from the phone to find a map of that small country on the television with a dramatic arrow pointing at Suwan; the image flipped to an imposing building with barricades all around it, emergency and military vehicles beyond that, and an ambulance speeding away from the outside edge of it all. *Berzhaan* was the special news flash. Berzhaan and a sudden surge of violence across the country, killing people, destroying their livelihoods. "No one knows the Kemenis' exact goals or what drove them to this move just when their arms dried up..." And the building was the Berzhaan capitol, only a few blocks from the embassy out of which Selena worked. The embassy that had apparently been evacuated as soon as the siege of the capitol began.

Then where's Selena?

Selena pinned her hopes on finding a master key on the stolen key ring, and sighed with relief when the fourth key she tried snicked neatly into the well-lubricated lock of the room at the end of the guest quarters hall. No one answered her quiet knock, but she found the room littered with signs of use and tried the next door down.

This room looked ready for guests—or at least, ready to *be* ready. There were no flowers on the table in the suite's first room, and when she found the bedroom she didn't see any dents on the pillow. But it was clean and ready for whatever final touches were deemed appropriate for its next occupant.

She didn't intend to stay here long. Sooner or later the Kemenis would do a room-to-room search, rounding up anyone they might have missed the first time through. She'd give them enough time to settle down…but not so much they'd entirely have their act together. And even though her inclination to rush down and check out the situation drove at her, she forced herself to brew a cup of tea from the supplies in the kitchenette. Her stomach hadn't been more than grumbly, but tea might well calm it further.

And then she sat cross-legged on the floor on the opposite side of a plush chair, giving herself a good view of the double-locked door while remaining discreetly tucked away, her briefcase at her side. She sipped tea and she considered the situation and how little she knew of it so far. *Kemenis.* They seemed to have based themselves in the public part of the capitol. The ballroom, perhaps, where the students would have been. She still needed to discover their intent. If they were holding hostages, to what purpose? What demands would they make…and how soon would they start killing people to achieve those demands?

For the Kemenis had never demonstrated a reluctance to kill people.

Quiet moments later, Selena set aside the tea, pulling her knees up to briefly rest her forehead there. Her stomach felt better…soothed. Her mind still whirled with unanswered questions—was she actually, truly pregnant? So hard to tell with her whimsical cycles… Had Cole actually, truly faked an assignment to have an affair? So hard to tell with his astonishing ability to play the moment…to play *people*.

But it shouldn't have been. She should have *just known*. And he was sending e-mail from their home computer, returned sooner than expected. Not surprisingly—he obviously hadn't had far to travel. Selena pulled her phone from the leather pocket on the side of her briefcase and turned it on. Its pale blue LED screen informed her she had voice mail, and that she had less than half the battery life left. She stared at it, tempted.

No. She'd wait until she had answers to her other questions—the Kemenis' intentions, their manpower.

Answers it was just about time to find out.

In her hand, the phone vibrated. Selena jumped, chided herself for being nervy and checked the incoming number.

Cole. Of course it was Cole; the message was probably his, too. It'd been forty-five minutes, maybe even an hour since the Kemenis had made their move on the capitol. By now CNN had a live feed going. He'd be expecting to find her at the embassy...and he'd be wrong.

The phone gave another hopeful vibration, and this time Selena thumbed the on button, resolutely putting the phone to her ear. "Hello, Cole."

"Selena!"

She'd never thought to hear Cole frightened. Of anything. But the fear tinged his voice even through this staticky satellite connection. *Cole's voice.* It was a wonderful, smooth low voice that triggered a flush of the very emotions she'd been trying to avoid—along with the usual warmth she felt in his presence.

The very reason she had to run so far away in order to sort out her feelings.

She'd always responded to him that way—the first day she met him, the day they'd gotten married, and each and every time he turned that smile on her. With effort, she managed to avoid blurting out her suspicions about being pregnant—because he really didn't need to know it. Not now, when she was trapped in a building under Kemeni siege. For whatever he'd done, whatever potential affairs he might have conducted, she knew he cared. Right there in his voice, she could hear how much he cared. She just wasn't sure if he cared in the way that she needed—or if he even could. He was so good at filling so many roles...maybe he simply couldn't limit himself to one relationship role.

You believed he could when you married him. That he had.

"Lena?"

Selena blinked. *Battery time. Don't waste it.* "Listen," she told him, moving up to her knees so she could react more quickly if anyone came to the door during this time she couldn't hear them as well. "I've got to save this battery, so I only have a moment. I'm in the Berzhaani capitol building."

He swore a blistering oath, but cut it short. "What's your situation?"

"At liberty. As far as I know, I'm the only one. I'm about to go down and scope it out, but I think Allori, Razidae, the staff and a whole busload of college students all picked the wrong day to be here."

"Fits what I've heard." Cole swore again, more softly this time. "Any chance you can get out?"

"I don't know yet. I doubt it. They know I'm here." Selena hesitated, hunting the best words. Businesslike words. Orderly words. "What have you heard? What do the Kemenis want?"

"Razidae's resignation," Cole said promptly. "Along with all his advisors, support staff, any capitol employee who ever touched the hand of an American in peace and all dogs who've wagged their tails at Americans. The cats can stay, because everyone knows they're notoriously fickle anyway."

Selena closed her eyes, touching the bridge of her nose. "And the threat? When do they start killing people?"

"That part's not clear. At least, not as it's coming over CNN. The truth is, no one out here knows what's really going on in there. They issued that short statement of demand, and—"

"Then I'll find out," Selena said. What the hell were the Kemenis up to? The other members of Razidae's government would never step down, not even to save Razidae's life. Those were the prime minister's own

well-known instructions, leaving the Kemenis very little to gain even if they survived. From the tone of Cole's
voice, he felt very much the same. She told him, "I'll
call you back as soon as I can. Stay off the landline." It
was more secure…he'd understand that.

"I'll be here." Cole hesitated. Even through her own
unexpected relief at this reassurance—she'd rather have
no one else handling details on the other end of the
phone with her life at stake—Selena could practically
see him wrestling with himself. She wasn't sure if he
lost or won when he spoke again. "Lena, I know you're
upset about something—"

At home, he meant. At him. What had given her
away? How unfair that he could be so certain of her
when she couldn't manage the same in return.

"—and I know we can't go into that right now. But
don't forget…" He hesitated, trailing off in a way that
meant he was hunting for better words. "Just don't forget how much I love you."

She hadn't expected it. She didn't know what to say.
She let noisy static fill the air between them—wasting
time, wasting battery power, but too surprised at the way
her heart snatched those words to do anything else.

"I mean it," Cole said, growing fierce. If he'd been
there, he'd have pulled her close by now. He'd be looking down at her, arctic-blue eyes intense with the meaning behind his words, close enough for her to see that
quirky dark blue spot on his left iris. "Whatever upset
you, whatever goes on there, don't you dare forget how
damn much I love you!"

She couldn't get her voice above a murmur. "I'll
keep it in mind."

"Good," he growled. "Now go save the day, will

you? I'll be waiting by the phone." And he cut the connection before she could.

Selena flipped the phone closed, turning it off; her movements came automatically, and she gave them no thought at all. Instead she dropped her forehead back down on her knees.

...how damn much I love you!

It was a lifeline. He knew she'd run, if not why. He knew the peril she faced—if the Kemenis found her, they weren't likely to escort her to captivity. She'd already caused too much trouble. *Come back to me,* that's what he meant. What he wanted.

She gave herself the moment...let herself feel what his voice did to her—what his emotions did for her. Selena, orderly and logical and everything in its place... unless she was with Cole. Unless he sparked the unpredictable in her as he so often did. In the outside world, she wore her precision like a shield; in their apartment, she was just as likely to strip in one room so she could surprise him in another. Like the evening the week before he'd left, when she'd walked into the bedroom during his workout, bare as bare came, and straddled him on the exercise bench.

He lost all the air in his lungs in a surprised gust of exhalation, both arms dropping away in mid butterfly-curl, his chest beautifully exposed and ripe for touching. She moved against him, sighing happily, and by then he was hissing through his teeth, his hands fumbling free of the weights and only making it as far as the bench press bars, which he clutched in helpless reaction.

They'd only been gym shorts. They hadn't lasted long. Selena ached to think of the moment, in her heart as well as her body. For as physically sweet as it had been, the memory only hammered home what he meant to her. What he gave to her.

Spontaneity. Unpredictability. Outrageous daring. And right now, if she was going to survive, she needed to find it all within herself, too.

Chapter 6

Selena took her outrageous daring back into the fray, leaving her briefcase under the bed and rinsing her teacup so as to leave as few signs as possible that she'd been here. She found a service elevator and tucked herself against the front wall beside the door. When the old doors clunked open on the first floor, she eased a hand over the *open door* button and held it there, giving any curious terrorist passing by plenty of time to check out the conveyance.

But no one approached. No one so much as grunted out a demanding question. Selena edged around the opening to find an empty hallway with a decidedly more utilitarian look than the other areas of the capitol she'd seen so far. The painted walls needed a new coat of their flat eggshell color, and the carpets needed cleaning—or better yet, replacement. A rolling cloth laundry bin sat at a haphazard angle against the wall, and the thick, steamy smell of food permeated the air. Roast lamb overlaid by all the spices of *baharat*—cloves and cinnamon and cumin and the sting of curry powder.

She held her breath, waiting to see how her stomach might react to the invasion of odors, but either the tea had done the trick or she'd gotten the problem out of her system. It was undoubtedly coincidence that as she held her coat closed with one hand, it rested low over her flat belly. *Flat for now?*

Stop that.

She stepped out into the hallway, moving swiftly to the first inset door to consider what she'd seen along the way. A door at the end of the hall with a mop and bucket sitting outside it. Double swinging doors not far from her current position, which seemed to be—she peeked inside to be sure—a linen closet, full of napkins and silky-fine linen tablecloths. Not of any particular interest. The maintenance closet and the kitchen, on the other hand…

She listened, heard nothing but the ping of a water pipe, and headed for the swinging doors, quickly scanning the interior through the small windows before she invited herself in.

Fancy. Lots of gleaming stainless steel, a bank of gas stoves against the wall, a column of ovens butted up against them. Cutlery, pots and pans and obscure devices whose purpose Selena could only guess.

Bullets riddled it all. Blood smeared the floor, thick trails leading to a walk-in freezer. Food sat half-prepared, congealing over cold burners.

Selena raised a critical eyebrow. If she were going to stage a government takeover, she'd want to make

sure her people had food available—not to mention a
place to prepare it. As it was, she hoped the Kemenis
had brought MREs along, because otherwise everyone
would get pretty hungry before this incident was over.
And a hungry terrorist was a cranky terrorist.

Still, no assumptions. Perhaps whoever ran this show
wasn't all that stupid after all, but had merely encountered a minor rebellion he'd had no choice but to quell.

Selena walked the kitchen, stepping over the blood
trails…walking through them would only betray her
presence here when someone inevitably came back to
see just what could be done about the food situation.
She helped herself to a lovely little paring knife, something she could stick through her belt without worrying about inadvertent stab wounds. *By all means, no
inadvertent stab wounds.*

Ice pick. Oh yeah. No easy place to put it; with regret Selena jabbed it through the bottom of her coat
pocket, leaving the knobby handle within easy reach.
Corkscrew? Too bulky. *For now.*

Besides, she could always come back. A good iron
frying pan upside the head did as much harm to a terrorist as to anyone.

A scuffle of sound alerted her, sending her up against
the wall beside the double doors. When it came again
she pinpointed it to the freezer, and immediately realized that not everyone thrown in that convenient storage had been as dead as assumed. She opened the door
with much caution, ready for any survivors who might
assume she was Kemeni.

In the glare of a naked lightbulb, a man stood totter-
ing on his feet, his whites splashed with the blood of
others and liberally soaked with his own. The impres-

sive fillet knife he clutched wouldn't have done him much good against Kemeni rifles, but he held it with much determination regardless. The equally determined look on his face faded to confusion as he took in the sight of Selena in the doorway, all her borrowed weaponry in concealment, an American woman in informal clothing who should be screaming at the sight of the grotesquely piled dead before her. Men in kitchen whites, men in green jackets.

Selena didn't scream. She said in Berzhaani, "You'd best sit before you fall. I'm not going to hurt you."

"The Kemenis have already done *that*," the man said. Short, stout enough to fill out his whites without slopping over the edges, he carried a cynical air and a nose generous enough to have provided for two men. He eyed her, taking hold of a shelf to steady himself. Before him, the pile of dead; around him, shelves of the highest quality food products, arranged in meticulous sections. "Are you a crazy woman, coming here? If they don't have you, why don't you run?"

"They know of me," she said, letting her voice take on an absent tone. "They just don't know where I am. I'd rather they not find out—just as I'm sure you'd rather they not know you still survive."

He made an emphatic gesture with his free hand. "I do believe we are allies, whoever you are—the enemy of my enemy."

"That last part's accurate enough," she murmured. "Are you badly hurt? There's not much I can do for you…tablecloths, maybe."

"I know only that I'm not dead." He glanced at the others from the kitchen, and sorrow flickered across his features, settling in at the flare of his substantial nostrils and the press of his lips. "I have been shot in the arm, which does not work very well. Otherwise, I am only cold."

"Tablecloths should help with that. We could raise the temperature—"

"And sit here in the middle of rotting food and the decomposing bodies of my friends?" He shook his head, sharply. "They brought their weapons in through the kitchen, you know. Mutaa turned out to be one of them. They came running in here and he handed out rifles like kitchen treats. And who are you again?"

"Someone who wants to get us out of this mess." Selena knew he wouldn't quite be able to understand, and he didn't. She left him with a baffled and wary expression. "I'll be right back."

Retrieving a pile of tablecloths from the linen closet took only moments. She brought him as many as she could carry, and used several to cover the dead. The others she draped carefully over the man's shoulders, and then she found a plastic crate full of cabbage and flipped it upside down, disregarding the rolling cabbages. "Here. Sit." And as he complied, looking more bemused than ever, she asked, "Have they been here since they did this? Have you heard them checking out this area at all? Did you overhear them say anything about their purpose?"

He raised a hand, along with both eyebrows. *"Ai, ai,"* he said, the Berzhaani equivalent of *hold your horses.* "They came, they killed, they left. I've been in here with the others since then. I've heard nothing. And they did not take the time to explain themselves before they killed."

Selena tucked her lower lip in her teeth for a thoughtful chew. Not helpful. Not helpful at all. She'd gained a few useful little defensive weapons here, but no information to speak of. She knew from Cole that the Kemenis were demanding Razidae's resignation, but she still had no idea what the terrorists truly wanted. Oftentimes the public demand and the private intent didn't match very neatly…and until she knew the Kemenis' true goals, she couldn't assess the situation properly. Act on it properly.

She found the man watching her with some curiosity, and saw his dawning realization that she wasn't merely calculating her best options for escape.

Not yet, anyway. Someone had to stop this. And just like this morning at the shrine village, Selena didn't see anyone else around with the means. *Just me.*

She'd jammed several spotless linen napkins into the cargo pocket of her coat, where they cohabited with the ice pick handle. Now she pulled them out and crouched beside him. "This'll hurt."

He grunted as she took his arm from beneath his tablecloth cloak and propped it against her leg, shaking a napkin out and efficiently rolling it into a tube. "It already hurts." But he winced as she tied the tube around his wound, not taking the time to remove the white chef's uniform shirt that showed the blood so well, and admitted, "That hurt more."

She grinned at him, finding herself drawn in by his cranky charm. "My name is Selena." She knotted the ends of the napkin, barely long enough as they were. "I'm a pushy American from the embassy and I'm going to do something about this situation. Would you like to help?"

He eyed the bandage as she released his arm, opened

and closed his fist with enough vigor to make himself wince and carefully tucked the limb away beneath the tablecloth. "I am Atif. How do you think I might help you?"

"Who knows this section of the building better than you do?" Selena shrugged. "My guess would be *no one.*"

"And in that you would be right." He gave his co-workers a pensive look and closed his eyes in resignation—an acceptance that his part in this crisis wasn't yet over. "What is it you need to know?"

"I think the Kemenis probably have everyone gathered in the ballroom, or at least one of the function rooms nearby. I need to check them out. *Quietly.*"

He smiled. Partly it looked gleeful, as though he had just the right answers for her. And partly the expression looked…predatory.

And so Selena found herself in a small, barely lit corridor sandwiched between the ballroom—currently in dining-room setup, Atif explained—and the hallway behind it. The corridor ran the length of the function rooms, providing discreet entry for maintenance, food service and even the occasional escaping Berzhaani diplomat who'd had enough of Western arrogance. The divider between the corridor and function rooms was a flimsy one, but it was enough. Selena counted the function rooms by the seams where outside light leaked through, just as Atif had instructed. And she kept an alert ear out for any indication that she wasn't the only one inhabiting the narrow warren. It took no key to enter this place, only the knowledge that it existed.

Not far from the kitchen, Selena herself had merely

opened the door Atif had identified for her, discovering what looked like a linen closet but what was in truth an exchange area. On one side, used dishes, burned-out table lights, candle stubs…some of them still waited for cleanup. On the other, shelves for supplies and trays and pitchers. And out the back, beyond the thick black curtain…this lovely little corridor.

Atif's brow had wrinkled slightly as he told her of the hidden access, and now that she was here, Selena had no doubt why. Each room had a number of tiny spy holes, no doubt so the servers could keep an eye on the needs of the diplomats and functionaries without intruding into their events. Selena peered through one into a small empty room meant for one-on-one discussions, and considered how easy it would be to observe such proceedings—or better yet, to observe the private discussion between two officials from another country who thought themselves alone. Was there a similar arrangement in the room where she and Ambassador Allori had habitually waited for the prime minister? Selena routinely and discreetly swept such waiting rooms for recording and listening devices…but she couldn't check for warm bodies lurking in narrow passages.

From ahead, a voice rose in sudden but short-lived fright, muffled enough to come from outside her little personal hallway. Selena moved quickly toward it and found the peephole by its light. With her own breath loud and revealing in her ears, she put her eye to it.

Bingo. A function room crammed with people. She found Allori; she found Prime Minister Razidae and his deputy prime minister, Amar bin Kuwaji—all under the careful eye of a tan and olive green dressed guard. *The*

Kemenis must want the entire government to step aside, or they'd just kill Razidae. Regardless, she doubted Razidae would survive. He was the most significant unifying leader this country had had for generations, and as long as he lived, the people would rally around him. Any Kemeni government would hold only temporary rule.

The others, they'd keep as leverage. As a way to induce Western and European countries to pressure Razidae's people into stepping aside.

The others.

As if those lives could be summed up so simply. There they were—the two chaperones who'd accompanied the students. The woman Selena had seen in the lobby, but not the man. A handful of diplomats who'd been unlucky enough to choose this day to conduct their business. The glamorous but modest events coordinator. Three young women in green jackets.

And the students.

Terrified, pale…they huddled together against the walls and around the few small round tables available. One girl had her legs crossed so hard Selena was sure she'd wet her pants before she had a chance at a bathroom. Two other girls comforted a third who cried softly, and when they looked across their friend's bowed shoulders, their expressions turned grim. And there, in the corner—the young man who'd given Selena such an openly appraising look and the girlfriend he'd annoyed, holding each other with a desperate affection.

The hostages had none of the small comforts this opulent room was meant to provide—no water, no finger sandwiches, no veggie plates with exotic dips arranged on expensive glass and silver serving ware. They weren't being attended, feted, or even being fed the propaganda they'd come to hear. Their lives, in an instant, had turned into terror.

Dammit. It wasn't right. These were young people; they hadn't even started their lives. They had nothing to do with Berzhaan's problems; they had done nothing to offend the Kemenis. They were here to broaden their horizons, to learn acceptance of this very culture. They had not, like Selena, willingly accepted a career that on occasion turned her into a target and at the least kept her in restless countries with high incidents of terrorism. They hadn't made those choices at all.

Like Selena, pregnant though she might be. Or like Cole. God, she wished he were here. And she realized the sudden irony of it, that she would trust him with her life but not with her heart.

As these young men and women were now counting on Selena.

They just didn't know it yet.

She wished she could give them some reassurance, some sign...*you're not alone.* But it wasn't time for that...far from it. By the time they knew she was here—working for them, fighting for them—things would probably be over one way or the other.

Selena closed her eyes against the sight of them, fighting a terrible wash of anger. She'd get nowhere with a paring knife and an ice pick if she didn't use her anger wisely—drawing on it for strength when she needed it, leaving it behind when her thinking had to be crystal-clear. Her entire purpose as an FBI legate was to fight terrorism. It was why she was here.

She'd just never faced it on such a visceral level before.

Surprise. Get over it. Move on.

And that's exactly what she did. She'd found the hostages; she'd seen that Allori looked as composed as ever and Razidae remained alive. For the moment there was nothing she could do for them. Now she had to find the terrorists.

She didn't have far to go. The next little peephole showed her just what she was up against. Just who. And as startled as she was to find the American fugitive, Jonas White, in deep discussion with a small grouping of the men sprawled around the room— cleaning weapons, holding weapons, staring fiercely at nothing in particular, and even in a few instances bleeding—her gaze skipped over the aging international player and settled on none other than the man from the lobby. The one who'd stepped from the cover of *GQ*, handsome and finished and sleek. Dark hair, sharp aquiline lines to his face and a broad-shouldered body made obvious now that he'd discarded his jacket and wore only the silk T-shirt; it followed every plane and long line of muscle, highlighting the elegance of his carriage. And his eyes…they flashed at Jonas White's words, a dark and simmering glower. Eyes to die for.

Except Selena didn't intend to.

She did step back a moment, taking a deep breath. Jonas White was one thing. He was a player, a man who liked to wield power and who liked to win—but a man whose most important considerations were his own skin and his own interests. His presence here no doubt represented some last-ditch effort to rescue his faltering influence and rebuild the empire that his adopted daughter, Lynn, had destroyed when she learned the true nature of his activities. And though Jonas was not to be underestimated…

It was the Berzhaani man who worried her. The one who'd been in the lobby…the one who'd probably started this whole mess, killing the guards so his people could storm the building. Unlike Jonas, this Kemeni leader burned with purpose. He'd see this crisis through to the end, and Kemeni interests would come before his own. Selena wouldn't be surprised if she'd been looking at the reclusive Tafiq Ashurbeyli himself. It would take a man such as this to drive the Kemenis to such risky action when they were in fact close to defeat in the wake of Frank Black's death and Jonas White's financial collapse.

What had White told Ashurbeyli? Not the truth—not that he'd been behind Frank Black all along. But somehow he'd tied their fates together.

Just call me *fate.* Selena smiled grimly in the dimness of the corridor. *Because I'm the one you're about to meet. Together.*

Having absorbed the implications of the room's occupants, she returned to the peephole. She found the door leading to the function room that held the hostages. Guarded, of course. She had no doubt the main exit from that room was guarded, as well, and she'd already seen the interior guard. The hostages had nowhere to go unless she could cause enough diversion to get them out through this corridor. The ceilings were high and original; the heating ducts primitive and usually merely grates between the rooms. The same factors meant there would be little opportunity to beard the terrorists in their chosen den. She had no intention of revealing she'd discovered this passage until she had no choice.

Well, then. Perhaps she'd have to nibble at them from the edges. They might know she was here, but they wouldn't know about her Athena Academy background. They wouldn't know she hadn't run to the darkest, most distant corner of the building to tremble and wait out the crisis.

But before she took any action at all, she needed to relay the details of the situation to someone on the outside. *Cole.* And to judge by the impact his voice had had on her the last time, she'd best get her head together before she made that call.

Cole crossed his arms and stared at the kitchen phone. Glared at it, truth be told. He'd already snatched it up once on the first ring, only to find himself at the other end of a useless conversation with someone at the FBI. Someone apologetically informing him that Selena might be involved in the current Berzhaani crisis. "Of course she is," Cole had snapped, adding the instant follow-up, "What're you doing about it? Has HRT been called?"

And the young man on the other end of the line had fumbled his words; Cole clearly hadn't followed the script. Then he'd admitted he didn't have any information about the Hostage Rescue Team and he couldn't tell Cole even if he did. Typical. Cole had darkly warned the young man that they'd best stay out of Selena's way. And then he'd hung up, leaving the line free for Selena.

He uncrossed his arms long enough to stalk from one end of the apartment to the other, then dropped for a quick series of push-ups. It didn't do much to ease his explosive tension; he grabbed his cell phone and considered calling the special agent who'd recently borrowed him from the CIA. *It's not* what *you know, it's who...*

But he didn't yet have anything to say, not really. And the woman wouldn't be at liberty to reveal any information even if she had it. Nope, he wasn't sure the FBI connection was the way to go, no matter that they signed Selena's paycheck. And the CIA? Not likely to be any better. They might well have a special ops team on the way; they might even be working with the military to get the SEALs sent in. They might well be engaged in a turf war with HRT.

That didn't mean anyone would tell Cole.

He considered the phone in his hand, one hand rubbing the back of his neck. There had to be someone he could contact...strings to pull, favors to call in. He had plenty of both...just not anyone in a position to siphon him this particular information.

He flung himself into the creamy leather recliner opposite the television—on, but muted. The UBC station had only been repeating the same old phrases, the very same words they were running across the bottom of the screen. But now...now they switched to an image of Tory Patton. Tall and elegant, sleek black hair sweeping the length of her chin, green eyes piercing even across thousands of miles of satellite feed. Tory Patton. More than just a pretty star reporter face. She, too, had been to the Athena Academy.

Selena said little of her former schoolmates even when pressed, but Cole had no trouble seeing her fierce loyalty to them; he had no trouble spotting her pride these past few months. Athena grads Kim Valenti and Diana Lockworth had each saved President Gabriel

Monihan from assassination attempts. Air Force Captain Josie Lockworth, Diana's sister, had done recent breakthrough work on the Predator spy plane. And then there was Tory herself.

He wondered if she'd take a call from a man who had an inside scoop on this story.

But first he needed his scoop. *Call me, Selena.* Call. *Trust me.*

Distraction almost did her in.

Selena stopped to look into the hostage room on her way out of the not-so-secret passageway and almost betrayed herself with a curse. For just as she peeked, several guards stepped into the room, grabbing Deputy Prime Minister bin Kuwaji one to an arm and dragging him toward the door without giving him a chance to fully catch his balance. The man Selena had privately identified as Tafiq Ashurbeyli stepped into the doorway, just far enough to snap a command. The rebels stopped long enough for bin Kuwaji to reclaim his feet, their expressions resentful. Then they marched him out the ballroom door—and, when Selena hurried back to the ballroom peephole, she was just in time to see the deputy PM being hustled through the double-doored entrance.

This can't be good.

Selena hesitated. Any influence she had would be used up in one great big splurt of glory if she was caught following them—and she was very likely to be caught. And meanwhile she could stay out of sight, taking the long way back to the prime minister's office and his private phone, where she could pass along what she knew. She had a preliminary insider's view of the situation no one else could provide.

Unless, of course, she died before she made that phone call.

Make the call. She tendered mental apologies to the deputy prime minister, hoping the best for him. And she was halfway back down the corridor when something bumped the wall, making a loud noise in a small space.

As in, I'm no longer alone.

She wasn't ready for a confrontation. The Kemenis knew she was here, but they didn't yet know how much of a problem she intended to be. They hadn't placed a high priority on locating her—or else the ballroom would have been empty, and the rebels would have been out combing the building for her. Instead here came a clueless clod of a Kemeni, probably confident he wouldn't run into anyone within this serving corridor. They were two trains on the same track, heading for a wreck.

She would have rolled her eyes if she'd had time. She didn't. She fumbled for the recessed push-ring for the thin door to the adjacent function room and slipped through, closing it as quickly as she could while remaining silent. Even so, there was the slight snick of the door settling back into place—little more than reinforced wallboard, it had no latch, just a snug fit—and if he was closer than she'd thought, he could well have seen the brief spear of light shafting into the corridor.

Be careless, she thought fiercely at him—but she reached into her pocket and withdrew the ice pick, fitting it through the center of her fist so the knob settled into the natural depression between the wrap of her thumb and index finger. It wasn't a kubotan, but it would do.

She barely settled herself into place against the wall

beside the door when she heard blunt fingers scrabbling against the inset latch on the other side. Great. Just once, she wanted a careless one. She slid down to crouch against the wall as he pushed the door open to scan the interior of the room.

Selena drove up from beneath, whipping her arm up from the elbow to slam the side of her wood knob-enhanced fist into the man's temple. Right on cue, his eyes rolled back; he dropped heavily to the floor. "Shhh!" she hissed at him. "Be quiet!"

But she didn't hesitate to see if the noise had been noticed. She shouldered his assault rifle and dragged him back into the corridor, closing the door firmly behind them. Without much care for his already insulted head, she grabbed his ankles and hauled him toward the kitchen, stopping frequently to listen for other incursions. At the converted linen closet she hesitated even longer, listening hard before sticking her head out to do a quick visual check, then quickly hauling her prize off to the kitchen.

Atif looked up, startled and concerned, as she entered the walk-in cooler, but his expression cleared by the time she'd closed its substantial door. "Already!"

"He got in my way." Selena let her annoyance show. "At least he doesn't have a radio—they won't be expecting to hear from him. And they're just getting their routines squared away, so if I'm lucky they won't notice he's missing for a while." She found a cone of butcher twine on a shelf near the door and yanked off a furious length of it.

"He's not dead?" Atif looked at the terrorist in surprise. "He looks so nicely limp."

"He's a deadweight, but he's not dead." Selena tested

the butcher twine and tossed it away, then spied an industrial-size roll of cling wrap. She smiled. Atif followed her gaze, and then he smiled, too. Within moments Selena had the man wrapped in enough layers of clingy plastic to all but immobilize him, with separate, twirled wraps around his wrists and ankles. She dragged him off toward the back of the cooler— "We need to leave room for more," she told Atif, who only smiled—and propped him up against the back shelves just as he opened bleary eyes. "Behave yourself," she told him, putting herself squarely in his unfocused vision.

"You…" The rebel couldn't seem to wrap his brain around the nature of the person who'd taken him down so neatly. "No woman tells me—"

"Okay," Selena said readily, and handed the assault rifle to a surprised Atif. "Then he'll tell you." She hadn't meant to leave the rifle here, but Atif had no other weapons…and he was wounded. If Selena brought more disabled rebels this way—or if someone thought to check this cooler—Atif would need the rifle more than she.

She'd just have to get another.

"And be quiet," she admonished the rebel as Atif fumbled the rifle with his wounded arm and finally got it pointed in the right direction. "Because there's plenty of cling wrap, and if you make a fuss, Atif is going to wrap up your face. I very much imagine that would make it difficult to breathe."

Atif looked intrigued by the thought, his expression just a little over the top. Selena's heart went out to him. He was hurt, he was surrounded by his dead friends, and he was doing his very best to rise to the unexpected role she'd assigned to him.

"I won't be long," she told him.

"But where—?" Even with the rifle, he clearly preferred to have company in his guard duties. Still, he didn't wait for her to respond. He cleared his throat and straightened his shoulders. "Never mind. Of course I should not know."

"I'm trying to help." Selena nudged the clingwrapped terrorist as he started to tilt; the man didn't acknowledge her. To all appearances, his intense embarrassment had inspired him to pretend she wasn't there at all. "That's enough, don't you think?"

Atif gave her a canny eye. "I'm not so sure. Over the centuries, many people have tried to *help* my country. The Russians, for instance. They almost helped my culture into oblivion, as I'm sure you've seen. And lately, there are many Westerners trying to help themselves to our oil."

"Can't argue with that." Selena headed for the door, pulling back on the heavy lever as quietly as possible and then listening through the crack she'd made. "In this case, all I want to do is help myself right back home, and help these Kemenis into a nice strong cell. After that, it's up to you."

Atif nodded, short and dignified. "Then I think we can work together well. Bring me back more Kemenis, and I will entertain them with lectures on fillet methods." He eyed his current prisoner. "I am prepared to provide a practical demonstration."

After that, Selena simply had to take the time to find Atif's fillet knife—and indeed, he appeared more imposing once he had it. Imposing and assured. So she left him that way, and took the stairs back to the fourth floor, heading for the opposing stairs in a series of forays with plenty of time to listen for Kemeni activity between movement. Back down the stairs she moved even more cautiously, and on the first floor she barely missed a patrolling Kemeni duo. Shortly after that she slipped back into Razidae's office, closing the outside doors to both the waiting room and the admin's office, so when she entered the office again, she had double doors on both sides.

She took a deep breath. Sat in Razidae's chair. Listened.

Silence.

Just watch out for that alluring sense of false security, she told herself. That's all it would take—one moment of carelessness. She was literally surrounded by the enemy, and the enemy had proven to be ruthless. For where, she wondered, were the capitol staff? She'd found none of the security personnel; none of the support personnel. None of the maids or maintenance people.

Maybe some had escaped—but why let them go and slaughter the kitchen staff?

She doubted any lingerers had been left alive. They didn't have the leverage value of the chosen hostages, but they were too problematic to release. They'd have been able to give numbers and weaponry and any other tidbits they might have overheard.

The Kemenis' own countrymen, innocent of any wrongdoing…slaughtered.

Maybe I'm wrong.

She didn't think so. She took another breath and picked up the phone. *Be there,* she thought at Cole. She might be mad at him, she might even not want to be married to him anymore, but she was definitely counting on him.

Chapter 7

Be there, be there, be there—

"Cole!"

"Where else would I be?" he asked, playing off the relief in her voice. The distance made him sound a little tinny, albeit without the static of the cell phones.

"Leading your own rescue effort?" Selena took a deep mental breath, surprised by how much hearing his voice meant to her. She was here, she was tough, she was doing what needed to be done…but she was grateful for the emotional anchor all the same.

That's not how you felt when you took this post.

As if she could afford to get tangled up in such thoughts just now.

"You all right?" he asked, and he didn't sound quite as cool anymore.

"Just…distracted." And far too acutely aware that

this might be her only chance to get tangled up in such thoughts at all. "I'm in the PM's office…I don't think they're hunting me yet." *Yet.* When they realized one of their men had gone missing, they might start taking her more seriously. She needed to finish her recon before then. "You ready for details?"

This time he was the one who sounded distracted. "Yeah…hold on…okay, shoot."

"Let's not use that phrase," she said dryly. "Here's what I've got so far—the hostages are in a function room east of the ballroom. They've got a whole busload of college students, their chaperones, a handful of diplomats…and they've got our ambassador."

"Allori?"

"That's the one. And they've already made it clear they have Razidae. They've got bin Kuwaji, too."

His voice suddenly held an odd distance. "And…?"

"You have something more important going on there?"

"Selena," he responded, an understanding warmth beneath the response that meant *get real*. Then he added, "Is there a television in that office?"

"Here?" She glanced around the room, not expecting to find any such thing in this dignified place of historic decor and presence. And so she almost didn't recognize it when her gaze swept past, a classy little flat screen tucked on the bookshelf between two rows of books. With the phone still tucked at her chin, she tugged the center desk drawer open, surprised when it yielded. No remote control, but she found it in the next drawer over. "So there is."

"How'd you assess them?" Cole asked, his voice strangely flat.

"In terms of intent?" Selena hunted for the power button. "They left a cooler full of dead people who didn't need to die. They had the lobby guards killed and the place full of tear gas in the time it took me to—" *Barf my guts out.* No, not that. Cole was no dummy. He'd start counting weeks, too. "I had water running in the bathroom. By the time I stuck my head out, it was all over. And Cole—I've seen their leader. Jonas White is there and there's no way he didn't have something to do with this, but this man is…he's a hawk. I think it's Tafiq Ashurbeyli."

"Great," Cole muttered. "He'll kill them all just for having seen his face. You have that TV on yet?"

"Getting there." Selena scowled at the strange little remote and started pressing buttons at random. The television powered up, the volume already low, the station already tuned to UBC's ubiquitous international news.

Selena didn't need volume to understand what was happening to bin Kuwaji. "Damn…they just took him from the ballroom. I *saw* them."

UBC's live cameras showed bin Kuwaji standing in the dark cavern of the building's main entry, gleaming white pillars on either side. He held himself with stiff dignity, and his expression showed not fear so much as acceptance. *"No."* Selena said. "It's too soon! They just got here—no one's had any time to respond to—"

Bin Kuwaji's head exploded in a spray of blood and brain, and he crumpled. *Oh, my God.* Those fools. Berzhaan's current Powers That Be would kill them all before they let the Kemenis go after this. From this isolated office, Selena had heard nothing. But right outside this very building, right this very moment, a man had died.

Making a point no one in the world would now doubt. The Kemenis were ruthless, and they wanted this government—this progressive warm and fuzzy, West-loving government—destroyed past reclamation.

"You saw." Cole's words came not as question so much as confirmation. "These are the people you're dealing with, Lena. Be damned careful. If nothing else, we've got a conversation going unsaid between us...and I want the chance to have it."

"Conversation..." Not the wittiest response, but Selena found herself unable to tear her eyes from the screen where a rebel had exposed himself just enough to nudge bin Kuwaji's body the first step of a long roll down the capitol's entry stairs. Arms flopping, body limp, the deputy prime minister landed at the base of the stairs and lay there. The UBC camera panned back, showing the barrier of police and military vehicles between the capitol and the law enforcement personnel, all of whom had made some initial move toward bin Kuwaji, only to hesitate at the thought of exposing themselves. Someone ran back behind the long line of uniforms and flashing lights, spurred to action on an unknown errand. An air of helplessness pervaded the scene.

"You ran," he said. "From me. We need to talk about it. But I'll be damned if I'm going to do that with an ocean and half a continent between us."

"How—" Too much to take, all at once and from all sides. How did he know? And could she have saved bin Kuwaji, if she'd thought to follow him? She thought so, but at what price? Her silence, perhaps, if she'd been hurt or killed before passing along what she knew.

"Your note, among other things. A feeling. I know

you, Selena." Cole let the silence stand a moment.
"Now's not the time, but it's foolish to pretend there's
nothing going on. Better to say it's there and put it
aside—as long as you believe I love you. *Believe* it, I
mean."

Believe? There was more to it than that. He could
very well love her with all his heart, but that didn't
mean his idea of love was the same as hers. Some men
had no problem loving more than one woman...but Selena wasn't made that way. And yet Cole waited, and
she couldn't linger here, and now was indeed not the
time because if they started talking about them, she'd
never keep her silence about her recent fatigue and illness and what it might mean. "I do—"

With a click, the phone went dead. Selena toggled
the flash button, hunting a dial tone.

Nothing.

Cut lines. Time to—

The door from the waiting room swung inward. The
man she'd described as a hawk stood there with gun in
hand. He looked so relaxed and self-assured she had no
doubt he considered himself to be in full control.

And why not?

He didn't say anything right away. He eyed her as she
stood behind the desk, not foolish enough to make any
sudden moves—just standing, trying to avoid the whole
deer-in-the-headlights impersonation. He looked her
over from head to toe and nodded, approving. Then he
gestured at the phone. "Very nice, but did you really
think we wouldn't have people monitoring the lines
from the security office?"

No point in lying; she responded in the Berzhaani language he'd used. "I didn't think this line showed up there."

He shrugged with one casual shoulder, as if to say *and you were wrong.* "Who did you call? Your embassy? They already know the situation here, of course."

Along with the rest of the world. He'd made sure of that when he'd executed bin Kuwaji on the steps. And she still had no reason to lie. "My husband."

His voice matched the rest of him—cultivated. Smooth. Offering a hint of darkness. He smiled, and didn't look amused at all. "You don't strike me as the kind of woman who goes running to her husband for help."

She imitated his one-shouldered shrug. "You don't strike me as the kind of man who does errands."

That *did* amuse him; his deep-set eyes widened slightly with his whimsy, one brow quirking. "I saw you come in. When my men described a Western woman in a long black coat…well, you can imagine there aren't many such here in the capitol. Very smooth, your work in the lobby." He lifted the hand that wasn't already occupied by his gun; her AC adaptor dangled from it. "A shame you had to give up all your weapons when you arrived."

She made a scornful noise. "Says who?" She didn't glance down. She knew the drawer was still open; she knew it held a thick sheaf of papers. Her fingers rested on them. Not your conventional weapon…

Then again, not your conventional situation. And while taking down Tafiq Ashurbeyli might be the perfect antidote to this crisis, right now she'd settle for getting out of this room unscathed—and unimprisoned.

He tossed the adaptor aside, a dismissive motion. "You have been valiant. I understand the desire to fight for your people—it is, after all, why *I'm* here—but you can accomplish nothing more. Come with me. Join the others. We will not take retribution for those things you have done…until now."

In other words, if she made him work for it, their next encounter wouldn't be quite so civilized. She looked him in the eye, her voice lowering. "I'll make you the same offer. You'll accomplish nothing here, no matter how many people you kill. Release the hostages. Come with me. I'll make sure you're not killed before you make it to the bottom of those same steps you covered with bin Kuwaji's brains."

"Ah. You saw that, then." He nodded at the flat-panel television.

"I saw," she said flatly. "I wasn't impressed. If you're worth anything, it's only that you're worth stopping."

He laughed. He laughed, and she snatched the moment. She whipped the thick stack of paper at him edgewise; the pages separated and fluttered at him like manic birds on the attack. He flung up an arm to protect his face, off balance, and Selena dived beneath the line of his gun, rolling to come just beside him, snapping her leg around behind his knee.

Tafiq Ashurbeyli, Kemeni rebel leader, went sprawling. His gun skittered across the floor; he hit hard, grunting with the impact. The gun didn't go far, not on the thick carpet. Papers settled around them, their susurrus the only sound in the room.

Both of them lay stretched out on the carpet; neither could reach the other. In that instant, they froze in place, hesitating in an uncanny moment of locked gazes—of mutual respect, equal determination and the acknowledgment of an enemy worth fighting.

But not for long. Selena's gaze flicked to the gun and

back to Ashurbeyli; it didn't take a genius to see who was closer to the weapon and who would reach it first. *He would.* Selena scrambled to her feet as Ashurbeyli scrambled for the pistol, both of them slipping on loose papers, and she glanced over her shoulder just long enough to see him bringing the weapon to bear as she ducked around the door.

She thought he'd been smiling.

Chapter 8

Now it's personal. Now he knew her face, and she knew his. Now each knew the mettle of the other. There was no going back from that...no changing it.

And it changed everything.

Except for what Selena did next: she hid. She crawled into the best hole she could imagine and, with the patience of a big cat stalking prey, she lay low. She nursed her rug burns, considered the apparently quiescent state of her stomach and floundered back and forth about the cause of its former rebellion. *Pregnant? Bad food choice? Pregnant...?* That quickly took her nowhere and she flushed the inner debate to instead contemplate what she knew of the capitol's layout. Maintenance closets, kitchen supplies, laundry...

Escape.

No, not yet. After bin Kuwaji's death, the hostages

were in more peril than ever. Not so long ago, not so far away, the Russians had gassed a theater full of innocents in pursuit of terrorists. Selena knew the mood of Berzhaan's leadership…their need to take a stand. She was the only wild card factor standing between these innocents and another hostage disaster.

She turned her attention back to the situation at hand. The basement laundry was particularly easy to contemplate, surrounding her as it did. Silent machines with their round glass doors and mounds of partially processed sheets and tablecloths stood guard as she stretched out on a sturdy shelf behind stacks of freshly cleaned towels. Washcloths at this end, bath towels at the other, bound for the fanciest of the bathrooms and the abruptly unoccupied guest rooms. Should she be discovered, Selena was perfectly positioned to bring this tall set of heavy-duty shelves down on whoever found her—but only one rebel had come to look, and his eyes didn't even hesitate on her.

So she relaxed, quiet and darned near to comfortable, pleased with the amount of space she had to herself. *Cole would fit here, too.* Right here. Right up against her, where he'd no doubt nibble her ear and clamp his hands firmly on her bottom and pull her close. Very close. Very…*ohsoright.*

She closed her eyes, adding in a big sigh. Tempting thoughts. Tempting to think about how well she and Cole suited one another in so many ways, now when she was forced to depend on him. It removed the doubts caused by that which he had no idea she'd seen. Him. The woman. The kissing. When he wasn't even supposed to be in the country, for God's sake.

Except that part didn't matter. She could trust him

to handle this situation. He'd make the right calls; he'd spread the information he had. And it was her job to keep feeding details to him. She had her cell phone; she hadn't wanted to use it because of the hinky satellite connections and the insecure nature of the beast—some poor confused city woman might get an earful through her baby monitor. She had no doubt it would go dead at the worst possible moment. Didn't they always?

So she wouldn't call for a while. Not until she had information worth calling for. Her laundry hideout wasn't it. Her generous collection of bleach didn't do it, either. Nor would the ammonia-based products she hoped to find in the maintenance closets, the mop decoys, fire extinguishers…not newsworthy goodies. But useful, oh yes.

For now she didn't plan to collect the material in a single spot. It'd be too obvious to anyone who saw it. But she'd bring it all within proximity of the kitchen.

In the kitchen, she planned to cook up trouble.

After forty-five minutes, the ruckus caused by her escape slowly faded. No more voices shouting along the hallways, no more running footsteps…they had enough to deal with, really, given the repercussions of bin Kuwaji's death. Posturing, imparting ultimatums, perhaps brandishing a second, less valuable hostage as a reminder for the looming security forces to keep their distance. The busy, busy day of international terrorists at work.

They probably wouldn't threaten Allori or Razidae just yet. Poor bin Kuwaji had been their sacrifice, just to show they meant business. Now they'd hold the other two back for more desperate moments.

Or so Selena thought. But Ashurbeyli was canny—canny enough to have escaped being photographed all these years. Canny enough to get into this high-security building and take out that security while rounding up hostages. So she wouldn't underestimate him. She'd just…

Guess.

Reassuring. She slipped down from the shelf, inspected her chosen gallons of bleach and made sure the lids to each moved freely. Good enough. She very much hoped to find ammonia in the maintenance closets, and from those two alone she could manufacture several types of mayhem. But she wasn't ready to leave evidence of her plotting just yet, so she left the bleach where it was.

She knew where to find it.

The basement also yielded a lovely maintenance area. The cordless drill held promise, but someone hadn't charged the battery pack. Selena plugged the thing in; it might yet be useful. Metal shelves, their lower legs rusting slightly on the clammy, unpainted concrete floor, held a variety of paints and shellacs. Selena acquired a hammer, hefting it lovingly. She tucked a pair of pliers away just on principle, and gathered several fire extinguishers for easy retrieval. A number of them already waited in the kitchen, but one could never have too many fire extinguishers. She hauled one along with her, and on her way past the kitchen collected a chunk of dry ice from a special storage freezer, dropping it into a towel sling along with the nearly empty giant mayo jar she'd put it in.

Selena moved past the first floor quickly, for the terrorists were most active here. On the third floor she raided a cleaning closet for ammonia and crept back down to the basement to store it with her bleach, tucking it thoughtfully away under a pile of dirty towels. She quietly sacked a few guest rooms and came away with a planter full of decorative marbles.

Sometimes the old tricks were still the best.

After stashing her remaining goods in the guest room she'd chosen, she spent some quiet time on each floor— observing the terrorist activity, confirming that they did only occasional sweeps through the upper floors, concentrating their firepower on the first floor. She heard a pair of men tromping up the stairs to the roof, and a moment later a second pair coming back down, relaxed and chattering about how the various women they'd used compared to the ones they hoped to marry.

So. They were watching the roof. She would expect no less from the man she'd encountered in Razidae's office. He probably had at least one other pair of men up there, their watch schedule staggered with the ones who'd just changed shifts.

But for those floors between top and bottom... Selena had the impression those sweeps were just for her. They lacked urgency but the Kemenis seemed to be looking *for* something—someone—as opposed to simply walking their rounds.

They didn't find her.

At least, not until she ventured back into the kitchen area.

There, a little rummaging in a back corner netted her a huge can of oven cleaner, and she was beginning to feel downright well equipped, and ready to check on Atif in the freezer. But she'd set her hammer down to do the rummaging, and when she looked up from the list of warnings and ingredients on the can, it was to discover a young man in dark olive and tan stopping short in shocked recognition of whom he'd encountered.

It could have been all over right then. The man—and young he was, barely any older than the college students he helped hold hostage—could have and should have shouted for help. He could have and should have shot Selena as she slowly rose to her feet. *Hammer out of reach. Distinctive Abakan rifle pointed this way. Best chance...fake it.*

She gave him the slightest of shrugs, and a feeble sort of oh-well-you-caught-me smile, all the while thinking of the Abakans, and how so many of the Kemenis had what the Russians used only as an elite troops rifle—a rifle that was widely considered user-unfriendly, and effective only in the hands of an expert. The pistol grip was uncomfortable, the angle of the magazine awkward, and the operation of the thing was far from intuitive.

She doubted the young man before her truly knew how to use it—how to accommodate its odd recoil characteristics, especially when in two-round-burst mode. On the other hand, she didn't really want to find out. Not at point-blank range, and not when even a wide miss would draw the attention of every other Kemeni in the building. So she gave him the smile, and when he hesitated, she said clearly in his own language, "Please don't shoot."

He absorbed her use of his language easily. He might have even been prepared for it. He lifted his chin, looked down along his nose at her as though he just might possibly be taller than she was—wishful thinking, at that—and said, "Ashurbeyli wants you."

"I'll just bet he does." He'd probably expected her to be flushed out in that first forty-five minutes of intensive searching—as much as he'd seen of her already, he probably still hadn't thought she'd be able to hole up and hold her ground without breaking like a frightened rabbit the first time someone stomped into her hiding place and glared around. Now…every hour that passed, his resentment of her would build—because the longer it took to get her, the more obvious her challenge of him. Woman to man. Immodest Western woman to self-appointed manlier-than-thou terrorist leader.

The look on the young man's face changed, becoming what he probably thought to be canny. "Alive, he said. But nothing more." He eyed her from head to toe, a clumsy parody of the way Ashurbeyli had assessed her.

Selena refrained from rolling her eyes. So it had occurred to him that he could now taste a Western woman. It wouldn't even count as brutality, because Selena herself had already been tainted and exposed by her bold and unacceptable ways. What an astonishing and unexpected development that this should enter his mind.

Looking at the way his pants scrunched up under the belt high on his waist and the rolled cuffs at the bottom, she thought she might be able to wear them. But the shirt was a better bet, oversize enough so that although she and the young man had about the same shoulders, there should be plenty of room for her breasts. And it was the olive-green color she coveted…after all, she'd need to ditch this coat soon. No doubt every one of them knew to look for it.

He frowned, an exaggerated scrunch of brow. He

sensed her mind was elsewhere…and couldn't fathom it. Selena ever-so-subtly lifted her chest, letting her breasts push against the fine fabric of her black turtleneck.

He took a step forward. He probably didn't even realize it. His too-big pants bloomed with the evidence of his intent, and he probably realized *that* with much acuity.

Overconfidence. A wonderful thing. She let herself look trapped. She let herself look frightened, and took advantage of the chance to make her chest heave with her panicked breath. He'd quit watching her face at all. He took another step, and the Abakan's muzzle with its oddly shaped self-cleaning muzzle brake drifted away from Selena.

She still didn't want the rifle to go off. But she wouldn't mind quite as much if it did.

As he hesitated on the verge of the step that would put him within range, she put deliberate revulsion into her voice. "You have no right to touch me."

His expression flickered into empowered outrage. "You are in *my* country! You play your political games with *my* people! You should have stayed where you belonged!" He took those last few steps in a rush, eager with assumed victory.

Selena dropped into a balanced crouch, thrusting the oven cleaner in his face and spraying with steady aim. By the time she hit the crouch, his victory had turned to boyish cries of pain. *Only a youngster, at that.* It wasn't hard to take him down, levering him around her hip as she bounced back up to her feet.

He landed hard, air knocked from his lungs with a grunt, cries of warning silenced—at least, until he caught his breath. She wrenched his rifle away and tossed it aside, and as the air whooped back into his lungs he rolled in pain, his hands clamped over the lye-infested chemicals she'd sprayed in his eyes, Selena targeted the nearest sink. She'd rinse his eyes, bundle him up, and stick him in—

Out of the corner of her eye she saw movement, and she had only enough time to think how stupid she'd been, that she should have been prepared for a second Kemeni. This one was bigger, heavier and wasted no time—he slammed into her hard, knocking her back against the gleaming tile wall. She groped for her pocket as he literally picked her up off her feet and flung her against the wall again. Her vision turned to sparks and darkness, and still she hunted her pocket. He backhanded her, knocking her aside; she crumpled to the floor.

But she found the pocket. And as he lifted her up to start all over again, she pulled the ice pick free and jammed it into his ribs, aiming for the heart.

He grunted when the wooden knob hit his ribs and twitched off the blow to shove her back against the wall, one hand pulling back to hit her again.

Die, dammit!

Incredulous, Selena withdrew the ice pick to try again, but suddenly understood—he was a big man, a huge man, and even if she'd hit his heart, even if she'd holed his lungs…the holes were very small indeed. He could do plenty of damage before keeling over, and he might well cause enough ruckus to bring others—and enough damage to Selena that she could no longer continue this self-appointed mission.

With a snarl, she took his next blow, another to her

already burning cheek and brow. This time she rolled with it, though it stunned her all the same.

She drove the ice pick home at the base of his skull.

He stiffened. Selena squirmed, still trapped, her vision prickling back to show her the stunned astonishment on his face and the already dead look in his eyes. She wiggled the ice pick around just to be sure. He spasmed and went utterly limp, collapsing so suddenly she had no chance to find her feet; she went down with him. But she bounced back up, staggering and mad about it. *Shake it off.*

When she had her balance she stood over him and glared down. "You really shouldn't have pithed me off."

The young Kemeni's groan came right on cue, but before she dealt with him, Selena yanked the rifle away from the dead terrorist and went to the double swinging doors, glancing out the small windows. She saw no one. Maybe she'd gotten lucky…but she wouldn't count on it. She wouldn't dawdle. She hauled the unresisting boy to the kitchen sink and shoved his head under cold running water. He quickly realized the benefit of it and stayed there on his own while she grabbed a kitchen towel and soaked it. When she pulled him away from the sink and aimed him at the cooler, she stuffed the towel into his hands and said, "Keep that over your eyes."

He readily complied. Definitely one whipped terrorist. Not that Selena blamed him…she didn't know if he'd taken corneal damage from the lye in the oven cleaner, or even if he'd inhaled the fumes, soon to choke on the fluids of his damaged lungs. But while she'd offer him what ease she could, she couldn't make herself be sorry. Not when she remembered the look in his eyes as he attacked her. Not when she had reason to wonder how many people he'd slaughtered in this one day alone.

Now he was out of that game.

She pulled the cooler door open with some caution—and a good thing, too, because Atif met her with a steadily aimed rifle. He quickly lowered it. "I was hoping that was you. You've been busy, I see."

"Exercise keeps one young," Selena told him. She prodded her captive into place beside the man already so carefully bound in plastic wrap, and proceeded to restrain his ankles and wrists—except she left his hands in front of him so he could hold the towel to his distinctly reddened face. Just for a moment she pulled it away; he looked at her through the slits of his swollen eyelids and she doubted he could actually see her. "If you cause trouble, any trouble at all, you lose the towel and I truss you up like a roast lamb. You got it?"

In testament to his misery, he only nodded.

When she returned to the kitchen, she checked the double doors again, found them still clear and dragged the dead terrorist's bulk into the cooler, leaving him well to the side of Atif's decently covered friends. He nodded firmly at that arrangement, and then again at her face. "Are you hurt?"

"Just my feelings." Selena ran careful fingers over her cheek and the edge of her brow line, finding puffy, hot skin and a trickle of blood. The hefty one must have been wearing a ring. Jerk. "They made me feel downright unwelcome."

Atif snorted. "And have you brought more weapons?"

"Let's just see." She pulled the bolt back on the first

rifle, found it sticky, and took a much closer look. "We're *both* lucky you didn't pull the trigger on this one, kid. They didn't give you much training on this thing, did they?" She wasn't expecting an answer; she didn't get one. She pulled the magazine out of place and handed it to Atif, then pulled the oval pin on the side of the stock to release the joint there and folded the stock back on itself. Storage and transport configuration— and in this case, a signal that the weapon wasn't to be used, at least not until it was thoroughly cleaned. She set it aside to inspect the second weapon, which proved to be in much better shape. "There we go," she murmured. Not much in the way of ammo, but she had an idea just how she'd use it.

Atif watched as she took a moment to remove the shirt from the dead terrorist, doffing her coat and pulling the shirt on over her turtleneck. "Lemon juice," he advised as she pulled the shirt out to inspect the blood dot she herself had created. Amazingly small…all the bleeding had been internal.

"If they're close enough to wonder about it, they're already too close." The olive-green shirt over her khaki cargo pants would merely allow her to draw less attention at a distance. They presented a color combination the terrorists were well trained to see as friendly—at least until they noticed her hair and the fact that she sported breasts. This particular shirt went a long way to hide those pesky giveaways, as ill-fitting as it was.

She would have cleaned up the mess in the kitchen, but the terrorists had already created plenty of their own blood trails and her own efforts barely added to them. So she left it alone, and rummaged in the cooler for things she'd seen here earlier. Butcher twine, very nice. Candle stubs and matches she'd find in the entrance to the service corridor.

"May I ask," Atif said, clearly prepared to ask regardless, "your intent? You are just one woman. They are many men. You cannot defeat them all."

Selena tucked away the twine in a thigh pocket, and yanked the ice pick free of the dead terrorist, squinching her face up in matter-of-fact distaste. *Stay strong, stomach of mine.* She cleaned the pick and threaded it between her belt and her hip. "You're right. I can't defeat them all. I'm not sure that's my job."

"Then—?"

"Keep them off balance. Keep them distracted from the hostages. Make it personal to Ashurbeyli, so he loses perspective." *Check. Been there, did that.* "Make them think I *am* important, so they're caught off guard when the real rescue comes along." And there'd better *be* a real rescue. She had to count on Cole…had to believe he'd see to it, whatever he had to do. Meanwhile… she looked around the room, from the dead Kemenis to the live ones. "Three down. And the rest to go."

Chapter 9

The condo closed in around Cole. It surrounded him with *Selena,* with her belongings and her style and even her scent. And with UBC muted, it surrounded him with memories of her voice on the phone. He wasn't used to the uncertainty he'd heard from her only hours earlier—uncertainty that underscored the problem between them.

He'd been on assignment; he'd come back. Somewhere in between, something had hit her hard.

He just needed the time to find out what. The chance.

He understood her request that they use the hardwired phone—it didn't crackle with static, nor drop every other syllable in a whimsical verbal word game. They wouldn't be overheard by those baby monitors—or by the various intelligence communities of the world. But if he only could leave—

What then, Jones?

Nothing, that's what. He'd called his office; he'd been shuffled all the way up to the deputy director himself. He'd passed along what he knew, the tidbits Selena had given him, and he'd been admonished to do the same with any further information she gave him. But what had he learned? Nothing. What had he gathered by way of reassurance that the CIA would immediately share this information to best benefit Selena? Nothing. And if there was one thing Cole had learned in his years of covert operations, it was that the various intelligence agencies jealously guarded their information. They talked a good game, and on some levels the situation had improved immensely—his recent assignment had proven that much—but cooperation was a boon, not the norm.

Call the State Department.

Yeah, he could do that. And they'd play the same games with him, and he'd still have no assurance they wouldn't lose Selena in the big picture.

He caught sight of Tory Patton, gesturing at the Berzhaan capitol building, her classically beautiful features tight with concern. The bottom of the screen held a scrolling tally of the damage and death tolls caused by the terrorist activity since it had kicked off in the village of Oguzka.

Go to the news station. Call UBC, spill everything he knew…dangle his inside source. That would light a fire under the CIA, the State Department and even the FBI. It would bring the troops circling around, forcing them to share intel…forcing them to act.

And he'd give it about thirty seconds before the CIA came and lit a fire under *him*. They'd haul him away for questioning, and he wouldn't be here to answer that phone at all.

Everyone else had their eyes on the student hostages, knowing that along with a tragedy, it'd be a publicity nightmare if those kids were hurt. They had their eyes on Razidae and Allori, both men that the region—and their countries—couldn't afford to lose. It was Cole's job to keep his eyes on Selena. To make things happen in a way that included *her* best interests. For neither the U.S. nor Berzhaan might realize it right now, but she was their best chance of coming out of this mess with survivors. She just needed the right kind of backup....

Cole paced behind the couch, down the hallway to the bedroom where her scent tortured him, a precise turn on his heel to stalk back to the living room where her beloved quilt squares reminded him of her well-hidden sentimentality. Complex, that was Selena. And every bit of her had called to him on that evening they'd met four years earlier—some state function he didn't even remember now, because all he could think of was the way she'd smiled at him and how he'd been so certain she'd had hidden fire under that cool, lean exterior.

He'd been right, too.

He realized he'd hesitated by the couch, that he ran his fingers along the cool leather. Not so long ago she'd stopped a similar pacing jag by pulling him right over the back of the couch and into her arms. He groaned at the thought, resting his forearms on the couch back and dropping his forehead between them. *Dammit!*

Go ahead. Torture yourself. Think about the way she'd been lurking under the comforter with her eyes closed and only a thin cotton camisole and sporty briefs covering freshly bathed skin. Think about the play of lean muscle covered with just enough padding to make her soft to the touch. Think about how she'd drawn him close and wrapped herself around him and whispered something about making babies he'd just barely had the remaining concentration to hear. Think about how she'd taken him so fast and hard that even now the memory dazed him.

Yeah, go ahead, do that. Get lost in it.

In how much you're afraid of losing her.

Slowly, he pounded his head against the couch. Not hard enough to do damage…but hard enough to interrupt himself. To try to get his thoughts back on a track that would do him—and Selena—some good.

When he looked up, there was Tory Patton.

Don't go to the news station.

Go to the reporter.

And go to her not as a reporter, but as a graduate of Athena Academy, and a former classmate of Selena's. For the Athena graduates didn't lose touch. They might go on to their individual achievements, but first and foremost, they were women of Athena.

And like Tory Patton, they had strings to pull. Influence to wield. And a noted track record for saving the day.

Selena crouched in the back stairwell, head tipped back. Thinking.

Unlike the posh main stairs in the front part of the building, this set was made of painted steel and concrete—and not recently painted steel at that. Tubular railings ubiquitous to stairwells everywhere, stained and worn texturized concrete…your standard ugliness.

Gunfire would echo magnificently.

She'd sacrifice the rifle, but it had little in the way of ammo—and like any soldier untrained in the use of this particular weapon, she found it unwieldy and a little counterintuitive. Not a combination she wanted to depend on in a tight spot. If things went right, she'd gain a few moments with the hostages—and maybe even an extra moment or two to cause inconvenience for the Kemenis.

That would be nice.

So yeah, she'd sacrifice the rifle.

But for now, she sat in the stairway, head tipped back, thinking. Making sure she had a clear idea of her purpose here. Given that she didn't intend to leave the embassy—an excursion that would no doubt be more dangerous than staying here—and that she didn't intend simply to hide in the basement, and that she'd already passed along what little she knew to Cole...then what could she hope to accomplish?

Free the hostages?

That, she knew, was thinking a little too positively. There were too many of them, too many Kemenis, and too few places to hide. The service corridor was a godsend, but the terrorists obviously already knew about it; she couldn't lurk there in safety or stash the hostages there, either.

Reassure the hostages.

A definite possibility, especially if things went to plan here in the stairwell. She didn't expect to draw anyone off their assigned post, but those who lingered in the ballroom...they were another story.

Nibble away at the edges of the terrorists. Another possibility. She'd already managed a few small bites. As long as she remained only an irritant, she didn't think

Ashurbeyli would divert too much effort to finding her. Why should he? He still had the control; he still had the hostages.

Stay alive. Now there was the question. She didn't think he'd have her killed outright, not at this point. No, he'd want to talk to her. Perhaps mistreat her. Make the point of his superiority, and salve the insults she'd already reaped on him—though she wasn't sure if he'd figured out the three men were missing. With all the rotating shifts and various patrol sweeps they were doing, it might well take time.

Stay alive. It hit her in an entirely different fashion. Not the analytical lawyer's approach to defining a problem, but the very personal, core reaction of a woman not ready to die. Not ready never to see the man she loved...or to learn if she'd be able to live the rest of her life with him. Or even to learn if her illness, her fatigue...if it had been more significant than a passing moment. Much more.

That fatigue washed over her again; she let it. A glance at her watch startled her and relieved her both. No wonder she was tired—she'd reached the far end of a long day in which she'd lost what little food she'd eaten. She'd started the day fighting terrorists, transformed herself back into her FBI legate persona, and now here she was facing terrorists again, disoriented by the lack of windows in the interior rooms and hallways in which she'd been spending time.

After this, she'd have to retreat to that laundry room and take more than a few moments' pensive rest. She'd have to grab real sleep. A few hours, that'd be all...and then she'd take to the prowl again, hoping to find the building quieter. Maybe even finding a moment to call

Cole—though after this she'd have to use her cell phone and chance being overheard. The phone lines were obviously not an option.

So. First step. Reassure the hostages. Second step... get something to eat. She'd need to check in with Atif in any event. Third step...a few hours' sleep.

Selena set the rifle on full automatic and leaned it against the railing halfway up the steps she'd chosen. Not only would the noise echo impressively from here, but she might even get lucky with a stray bullet if anyone from the roof came charging down in response. Quickly now—no telling when one of the Kemeni guard pairs might come through, and once she started work she'd be unable to dash away without leaving bits and pieces behind—she tied the rifle in place with butcher twine. A nice five-pound bag of dried beans hung beside it, and she used a second piece of twine to tie it to the trigger, leaving just enough slack so there was no tension between the two.

And then she set up the candle stubs, carefully positioned to burn through the twine holding up the bag. If everything went right—no drafts, no shifting—when the twine burned through, the rifle would discharge at least a handful of rounds before recoil broke the twine holding it in place.

If nothing went right, she'd give them a reason to hunt for her without gaining anything in return. That would suck.

Selena double-checked the setup, nudged the candles into better alignment and pulled the matches from the thigh pocket of her cargo khakis. The match flared to life against the worn concrete step, and once she touched it to the second candlewick, she hesitated only

long enough to see that the flame was a good height...
and then she ran. Down, down, down—ice pick in one
hand, hammer in the other, hoping she wouldn't run into
anyone but ready to leap if she did.

Sometimes luck ran her way.

She threw herself against the wall at the first-floor
exit just as the rifle discharged. A long, painful burst of
sound, far too distinct to be taken for anything but automatic rifle fire, far too loud to be missed.

Selena smiled, a wicked little smile that would have
raised Cole's eyebrows all the way to his hairline. Already she heard shouting, even through her ringing ears.
But as she pivoted around, reaching for the door bar, she
caught a glimpse of movement. She had time for nothing more than half a gasp as she flattened herself beside the hinges and then the door slammed open,
whipping back at her so she turned her face and sucked
in her breath, pressing the small of her back against the
cold concrete wall, turning her feet sideways—all to
make herself as thin as possible.

The door bar smacked into her hips, hard enough to
bruise but not hard enough to break. She snatched it, just
enough to make the door hesitate before starting to
swing close.

No one else came through. And those who had clattered swiftly up the stairs, leaped over the landing and
turned to continue upward.

Now she had time to curse. Silently but fervently, her
pulse knocking around her body with frighteningly
reckless speed. Too fast...not just adrenaline, but a tired
body desperately trying to rise to the challenge. She
knew herself...she knew she was pushing too hard.

No help for that.

She let the door close most of the way, caught it again and peeked out into the first floor, that back corner she'd come to know so well. Sound still came tinnily through her offended ears, but she didn't hear anyone else—just the growing ruckus up the stairwell. Selena took a deep breath and a big chance, and she ran for it. Down the side hall to the little false-backed closet, down the dimly lit corridor to the room that held the hostages. Nothing much had changed, aside from the establishment of one corner as a bathroom area— blocked with chairs, draped with tablecloths and as far from the people as they could make it. That, and it seemed to her that there'd been something shoved up against the other side of the wall. Blocking the servants' door?

She spied upon the table-filled ballroom beyond that, discovering that it held only one man. One disgruntled, impatient man who glared out the entrance closest to the main lobby—the closest set of stairs lay in that direction. With complete disregard for the history and the value of the building, he vented his anger by repeatedly stabbing an oversize survival knife into the wallpaper-covered plaster. Left behind and soooo unhappy.

Good. Because he wasn't paying any attention at all to the hostages.

Selena backed off, slipping out into the private function room where she'd not so long ago clocked her first Kemeni conquest on the noggin and dragged him away. She didn't want to startle them by appearing out of nowhere—distracted or not, the guard in the ballroom would hear such a reaction. He'd definitely hear it if she had to shove aside a table to get there. Then, too, the fewer people who knew about that passage, the better.

Surely Prime Minister Razidae knew of it, as well as the events coordinator, but the others…if they learned of it, they might be tempted to try for doomed escape.

No, if they were going to escape, Selena wanted to be in on it. But she didn't think escape was their best option, not just yet. Not until she'd picked off a few more terrorists; not until she'd heard more from Cole. If he could help her arrange a diversion from the outside…

For now, she'd settle for talking to them. Letting them know they weren't alone.

Selena checked the hall, ducked into it long enough to reach the hostage room entrance and hesitated there the mere instant it took to confirm the hostages were still alone.

She entered the room with a finger already to her lips, a plea for silence.

They froze, expecting any arrival to be Kemeni—and then Allori jumped to his feet, his astonishment turning instantly to concern. "Selena!"

He'd kept his voice to a whisper, but it acted as a release for the others; their voices tumbled over one another, low exclamations of surprise and pleas for help that accumulated to significance. Selena glared a warning, putting a demanding hand out to hush them, ready to run right out on them if she had to.

"Silence!" bellowed the guard in Berzhaani, and even the students understood the intent of it.

Allori, bless his heart, stood where he could look into the ballroom, and he gave Selena the slightest shake of his head. No, the guard wasn't actually coming this way. Not yet. She kept her hand raised, her expression full of warning, and then when they stood, silent and hesitating on her next move, she pointed at the college student with the steadiest demeanor and directed him with a gesture: *watch the guard through the door.*

He wasn't the most mature of them; he even looked to be the youngest, still short and slight, his need to shave still questionable and his chin too weak ever to truly firm up. But though he might have paled a little, he didn't hesitate. He put himself in line of sight of the guard and sat in the closest chair, and then he gave her the same slight nod Allori had given the moment before.

Selena nodded back, and then she gestured the others closer, a finger still on her lips.

The bold young man from the lobby was the first to speak up, though he remembered to keep it low. His girlfriend stood close beside him, a tentative hand at his arm. "I saw you in the lobby."

"And I saw you." Selena looked them over, found none of them injured, all of them scared. "Have they allowed you to talk?"

Razidae said, "Yes. At about this level. We should be all right unless something alerts them."

Allori got right to the point. "What's your situation? What can you tell us?"

"They know I'm in the building." Selena gave her sore face a rueful touch. "Tafiq and I...well, it's personal now, Dante. I don't honestly know how much longer I can evade them. But I'll do what I can, while I can. I'm in touch with Cole."

Who's Cole? The question stood loud on everyone's face except Allori's—and Razidae's, who knew it didn't matter, so long as Cole represented help. "I've briefed him on the situation on the inside. He'll keep an eye on our best interests. The important thing—the reason I risked exposing myself here—is that you should all know you're not alone. I'm here, and I'm working to get you out. Berzhaan and the States are working on getting you out." Probably not together, not to judge by Selena's own initial reception here in Berzhaan. "Be patient."

"What about that man they took?" The girlfriend, so close to Selena, looked her straight in the eye. "He was important, wasn't he? What happened to him?"

"Amar bin Kuwaji," Razidae said softly. "Yes, he's my deputy prime minister. *Was* my deputy, I should think."

Selena met his gaze and nodded. "I'm sorry."

"They used him to prove their intent?" Allori asked, immune to the little gasps of dismay around them. He didn't wait for Selena's confirmation before giving a little nod. "Yes, they would have. Eventually, another of us will be used the same."

"Not if I can help it." But Selena felt with keen guilt her inability to save bin Kuwaji, and her words reflected more determination than expectation.

The petite events coordinator caught her gaze. "You came through the hall. Do you know about—"

Selena nodded sharply, cutting her off. "It was the best choice. They know about the other, as you've probably guessed." The students didn't, to judge by their expressions. Imagine that, the Kemenis had been discreet as they'd blocked the wall. She came down on her next words hard. "And you should all *wait here until I say otherwise.*" After that she looked deliberately from one student to another, waiting for acknowledgment by each. The two businesswomen were quick to comply.

Razidae took longer. Long enough that she said, "Please, sir. Trust me. You know as well as I the mood of these people. They're desperate—and they're being guided by Jonas White."

"I've heard of him." Razidae ran a finger across his thick mustache. "If I'd known he was anywhere near Berzhaan—"

"None of us knew. And I'm still not sure what he's up to. But if he's behind this, he's put the Kemenis into a desperate situation—a last stand. Provoking them is the last thing any of us can afford. If things go badly, they have nothing to lose."

Allori glanced toward the ballroom. "I must agree, Mr. Prime Minister. If we act—*when* we act—it must be a coordinated effort. Selena is the only one of us in a position to represent our best interests to the outside world. We need to do everything we can to preserve her ability to do so."

Razidae grunted, eyeing Selena. "Then you shouldn't have come here."

"I had to." She shrugged. "Tell me you weren't already plotting the best way to slip some of you out. It would have tipped the Kemenis into action—I had to let you know I was here."

A sturdy girl with skin the color of a sleek brown seal and scarf-hidden hair pushed her way toward Selena. Scared, like all of them. But still thinking. "And who *are* you?"

Selena regarded her in return, and offered up a slow smile. "I'm a Kemeni collector," she said. "And I'm in the right place at the right time."

At that she got a few tentative smiles. Good. She'd done what she'd come for.

"This has to be off the record." Cole held the cell phone tightly, too tightly, and paced the length of the apartment. The flicker of the television provided the only light, inconsistent and often disconcerting.

Tory Patton laughed, light amusement that came short enough to reflect the nature of her current story. "That's what they all say."

But then, she didn't know much of Cole. None of the Athena alumnae did; he was too often gone, too often buried in secrecy. Tory had no reason to leap to compliance at a phone call from Cole. Not as UBC's star reporter, and not as the graduate of a school that taught its students to think for themselves.

"Listen." He stopped, cleared his throat to remove the growl and tried again. "Listen. I didn't dig up your private number on a whim. I need help, but it's got to be off the record."

"So that's two favors just to start." She wasn't making it easy.

Then again, he hadn't expected her to. He hadn't yet invoked Selena's name, and he wouldn't do it until he knew for certain he wouldn't compromise her. Tory had to suspect this call was about Selena, but she wouldn't take it for granted. For all she knew, Cole was at work a single border away, and not calling from D.C. at all. "Do it," he said. "Hear me out. You've got nothing to lose. Not even air time—they've gone to commercial." Silence hesitated between them, and he knew he was doing this wrong. Desperately, he added, *"Please."*

Another moment of expensive international silence. "I've got another fifteen minutes before my next spot," she said, and he could hear her stretch, completely at ease with her situation at the edge of hostilities. "You can have a couple of them. Off the record."

He didn't bother with introductory details. She knew them; she was *reporting* them. "Selena's in there."

This time the silence turned electric. He wished the camera was still on her, that he could read her reactions across the miles. Finally she swore, so softly he barely heard. "I was afraid of that. I wasn't able to reach her at the embassy, and now they've closed up shop. No one's been willing to confirm, though—they figure the Kemenis can watch the news as well as anyone, and they don't know if everyone in the building was rounded up. You know for certain?"

"I've talked to her. We were on the phone when they killed bin Kuwaji."

"That's pretty certain."

"Unfortunately, we were cut off. I'm waiting for her call. I damn well wish it'd come by now."

"I hear you there," she said. "She have any intel?"

"Some. Going for more. I've passed it along, and I've been patted on the head and told to wait like a good little husband. No one's talking to me—not even my own people. I have no idea if the agencies are sharing, or who's planning to take action...or if they're keeping her welfare in mind at all. Here's the thing, Tory—I want someone in on this who *will* keep her in mind."

"I hear you there, too. But I'm still waiting to hear why you called me."

Cole couldn't help it; he snorted. "Because I know you can help. You know it, too. You think Selena hasn't told me about the Cassandras? I know she wasn't one of them, but she was still Athena, and you're wasting time by making me spell it out. You've got connections, and Selena needs them. You've got someone by President Monihan's side, for God's sake."

"Yes," Tory mused. "I guess we do. And I'm sorry. I did want you to spell it out. I'm not in the habit of tak-

ing anything for granted. And of course I'll do everything I can to help. In fact…"

After another moment's silence, Cole couldn't stand
it anymore. All his cool under fire, gone. All his seat-
of-the-pants success, useless. This one wasn't up to
him.

At least, not alone.

So he broke the silence with his impatience.
"What?"

"Mmm," she said. "Not on this phone. We've said
enough, I think. Can you get out here?"

"Yes," he said instantly. He had no idea how, but he
had enough of his own favors to call in—he wouldn't
wait for a commercial flight. "I'm at liberty." Not
strictly true, but he didn't much care. "I'll be there."

A twelve-hour flight he had yet to snag. But he repeated himself. "I'll be there. I'll call you."

But he didn't know whether he'd be there in time. If
Berzhaan grew impatient, if the Kemenis lost their temper, if Jonas White meddled once too often…

Hold on, Selena. Just hold on.

Chapter 10

Selena hesitated in the servants' corridor, crouching behind the black curtain, hammer and ice pick in hand. Listening.

Hard to hear anything over her stomach growling. Not that she trusted its hunger; for all she knew it would turn on her as soon as she fed it.

Still. She needed food to stay on top of her game, so food it was. And she'd spent enough time with the hostages that those Kemenis she'd diverted from their ballroom ease were probably trickling back down to this floor. They'd be mad, no doubt about it.

Tafiq would know just who had set up the rifle. He just wouldn't know why.

He'd want to know why.

He'd have his people scour the capitol, hunting for signs of her presence, signs of that from which she'd diverted them. He wouldn't find anything—but only because she hadn't actually put any of her half-formed plans into play. She needed to talk to Cole first.

She needed rest.

She peeked out into the supply closet. No sound of searching. Did he realize he'd already lost several men to her? She'd be surprised if they were that well organized—a place for every terrorist and every terrorist in his place.

God, woman. You really do need sleep. How long ago had this day started, anyway?

She edged up to the door. Heard nothing.

Last week. This day started last week sometime. Last year, maybe. And if she let herself slow down now, she'd lose her edge. She couldn't allow herself to slow until she was ready to crash. Nice, safe laundry room. A few hours. That's all, just a few hours.

Selena slowly turned the latch, nudged the door open. Only silence. She opened the door another inch, just enough to peer out, not really enough to see anything, her hand still resting loosely on the latch—

The door jerked forward, out of her grasp. Without its support Selena fell, and she turned it into a roll, the hall a blur of olive and khaki all around her. Shouts erupted; hands landed on her, pinching and pulling and grabbing—

But not shooting.

Alive. They want me alive for now.

She wouldn't make it easy for them. She squirmed, striking out with her feet, lashing out with both the hammer and the ice pick; the aggressive shouts changed to pain and alarm. Still they came at her. She found her way to her knees. Someone snatched her hair; she lost the ice pick in his arm. She surged to her feet, now thinking only about staying alive and escape and the exit beyond the blood-smeared kitchen floor. Escaped, she wouldn't do the hostages any more good...

Can't do them any good in Tafiq's hands, either.

She went for it. She wielded the hammer like an old war ax and kept them at bay—were there only three of them?—and when she spotted an opening she went for it, pure fullback style.

And then suddenly she slammed into the wall. The hammer fell to the floor from her numbed arm and she looked up, bewildered and somewhat betrayed, to discover a fourth man holding his Abakan by the muzzle. He'd not been allowed to shoot her but he'd found a way to use the rifle on her nonetheless, and now suddenly her arm began to hurt, a deep, hot throb that told her just how hard he'd hit her.

Another figure stepped into the suddenly quiet tableau, a stained hallway full of panting combatants and their wounded prey, finally brought to stand. *Great. Just what I need.* Tafiq Ashurbeyli, only moderately more ruffled than the last time she'd seen him. Still fully in command of the situation. Of himself.

And now of her.

Ashurbeyli spoke into a quiet punctuated only by the heavy breathing of his men and Selena's own gasps, as much in pain as for air. "You should have run when you had the chance."

"Probably," she said. She didn't shrug, because it would have meant moving her arm. At least it was the right arm...at least she was left-handed. "Gave you a chance to find a decent use for those silly Abakans. Damn, you didn't have to hit me that hard!"

Ashurbeyli looked around at his battered men, at the blood splattering the walls from one of her particularly good hammer blows. Someone lay on the floor behind him, moaning in pain. "I think we did. Yes, you should have run. But I consider it our good luck that you didn't."

"More than *luck* that you were waiting for me here." She tested her ability to make a fist, found it distinctly wanting. Otherwise she remained still. Nonthreatening. Giving them no reason to hit her again.

Though she was excruciatingly aware that they weren't likely to need a reason.

Ashurbeyli merely smiled. Handsome…*beyond* handsome, with the sheer charisma of his presence. But predatory, oh, yes. And far too knowing. "Perhaps it was." He gestured at his men with paired fingers, and two of them stepped forward, hovering in overeager readiness as Ashurbeyli stepped in and gestured that she should raise her arms and submit to a search.

Resigned, she did just that. More or less, since her right arm had no intention of functioning just yet. The novelty of being searched by men had worn off long ago, and she barely paid attention other than to note Ashurbeyli was just as thorough as he needed to be, hands following her every curve—but he didn't linger, didn't take advantage. He retrieved the paring knife from her belt and the pens and Buck knife from their most recent cache in her back pocket, handing them off to a third Kemeni who stepped forward just at the right moment.

They worship him.

That would make it harder. Foot soldiers who *believed*…foot soldiers who were dedicated to both their leader and their cause.

She wouldn't waste her time exploring potential rifts between them. She'd give him the respect they felt he deserved, and now and then they might just see her as a person instead of a blank-faced Enemy Barbie.

It wouldn't be hard. He was a man who commanded respect.

He stepped back, having discovered everything worth taking, his hand hesitating only once—on the lower curve of her left breast, where the tiny blood dot from the ice pick interrupted the olive-green of her borrowed shirt. He met her gaze long enough so she knew they'd talk about it later, and then stepped back. "Take her to the ballroom. Don't harm her further unless she gives you reason—but I don't think you'll do that, will you?"

This time Selena did shrug. It was a painful facade of movement, hiding her fear and awareness. She'd be blind in the ballroom, unable to call Cole, unable to feed him information…unable to keep the hostages out of the line of friendly fire.

And mostly unable to hear the reassurance of his voice, the voice of a man who spent his time successfully doing exactly what Selena had just failed to accomplish. Seat of the pants. Casual, confident, ops-on-the-fly. What she wouldn't give to hear that voice right this moment, breaking up this little party and turning it into his own.

Damn. I'm in trouble. But she wasn't quite ready to admit—even to herself—that she was scared. So she shrugged again. "I'll be good," she said. "This time."

Ashurbeyli shook his head, a sharp, short motion. "It's too late to think beyond that," he said. "Your fate, I'm afraid, is thoroughly sealed."

She glared back at him, glad for the arrogance that had sparked her back into anger. "That makes two of us, buddy."

He might have hit her. One step and he could have smacked her head back against the wall. For a moment, she thought he would. And then, oddly, he inclined his head ever so slightly in her direction and then strode away.

She had to admit, they could have been nastier about that walk to the ballroom. Perfect opportunity to snatch her arm and yank her around, and she didn't think she'd stay on her feet if that happened. But one of them aimed his rifle at her midsection in a most casual manner while the other, the bigger of the two, clamped a hand at the back of her neck and guided her to the long hallway that paralleled her recently abandoned false corridor.

She tried to shake the impression he could pick her up like a puppy and snap her neck. She tried to forget him altogether. If it had only been the two of them, she'd have found the right moment to make a break for it. The closer they came to the lobby, the better her chances of diving out that door to freedom, even if it meant rolling right down all those stairs.

But it wasn't just the two of them. The entire ballroom contingent followed, and only two of them broke away to continue whatever guard duty they'd been about before she distracted them. And handcuffs…there were handcuffs, of course.

So Selena walked unresisting, arm throbbing, taking in the details of the men and their reactions to one another and to her, and all the time wondering how they'd been so ready for her.

You took too long with the hostages, that's how.

Maybe. They'd had time to disarm her little distraction, to search the area and realize it was nothing more than a distraction. They'd had time to trickle back to the ballroom, or to rush to all the potential exits on this floor and make sure no one was on the way out—or in. But to be waiting for her in silent ambush, at just the right spot? It's not as if she'd left muddy tracks to follow or even a handy little blood trail.

They took her to the main ballroom entrance just off the lobby, offering her a tantalizing glimpse of freedom—the ornate capitol doors with their hidden armor and the bright-as-day grounds, halogen lights shining through the tall, narrow windows fronting the lobby. An unexpected inner voice full of primordial fear shrieked *run! runrunrun!* She stiffened enough to draw her escorts' attention…and she didn't run.

At the moment, she was still alive. Still had the opportunity to work the situation. The chance to do some good.

Running would end all that. Ashurbeyli might want her alive, but the Kemenis would never let her near those armor-core doors.

They pushed her into the ballroom and shoved her in a posh padded chair in the haphazard group of chairs and tables that had been shoved aside to make way for pallets and blankets. On the way she got a glimpse through the open door to the next function room, and she caught the shocked reaction of one of the students. *Don't give me away!* she thought fiercely, although it hardly mattered now if the Kemenis knew she'd spoken to them.

Just instinct.

They left her to her own company and took up already established positions around the room. She didn't mistake their casual ease to mean they'd stopped paying attention to her. A quick count tallied one rifle and three automatics pointing in her general direction. She sighed, slumped in the chair with every appearance of resignation and tried to consider her options. Not that she had any. And not that she could think in the first place, given the throb of her arm and her general disgust with the situation. She flexed the arm, testing… pushing.

It bent. Barely, but fingers, hand and arm all moved at her command. Not broken, then. Not terribly useful, but no jaggedy edged bones messing with nerve and blood vessel. She wouldn't bleed to death internally without even knowing it. She'd just hurt a lot. Even through the layers of her turtleneck and borrowed shirt, her hand hovering over her biceps could feel the heat of the swelling.

Her stomach growled.

Knowing Berzhaani would never serve her better. "Hey," she said. "You fellows have anything to eat?"

They froze in group disbelief that she'd asked.

"Look," she said, "Tafiq might well decide to starve me, but then again maybe not. He might actually want to talk to me, in which case it would be good if I wasn't too faint from hunger to speak respectfully to him."

She didn't think they'd go for it. She thought she might as well put her head down on the closest table and catch some sleep while she could. She looked across the long, narrow room with a gaze so tired as to be entirely neutral. Most of them had camped out on the padded carpet of the raised section spanning the front of the room. A long table snugged up against the back wall, shoved there and now covered with supplies, including a stack of black hand-held controls of some sort and a pile of sturdy travel cases meant for electronics jarringly adjacent to prayer rugs. The cases left her puzzled, but the rest of it only reinforced her first impression—that they'd come prepared for the long haul.

At least, they'd come prepared with supplies. Looking at the faces of the men sprawled in chairs and on the floor, Selena wasn't sure they'd also come prepared for the emotional drain of holding the entire building hostage. Only eight hours in, and already she saw signs of strain and tension. How would they feel after a few sessions of Salat in this far-from-holy place—or worse yet, a few *missed* sessions? And sooner or later they'd realize the futility of this take-over. They'd get tired and careless and they'd leave an opening for the forces hovering outside in wait for just such a moment.

Not what she'd normally expect of any crew run by Ashurbeyli—except that the Kemenis had been at the end of their collective rope before this had even started, their funding cut, their people hounded.

And where was Jonas White? Off rifling government offices? It wouldn't surprise her. Ashurbeyli defied the Berzhaani government openly and brazenly, taking what he wanted, while Jonas White hid behind false names and front men and slunk around gathering secrets to use against anyone he could.

She looked over at the men; they looked back at her. Oh, well. She sighed, put her head down on the table and prepared to go hungry. But one of the men cleared his throat and said, "There's that batch of bad MREs. They're not halal."

Another snorted. "Filth for filth."

Oh, yeah, Selena thought. *Bring on the filth.*

And the filth was good. The filth went down quite well. Selena made a series of reality checks, but at this point her stomach didn't seem inclined to object. Just a bad day after all? She patted her tummy low between her hip bones, once again tugged through the series of conflicting emotions that came with the thought of pregnancy. All the overwhelming *not nows,* somehow balanced by that tiny little hope that it might be true.

Because she did want a child. And she wanted a child with Cole. But...*not now.*

Hard truth...she didn't know what she wanted. She just knew the hope of it made her ache in so many ways she couldn't begin to count.

And Cole... *Dammit. Why?* Try as she might, she couldn't reconcile his presence in the park with his CIA position. By definition, Cole's work was done on foreign soil. And foreign soil was exactly where he should have been—not right under her nose in D.C. Kissing.

Gah. She trusted him completely...and not at all. No way to start a family—no way at all. Not unless she wanted to continue the streak of the Amazing Divorcing Shaws. Grandparents, parents, aunts and uncles... siblings. A divorce-enabled clan.

Selena growled a little under her breath. When she realized what she'd done she swiftly checked the Kemenis, but they were busy showing each other pictures and telling exaggerated stories of their family loyalty to the Berzhaan that should be. Not so busy they didn't have an eye on her, but a little growling was apparently only to be expected.

She shoved the MRE trash aside, licked a last crumb of cookie from the corner of her mouth and cradled her head in her arms. Athena training had started her young…endurance courses, survival in the White Tank Mountains of Arizona…they'd taught her she could do more than she thought she could. Always. Always one more sit-up, one more mile, one more day. But now, with this very long day and several terrorists behind her, drained by illness and lack of food, she thought she'd just take advantage of the quiet moment she'd been given.

And then she'd find some way to get Allori, Razidae and the kids to safety. Poor, scared kids. They were holding up well….

But then, to judge by the Kemenis' supplies, this had only just started.

"—hadn't expected you'd trust us enough to sleep so deeply."

Say what? Selena opened her eyes, got an up-close-and-personal view of the tabletop, and discovered her head had slipped from her arms, her cheek mashed against the surface, her breath misting the lamination with each exhalation. She blinked, took a deep breath and lifted her head with as much dignity as possible. "You said you wanted me unhurt. I didn't think they'd dare defy you."

Besides, they probably figure they'll get their chance later.

She didn't know how long she'd slept, but to judge by the crick in her neck and her grumpy frame of mind, it had been a while. She rubbed the side of her face, swept her hair back and stretched as though she didn't have a care in the world. Huge mistake, because she had plenty of cares—and as soon as she moved her battered arm, pain swelled in protest. She couldn't help but wince.

His expression remained unreadable. "You're right about that much. They won't touch you until I say they can."

Until. Not *if*. Great.

"I would apologize for keeping you waiting, but I see you've made good use of the time." He nodded at the MRE trash as he reached for a chair, putting it opposite her and so close that their knees nearly touched.

"No problem," Selena said, carefully bending her arm so as to get a glimpse at her watch—5 a.m. A nice little nap at that. "I'm sure you keep pretty busy with all your terrorist things. You know, phone calls to Berzhaan to make threats, phone calls to various embassies to make threats, strangling puppies and boiling rabbits…."

The corner of his mouth twitched. Ire or amusement, she couldn't tell—and that imposing set of features gave nothing else away. Not even a smudge of fatigue…how unfair. She decided he must have had a nice nap, too, and felt better immediately.

Quite abruptly, he asked, "Who are you?"

She grinned. Her face had stiffened, but she grinned anyway. "Can't figure me out at all, can you?"

"American woman," he said. "You came with Allori, and the guards knew you. You speak Berzhaani as fluently as I've heard from any foreign tongue. No doubt you're from the embassy…one of their CIA plants, perhaps."

Selena snorted with such expressive spontaneity that

he suppressed a smile and said, "No, then. Their loss, perhaps."

"Thank you. For that, you can call me Athena." She hadn't thought ahead…it had just come out. But she supposed there was no harm in it. In fact, it bolstered her—made her think of the strength she'd found at the Athena Academy…the way the young women there never gave up. "And for the record, I also speak Russian, Euskara, Portuguese and probably any other language you care to name offhand."

"Athena." This time he downright smiled, as dry as it remained. "Appropriate."

She didn't respond. She let the silence stretch between them, tight as it was. Until he finally broke it, quite matter-of-factly. "You're going to help me," he said, and sat back in the chair as though it were a done deal, his knees still close to hers. He'd changed, she suddenly realized—he no longer wore his expensive suit, but blended in with the others in Kemeni chic—an olive-green military sweater that he wore like a cover model, and khaki cargo pants not unlike her own.

Quite reasonably, Selena told him, "No, I'm going to stop you."

He smiled, a tight expression but this time true amusement. "Unlike your government, you say what you mean. If you continue to do so, you might not find your death so unpleasant after all." He nodded at her, and his expression hardened. "What did you do with the man who once wore that shirt?"

She'd told Atif…*if they get close enough to see the blood, I'll already be in trouble.*

And she was.

"Does it matter?" she asked, thinking of Atif hiding in the cooler. Leading Ashurbeyli to the body would lead him straight to the injured cook. "He doesn't need the shirt anymore."

"And the others who have gone missing? Are they all dead?"

After a moment, Selena shook her head—a minute gesture. And then to forestall the next question, she raised an eyebrow at him. "You imply otherwise, but my country has been perfectly honest with you. We never supplied you with arms. We never supported the Kemenis with one hand and Razidae with the other. So when your funding dried up, that wasn't us, either." She nodded at the spot where she'd earlier seen Jonas White, a little huddle of chairs next to which still sat the remains of a substantial meal. "Where's Jonas White? Why don't you ask him about the way your supplies and funding dried up? Ask him about Frank Black, who also used the names Richard Dunst and Roscoe Dupree, especially when he was doing White's dirty work. Ask him, why don't you, about those ridiculous Abakan rifles. Why do you think you have them? Because he got his hands on them and needed to unload them, and he did it in a way that let him jerk the Kemenis around."

He sat straight up, his expression shifting from indulgent to furious before she finished forming the last word.

Oops. Went too far.

He slapped her. Backhanded, heavy…powerful. And then he sat back as though he hadn't lost his temper at all, the only signs of it lurking in his flared nostrils and the fire banked in his eyes. "Be respectful, or pay the immediate consequences."

"You want respect?" Selena found her hand on her cheek, the existing bruise reawakened, blood trickling anew. "Then earn it. Let those kids go. They don't have anything to do with your problems."

"They represent countries who have interfered with us. They'll stay." He flicked a hand in dismissal. "Now. You work for the United States. You work with Razidae and his government. You understand them both. *You* can make them understand how serious we are. Make this real to them. At the moment they simply play games with us. They watched bin Kuwaji die, and yet they don't take us seriously."

"Oh, they take you seriously all right," Selena said readily. "Let me guess—Berzhaan won't even respond to your communication. The U.S. is stalling and pretending not to."

Ashurbeyli pressed his lips together. Hard. Sensuousness thinned to nothing. "Essentially."

"It's like this," she said, and then hesitated, her thoughts tugged by awareness of the chaos on the other side of those halogen lamps—the discord between the countries involved, the struggle for control. Berzhaan capitol, U.S. personnel, hostages scattered across a handful of national lines.

She thought, too, of Cole, still waiting to hear from her…no doubt imagining the worst. *And probably close to being right.* As long as she'd been able to reach him, he served as her secret weapon. Her off-site backup. The man she trusted to cut through red tape and national barriers to get her the information she needed and to pass along the inside intel she provided, tidbits that would help keep them all safe.

The deep voice she'd counted on to fill her ears and

bolster her confidence. She didn't need it; she could depend on herself.

But she wanted it.

Ashurbeyli hadn't so much as cleared his throat...just the slightest rise of a single eyebrow. But it was enough to rivet her attention back where it belonged.

She said, "Berzhaan won't deal with you. They'll sacrifice all of us before they let this country fall into Kemeni control. I can't believe you don't know that. And Berzhaan won't ask for help from the States. The U.S. is planning something anyway...several somethings, probably. Things they can put into play and apologize for later. They'll claim it's for Razidae, but they can't afford the bad juju of losing those kids."

"Juju," he repeated.

She ignored that and added thoughtfully, "In fact, I really wouldn't touch the kids. There's not much you can do to rile up the U.S. more than picking on kids."

He tipped his head to send a sardonic look her way. "So you'd have me believe Berzhaan is prepared to let you all die, and your United States is playing quiet but ready to spring. That we're doomed either way. That if I take you to that front door and add your blood to bin Kuwaji's, no one will be moved by the death of a woman."

Selena wanted to swallow hard. She wanted to bite her lip. She wanted to make a run for it right then and there.

But she cleared her throat and said, "Essentially, yes. The success of your action here rests on the belief that someone with influence will bend to your demands. That's not the case. Berzhaan will either wait or have the Elite Guard storm the place, and the States will pick their moment and mow you down with SEALs."

He simply stared at her. Not startled, not angry. Just watching. Waiting to see if she'd hold on to those words.

But she'd meant it, every bit of it. She gave him the slightest of smiles, as though none of it was any concern of hers. In truth, she knew herself in the presence of a man so strong that little she could say would affect her fate one way or the other. He already knew his ultimate plans for her. With words, she might change the exact events that got her there...but only with action would she save her own life.

And the hostages. Those frightened children. Hadn't she gotten into the counterterrorism racket just precisely to prevent this sort of situation?

She just had to pick her time. She had to hope she lived long enough to find that time.

Ashurbeyli nodded, a precise gesture. "I see. This is your final assessment of the situation? Are you certain you wouldn't like to try some fancy Western lies to talk your way out of trouble?"

She snorted. "I don't lie very well. And frankly, I'm surprised you expected anything different." She hesitated, considering him—wondering just what he had expected, and what he truly hoped to accomplish here. "And U.S. policy is spread all over the news, every day. We've dedicated ourselves to taking down groups like yours." She didn't hide her regard, looking at him much as he'd looked at her. Thoughtfully. With much assessment. It seemed to amuse him. The byplay in general seemed to entertain him, a fact for which she was mighty grateful. As long as he stayed amused, he wasn't likely to throw her to his men. *Just a matter of time.* A matter of time, too, before another hostage died. But for now, she'd try to ride that thin balance of being useful and annoying and, yes, of being amusing…and just possibly, making a point. "Who talked you into this, anyway? White? What did he dangle in front of you? Something better than those rifles he provided? Better than the nonhalal MREs?"

His eyes narrowed. *Ah, struck a nerve.* He leaned forward; she had to steel herself to avoid reaction. Knee to knee, sheer charisma carrying between them like a direct connection…if only this man had thought to dedicate himself to *good*… With the first heat of the conversation, he said, "Those rifles came from *your* people. From the United States."

She raised a skeptical eyebrow. "You're kidding, right? Abakans? It's a Russian rifle."

He waved away the words. "Exactly. No ties to the States."

"Not only that, it's a *terrible* rifle for basic troop use." Selena crossed her arms, unable to suppress a wince but not hesitating over it. "No, those rifles came from Frank Black. The recently deceased Frank Black. At least, that's the name you knew him by, and far from being a U.S. rep, he actually spent his dearly departed days running errands and playing evil henchman for Jonas White. We've learned quite a lot about Frank Black lately, as it happens. It was Jonas White who gave you those nasty rifles, Jonas White who diverted those MREs your way. And then he lost his empire because sometimes life is good and just, and he came looking for a new power base." She nodded at him. "That would be you. If you're successful. But you won't be."

He stood so abruptly that the chair scooted away behind his legs. "That's enough." But he scowled, a definite and outright scowl over her words about White.

"Bring him in for a little conversation, just the three of us," Selena suggested. "See how hard he sweats."

"The time for talking is over." Ashurbeyli looked at the door separating the ballroom from the function room, and Selena instantly knew what he was thinking. *Another hostage...*

"No," she said, her cool calm dissolved into desperation. "Not yet. Not until you understand how you've been used—"

"Does it matter how we got here? We're here, and we want what we want. Worthy goals. Martyrs for our cause will find their own reward." He looked over his shoulder, a single glance, as he headed for his men. "I think you'll appreciate my choice."

Selena didn't find it likely.

She found it even less likely a moment later, when— after some minor fuss from the hostages—he returned flanked by two of his men, Atif the cook in tow. His hand clamped around Atif's bloody white sleeve in a cruel grip, his pistol pushed solidly between the cook's shoulders. Atif wouldn't meet her eyes; at first she thought he was embarrassed on top of his fear. He kept his gaze on the floor even when he spoke to her. "I heard the distraction you made." His gaze flickered, didn't make it all the way up and returned to his toes. "I thought it my chance to escape."

Selena had looked at Ashurbeyli with respect and even a certain understanding of his motives if not his methods. Now she looked at him with disgust. "Pick on someone your own size, why don't you?"

She wasn't expecting his wry grin. "You underestimate him, just as you underestimate the Kemenis. How do you think we had arms and supplies waiting inside this building? Surely you already considered that we entered through the kitchen—it was one reason the casualties there were so regrettably high. They hadn't yet had time to run, but we couldn't let them spread panic."

Selena blinked, surprisingly pained. "Atif?"

He closed his eyes, a desperate gesture. "I thought I could keep down the bloodshed. I let the guns in, packed in fruit boxes. *I* opened the door, yes! I thought it would make the inevitable easier."

"But you weren't so sure that you didn't have your hideout planned," Ashurbeyli observed. "And you were quick enough to offer up our Athena here, weren't you?"

This time Atif looked up at her, nakedly honest in his self-acceptance. "I know what I am. A weak man. I was trying to save my own life. Again."

She met his gaze. She understood his fear…she understood why he would waver before the Kemenis. He was, as he had told her, a cook. Not a Jackie Chan fighting cook, just a man who hadn't wanted to be involved in any of this in the first place. She said, "It doesn't seem to have worked out as you hoped."

"No." His face was tight with fear. "If I had stood my ground, I would at least have died in honor."

Ashurbeyli shook his head, short and tight. "And now you will simply die. You may hope it still counts for something."

Selena thought…in some small way, perhaps it would. For Ashurbeyli had still asked her about his men…and that meant that Atif had not given up the kitchen cooler stash. As a hideout, it still had some value. And while one man was dead and the youth disabled, the third could have reinforced the terrorist efforts and was best kept out of the game.

Not so weak as all that. Just not quite strong enough.

She found her eyes hot with fury and frustration and sorrow. "You helped me, too," she told him. "That still matters." He stood ever so slightly taller, and Ashurbeyli, as if realizing this encounter wasn't quite turning out as expected, shoved him onward, glancing back at Selena as if despite himself. She gave him a hard, unforgiving gaze, and then she crossed one leg over the other and looked away as if he were no matter at all.

His voice came harshly over his shoulder, directed at his men. "Watch her. She's probably prone to pointless gestures." But then he hesitated, and he looked again at her, this time more thoughtfully. "But bring her close to the door. I want to make sure she can hear."

Incredulous, she dropped her foot to the floor. *"Why?"*

"Because," he said, and his voice was as harsh as she'd heard it, "it's time you realized the hopelessness of your own situation."

She didn't have time for any kind of response, hopeful or not. Three of the Kemenis left their rest and descended upon her, and would have lifted her by the arms had she not snarled and smacked their reaching hands away with such purpose as to make it clear she'd have it out here and now if that's the way they wanted it—when she knew Ashurbeyli wasn't quite ready for that. Hadn't quite seen in her eyes the defeat he wanted to see. And indeed, he looked back again to give a short shake of his head, even as he escorted Atif out of the ballroom.

The three men stepped back slightly. Of varying olive-dark complexions, one in a *yashmagh* and the other two bareheaded, two with short beards and one clean shaven…she doubted they had much in common other than their defiance and their loyalty to Ashurbeyli. Years of rotating occupation had left Berzhaan a country of scattered influences and little cohesion…and had led to this moment, this incident. Atif's death.

Soon, her own. And that of the hostages, if she didn't manage to deal with things. For as she'd told Ashurbeyli, she had little confidence that Berzhaan would prioritize anything but stopping the terrorists…and that any attempt at rescue made by the U.S. would be hampered by their need to work around Berzhaan. She hadn't even mentioned the difficulty of coordinating the different agencies involved.

Up to me.

And that meant she had to hold it together through whatever came next.

Chapter 11

Ashurbeyli's men must have blocked the capitol's doors open, for his voice carried clearly to where Selena stood in the ballroom—not close enough to the door to make a break for it, not with one man's hand resting on her shoulder where he'd feel every shift of her weight and the other resting his pistol muzzle in her ribs. "Good morning!" Ashurbeyli said, his voice ringing clearly over the sprawling steps that led down to the courtyard, the halogen lights and the military vehicles ringed by press from around the world. Midwinter and still full dark as they approached 6 a.m., but Selena had no doubt that the right people were watching. Or that they would be, for the cameras were running, and this footage would find a worldwide audience.

Tory Patton might even be out there. Selena hoped so. It would take someone with Tory's heart to make this story as real to the world as it was to Selena.

As it was to Atif. First traitor, then Selena's silent partner in counterterrorism, then traitor again—but beneath it all, a man who had simply been caught up in something bigger than he was. Bigger than he was ever meant to be.

Ashurbeyli said, "Yesterday I made a very clear point here on these very steps—I can still see the bloodstains. No rain will ever be enough to wash them away, just as it cannot wash away the damage done to my country by those who have occupied and interfered with us over the years. Our current government is weak, and too open to the influence of those people who have previously enslaved us—or to those who would exploit us for the resources we have chosen to leave in the earth."

The oil.

And of course he was right. Everyone wanted that oil, and no one had qualms about taking every advantage of a people in turmoil to get it.

That was the hell of it. Ashurbeyli was wrong, so *wrong,* in what he did. But he was no fool. He had a clear vision of what his country faced, and that behind every proffered friendship lurked self-interest of some kind—including her own work here. She'd come to make his people safer, to start a partnership in counterterrorism. Her genuine drive to keep innocents safe from the random cruelty of terrorism didn't mean the United States didn't have its own agenda behind the FBI Legate programs—for once they became entwined, once Berzhaan depended on the States to help train their own, disentangling wouldn't be so easy. And in the end, Selena's mandate to stop the trouble here was a mandate to keep it from spreading to U.S. soil.

She closed her eyes and wished she could close her

ears. *I wouldn't be here if I didn't care. I wouldn't have saved those women yesterday morning...I wouldn't have stayed in the capitol when I could have tried to run. I would have stayed hidden in that room instead of coming down where I could be caught.*

She cared, all right. But that didn't mean those like Ashurbeyli wanted her here. Or that they were wrong to resent the interference of outsiders, no matter the motive.

The cold ridge of the gun muzzle prodded her ribs, demanding her attention. "Listen to him."

She didn't think she'd missed much. He'd either paused for effect, or he was repeating himself...the words flowed well enough. "Since then, we have heard nothing from our own government, and nothing from those of the people we hold." Did he have Atif in front of him, shielding him? Or did the snipers—for there were surely snipers—simply have orders to hold fire, fearing for the remaining hostages' lives should Ashurbeyli go down those steps himself? "We imagine that you think us weak—that we won't carry out our plans. Or that you think us unprepared, that we don't have the resources to wait."

God, he was good. No hesitation in his voice, no stumbling over words. Conviction ringing out to the world.

"You will find we have the strength to carry out these plans, and the resources. We have warm clothing if you should find a way to cut off the heat. We have drinking water enough to raise the level of the Caspian Sea. And we have hostages enough to continue killing one each day for quite some time. We have the prime minister." And they wouldn't kill Razidae unless they couldn't avoid it, for keeping him alive would keep everyone hopeful—and would keep every involved nation from storming the capitol at once. "What we *want* is for this absurd charade of friendly interest and false intentions to end. We want the government which has allowed things to come this far to admit defeat and to leave this country to those who will keep it safe. We want them to step down—every last lowly advisor. And until that happens, people will continue to die." There was a pause; some dramatic gesture, Selena imagined. Ashurbeyli's voice held a smile when he continued, albeit a cold one. "I don't refer to those inside this building. I refer to those out in the turmoil you have created for us. You who think you can find some way to control us for your own gains. Right this moment, you're killing my people. *Berzhaan's* people. So we invite those responsible to resign, and we invite the rest of you to go away."

And all this while, Atif waited to die.

Ashurbeyli seemed to think he'd made as much of his point as he was going to. "This man is a traitor to his government, and yet still too weak to be one of our own. He is my gift to you. The next hostage to die will be someone you cry over."

The scuff of leather soles against marble steps, a quick, futile protest—

Selena flinched at the sudden, resounding blast of the gun, muffled as it was by the back of Atif's skull. Nothing came close to describing gunfire in close proximity, *nothing*. Nothing came close to describing the aftermath, as she listened to the sodden thump of Atif's body hitting the first stair, rolling down to the sec- ond...the image of bin Kuwaji came to mind, flopping his way downward to lie on the long, narrow landing until someone took the risk to acquire his body.

Closing her eyes only made it worse.

Ashurbeyli found her there. "And what do you think? The drinking water enough to raise the level of the sea—was that perhaps too far?"

She glared at him in unabashed fury. "You went too far when you stormed in here yesterday afternoon! You went *too far* when you shot a man for being less complicated than you! And then you blame everyone *else* for the turmoil of your country—that's one hell of a case of self-delusion you've got going, buddy."

"Ah," he said, looking at her with an understanding that turned her fury to cold wariness. "You think that man was someone to cry over. And you would be the one to do it."

She hesitated, uncertain whether to admit to it—to show the weakness, or to get right in his face about it. Two men flanked him and blood splattered them all, a pattern so distinctive she could almost tell who'd been standing where. She could certainly tell that Ashurbeyli had pulled the trigger.

And two men flanked *her*, still jamming the gun in her ribs, only far enough away so they weren't impeding Ashurbeyli's conversation.

She got in his face anyway. "Yeah," she said. "I damn well would. Because of the two of us, I'm the only one with enough humanity to care!"

She grunted as the pistol barrel rode her ribs, bruising them, and Ashurbeyli raised a hand that put an instant stop to the rough treatment. "Leave her," he said. "Put her back where she was, and two of you will watch her at all times. See to her needs, and have her ready to move if Mr. White or I choose to speak to her in the back room. Soon enough you will see her die. Until then, we will not mark her." Touching her for the first time since he'd searched her, Ashurbeyli lifted Selena's chin in his hand, a proprietary gesture with complete awareness. "These marks already here will be perfect, I think. Not so much as to disguise her identity, but enough to heighten the poignancy of her death."

"Oh, *please*," Selena said. "*Now* you're going too far. Too much."

He shook his head, maintaining his firm grip. She somehow stopped herself from biting his fingers. "I'm afraid," he said, "that you underestimate the reaction of those with enough humanity to care. The stories they will tell about you…" He *tsked*. "A tragedy, really."

This time she jerked her chin free to glower back at full force. "There's a tragedy coming, all right."

She didn't have to say anything more; she saw his eyes darken. Not irked at her implication so much as at her continuing challenge…but she had to give him that much: he had patience. He had his schedule and his plans, he had other things to do and he had the patience to make her wait for her tragic end—to make it happen at a time and in a way that would do him the most good.

Even for that, she had to respect him.

But she still intended to stop him.

Cole stepped out into the gusty, spitting rain of the old runway. He pulled his shearling coat closed against the Berzhaani winter, a duffel bag slung over his shoulder and the cell phone—the silent cell phone—within easy reach. Selena called this his McCloud coat, reminiscent of the fictional Texas cop who'd been transplanted to New York City, and teased that he'd chosen it to disguise his adaptable and quick-thinking nature with a laid-back image. Cole thought he'd chosen it because it was warm and he liked the rough-out leather, but a second thought made him reconsider. Made him realize she was right, that he'd done it almost without thinking.

If she knew him so well, what had set her off? Sent her away to this turmoil? She'd as much as admitted he was right about that—but he hadn't even been home to put his foot in it. He'd been a lot closer to her than he'd expected, but she hadn't known that. *She should have.* He should have let her know; it was their long-standing agreement. But things had developed too quickly, too quietly…and she hadn't. And even if she'd somehow found out, it was hardly cause for…for…

This.

He shivered and turned his collar up. Nearly half a day in a noisy Lockheed Starlifter, keeping company with nine cargo pallets and one other passenger who was no more eager to introduce himself than Cole, and he'd come halfway around the world, from one winter to another. This small airstrip had made the pilots work for a landing, and the crew had given him no more than an amiable wave as they prepared to unload cargo—relief supplies for besieged villages, support gear for the small remaining military presence here. Berzhaan allowed no more than that, and gave the U.S. access to this landing site only for the relief supplies.

They definitely didn't want the States in on the hostage crisis.

"Sir?" One of the energetic young men engaged in unloading the Starlifter moved away from the rear fuselage to approach Cole beside one of the four under-wing turbofan engines, now silent. Even with the efficient bustle at the tail of the plane, after the extended noise of their travel, the whole airstrip seemed silent.

Cole's cell phone seemed especially silent. *Selena, where are you?*

Knowing Selena, she was simply busy. Or she'd very wisely taken the chance to grab some rest.

Except she should have called by now regardless—if she could—and he knew it. He couldn't talk himself out of knowing it.

"Sir?" the private repeated. "Can I help you?"

It was a polite way of asking whether Cole had any real business being here, and of warning that without a good answer, he could expect to be removed. Remarkably polite, under the circumstances. Cole eased his duffel to the ground. "I'm waiting for my ride," he said. "CIA. Would you like to see ID?" Sometimes he carried it…most times he didn't. But this trip, he'd use it to pull as many strings as he could.

The private gave a short nod, and Cole opened his jacket to the cold and fished the ID wallet from his inside coat pocket. Carefully. Letting the young man see that he did indeed have a pistol, a 9 mm Browning Hi-Power Mark III in a belt holster that wasn't meant to be the least bit hidden but which was carefully placed opposite to the direction in which he fished for the wallet.

The young man gave it a careful look, eyebrows rising at the sight of the eagle-topped shield, and returned it. "Would you like me to check on your ride?" His tone was perfectly respectful, but Cole understood his intent. To get Cole off this airfield, and away from military turf.

Cole shook his head. "Not just yet." If Tory couldn't

make it, she'd send someone for him. Their arrangements, made as soon as he'd snagged his transportation, had been quick but thorough. She was, he thought, quite a bit more habitually circumspect over the phone than he'd expected from her.

The young man shifted into conversational mode, obviously planning to stay for a while. He'd been sent, then; he had his orders. It made Cole wonder with just what kind of cargo he'd kept company. The private said, "You've been in the air a while. You hear about the second hostage?"

The second hostage? There were at least twenty-five of them as far as Cole knew. The second hostage... what?

Then he knew. His pulse hammered into overload and his shoulders stiffened and he said sharply, "They killed someone else?"

Taken aback, the young man frowned, expressively dark eyebrows bold in a face with such little hair atop. Cole had to stop himself from grabbing the fellow up and shaking the words free—he'd be useless to Selena if they detained him, or even if the cargo handlers all piled atop him with such force as to break every rib he had. But nor could he quite find the words to demand answers; his tongue tangled around things unsaid until he finally spat out, *"Who?"*

The soldier's eyes widened in sudden comprehension. "You know someone." The thought froze his expression, and then he shook himself free of it and said, "Sorry, sir. I don't know much. But it was a man—"

He said other words, but Cole didn't hear them. Too busy dealing with the sudden loss of strength all the way down the back of his legs and the flip-flop in his stomach. His heart, formerly pounding, now just raced in relief. He realized the soldier had hesitated, waiting for some indication from Cole, and he shook his head ever so slightly. Then he reached down for his duffel, just to be doing something. *Cool, Jones. Real cool.*

But this wasn't one of his assignments. This was Selena. The heart she carried under her controlled exterior had grabbed him the first time they met, had grabbed him hard. And she'd shown him that heart over and over again…right up until the moment she called him from hiding, quite typically refusing to leave that besieged building. The difficulties of their marriage, the thing that had almost torn them apart…

That same heart. Living apart from one another so frequently had turned them into the very kind of family that Selena feared…a broken family in physical fact, even if not emotionally. When they'd reconciled, it had been with the awareness that they'd have to try harder than ever—and that inevitably, something would have to change. Cole would have to take a Langley-based position or find work elsewhere altogether; Selena might simply travel with him for a few years, or she, too, might stay stateside. They just hadn't had a chance to come to any conclusions when he'd been called away.

So it had often happened. Things got left unsaid, and then when they rejoined they became too caught up in relearning each other's every favorite touch to tackle practical things until again, they received the call to arms. These past few years…the fears and chaos of the world had not been kind to schedules that had previously been workable. And now he could only hope they'd have the chance to change that.

"You okay, sir?"

Cole realized he still crouched by the duffel and straightened. "Just thinking," he said. "Any change in their demands?"

"I didn't hear the little speech the guy said before— well, you know—but I think it was just the expected stuff—do things our way or more people will die and next time you *really* won't like it."

"Time frame?"

Because Selena still hadn't called. They could still have her.

The guy shook his head. "Haven't heard they gave one. They didn't last time, either. Just showed up with a hostage—*bing!* Time's up!"

Great.

Cole closed his coat, squinting into a renewed gust of misty rain as he caught sight of the dark, boxy sedan headed their way. It couldn't have looked more out of place on the airstrip, and he very much expected it to be his ride. Enough so that he gave his unofficial escort a nod and stepped out to meet the car. The back door opened as the car stopped; the driver even kindly popped the trunk. Cole tossed his duffel into a space otherwise full of camera accessories and shoved it closed before diving into the refuge of the vehicle.

Even as he closed the door, Tory Patton murmured something to the driver; the car swooped away from the plane and across the tarmac, affording Cole a view of scattered hangars and a small control tower through the rain-streaked windshield. He shifted his attention back to Tory, who had also chosen the back seat—he presumed so they might talk. She looked just as she did on camera—calm, elegant beauty, set off by a natural poise—even with her hair tucked under a Sherpa-style hat with tassels hanging from the ties. "Brr," she said. "I haven't been warm since this started." She looked at him with something akin to surprise. "Only a day. Seems longer, doesn't it?"

"A lifetime," he said. "You told me to get here—I got here. Now let's talk about what you wouldn't say over the phone."

One winged eyebrow rose. "Wow. And here I thought you CIA guys were so good at finesse."

"I can finesse with the best of them—when we're not talking about Selena. You don't want to talk in front of your friend?" He jerked a thumb at the driver. "Then stop the car and we'll get out."

"Mmm." She pressed her lips together over the thoughtful noise and then shook her head. "Not a problem, or he wouldn't be here." She raised her voice slightly. "Isn't that right?"

The driver didn't so much as cast a glance at her; he turned between two hangars as if he knew just where he was going—and it didn't necessarily seem to be off this airstrip. "I'm sorry, Tory," he said, his voice full of studied innocence. "Did you say something?"

"So convincing," she told him, but turned back to Cole with a more serious expression darkening her brown eyes. "Here's the situation as I know it—and for the sake of argument, let's just say I've got the real scoop."

He nodded, short and impatient. "Just skip past the part where the CIA has a couple of SEAL teams on standby, desperate for intel. And the part where the Berzhaani don't want us here and damned sure don't want those SEALs going in—they'd rather see the hostages go down than find victory in U.S. assistance. Razidae is the only one who showed signs of softening on that stance, and he's out of commission. So we've got relief troops here waiting to swap hats and turn into peacekeepers. Just tell me what I don't know."

She pursed her lips slightly, thoughtfully. "That certainly limits the conversation. How about this—in exchange for some of the relief we've offered their Kemeni-damaged areas, Berzhaan had given us a little space to work from—and the air force already had a special Predator team in the area. They've been keeping an eye on things south of here, a certain much-traveled border where we're hunting a certain well-traveled terrorist leader."

Afghanistan. Of course.

"They've pulled the Predator back in—they've already done one pass over the capitol. We've got some of that intel the SEALs need—some close-ups of the roof, with all the hidey-holes and exits. They're still analyzing what they gathered up, and they'll be headed back for a second pass. I thought the operators might be just the contacts you need—the wild cards who'll not only keep Selena's best interests in mind, but who have the ear of the people on the other end of the intel."

Whoa.

She waited with patient amusement, watching him process what she'd said. The car eased to a stop, almost unnoticed, slotting in between several others of a similar make beside one of the smaller Quonset buildings.

Of course. The Cassandras. They'd actually come through.

"Josie Lockworth." He said it, and he shook his head, barely believing it. "You've got Josie Lockworth and her modified supersneaky remote-control spy plane here."

"Well, in point of fact the air force has her here. But what *I* have is ID giving you access to the building—not, mind you, that I think that would stop you, but we might as well do this the easy way—and Josie's got a keen interest in talking to you. For that matter, in keeping you close by in case you hear from Selena again. Have you?"

He didn't quite hear her last question, still full of relief at just how very thoroughly Tory Patton had come through for him. For her Athena classmate. He said, "I'm going to owe Selena an apology…I once implied she was exaggerating about the Athena grads."

Tory smiled. It had a secretive look to it. "Ah, she said you could be a charmer."

"She—you've talked?" *Great deduction, Jones.*

Her smile told him all he needed to know. Oh yeah. *Women.* She shrugged, a motion almost lost in her quilted coat. "You didn't answer my question. Have you heard from Selena?"

The answer sucked any vestige of the light moment from the air. "No. And I should have."

"Yes," she agreed quietly. "You should have."

Cole shook it off. As best he could, which wasn't entirely convincing even from his own point of view. "She knows how to take care of herself. She lost the landline the last time we talked…there's no telling what's up with the cell. She'll get in touch." He cleared his tight throat. "When she can." His throat had clogged right up again; he coughed, and then he held out a hand. "We haven't been properly introduced. I'm Cole Jones. And I'm very grateful for your help."

Worry lurked around her eyes, but her expression softened as she took his hand. "Tory Patton," she said. "And I'm glad you thought to call me. We'll all do what we can to see that Selena walks out of that building." She released his hand, tucked a lock of hair back into her hat. "Now. Do you want to go meet another Cassandra?"

Hours passed. Selena prevailed upon her Kemeni guards—a new set, as guard shifts changed over for the third time—to escort her to the ladies' room, giving her the chance to establish she was on her period. It wasn't a lie that would hold up, but it took some of the eagerness out of their eyes; as men who considered themselves righteous warriors fighting for a righteous cause, they leaned too hard on their spiritual beliefs to casually break the law against being intimate with a woman in her menses. In fact, they'd probably have to perform ablutions before their next Salat just for touching her.

They fed her more of the excess standard MREs— beef chili macaroni, the one that tasted good even cold. Even for breakfast. They allowed her water. She got glimpses of the hostages in the next room as they now occasionally made escorted trips to the facilities and shared rudimentary meals—was once even able to exchange a meaningful glance with Dante Allori—enough for her to send him a fierce message. *I'm not hurt. I haven't given up.* Not yet.

Other than that, they tolerated very little movement on Selena's part. She sat at her table, thinking about anything but the previous day's illness…trying not to wonder if it would happen again. She eyed the haphazard pile of cell phones along the wall—every one belonged to a hostage, and they'd all been turned off after the constant, plaintive ringing irritated the Kemenis beyond endurance. She sneaked in isometric exercises, she wiggled her toes, she quietly flexed her stiff arm. She would have preferred an ice pack, even in the chill of an obviously faltering furnace.

And every now and then such practical things made way for a burst of adrenaline from nowhere—demanding *action,* demanding *escape,* demanding anything but this *waiting.* It seized her with a strength akin to panic until she resorted to deep breathing, looking anywhere but at the terrorists...because if they knew how close she hovered to giving in, they'd come bash some sense into her. Or they'd simply shoot her outright.

That would be the smart thing to do.

She drew a deep breath, hearing again the shot that had killed Atif. Yeah, shooting her outright would be the smart thing.

But somehow, when Ashurbeyli walked through the door only moments later, she didn't launch herself at him. Her pulse pounded through her body, but she schooled herself back to the cool demeanor for which she was known, only one leg twitching to give away her impulse. It twitched again as Jonas White followed Ashurbeyli, looking well rested and refreshed enough to hold a press conference. She'd never guess his age at over sixty; his round face held deep grooves from nose to mouth and impressive scowl lines ridged his forehead, but his hair remained dark—just enough gray at the temples to deny a dye job. Unlike everyone else in the room, he'd clearly been getting enough food— and if he was worried about the success of this crazed new venture, it didn't show in his body language.

Perhaps just a little, right around the eyes.

Ashurbeyli caught her watching White and sent her a grim little smile that meant she hadn't been forgotten. He exchanged a few more words with his men, low murmurs that Selena dearly wished she could hear. They all seemed satisfied enough. She wasn't sure why...several hours had passed since Atif's death and there'd been no indication of change in their situation. The Kemenis were as they'd been, patient and prepared and not, somehow, quite as concerned as the situation demanded.

Then again, maybe he'd been smart enough to expect such delays...even the failure to gain the control over Berzhaan that he sought from this strike. Maybe he knew he'd have to go to the extreme of killing some college kids—or Razidae himself. Hell, for that matter, maybe he'd made contingency plans. There were any number of grand gestures at his disposal, and most of them involved death. If he had a Javelin anti-tank missile or two—even one of the old Dragons—he could take out a big chunk of Berzhaani troops right on the street, not to mention reporters from around the globe. Or maybe he'd just bring this building down around them while he made his escape in the mess—and in the resulting chaos, the Kemenis could strike elsewhere and strike hard. Strike with success.

Maybe he planned to bring this building down around them.

The thought sent chills up her spine, coalescing around every previous doubt she'd had. Those moments wondering what the Kemenis thought to accomplish, Ashurbeyli's calm lack of reaction when she'd said as much. Her incredulity that he hadn't figured out the futility of this pathetic coup attempt all on his own.

But he'd known better all along. He had another purpose here, a *true* purpose—and she had to figure out
what it was. She glanced over at the careless pile of
black devices. Remotes? Ashurbeyli might well have
turned this place into a death trap. She had no doubt
he'd do it if he believed it would lead to a successful
coup. Or that he'd sacrifice every single hostage in the
process, perhaps even many of his own men.

She had no doubt Jonas White would urge him on.

Something must have shown on her face. Ashurbeyli
lifted his head from his conversation and looked at her
with sharp attention. A few more words to his men and
he straightened, reaching into his pocket as he moved
toward her. So casual. He caught White's eye along the
way and White moved away from his own, less intense
conversation—by necessity, as he didn't seem to speak
Berzhaani.

Indeed, Ashurbeyli made his opening comments to
her in English. "You seem to be faring well enough,"
he said, an oddly innocuous opening. "Not too lonely,
I hope. We really must keep a better eye on you than on
the others."

"I'm fine, thank you," Selena said in her polite diplomatic party voice. "And have you and Mr. White been
having a nice chat? Did he perhaps explain those
Abakans?"

Jonas White cleared his throat with annoyance. "No
need for that," he said, "since I didn't have anything to
do with them."

Selena nodded wisely. "Sticking to the story, are
you? Haven't you figured out it's best to come clean
now? Because your Kemeni associates are going to be
really, really upset at you when they learn that you've

lied to them—lied to their *faces*. In their own way, they're much more honorable than you on your best day. And you'll hardly be able to hide your interest in their oil when the time comes, although I imagine you've already got a new henchman lined up to front your activity in that sector." She frowned slightly, thoughtful. "Then again, none of it matters, since this whole hostage business is going to blow up in your face."

She used the words quite deliberately—and she saw in White's eyes a flicker of smug reaction.

Oh God. Couldn't it have just been my overactive imagination?

A wave of queasiness washed over her.

No, no, NO.

But White didn't notice. He squinted at her, far too thoughtfully critical for her tastes. "Who is she, Tafiq?"

"She had no identification," Ashurbeyli said, watching White more carefully than he did Selena. Good. Maybe he'd see that she'd actually made White uneasy. *As much as he hid it, she made him uneasy.* Ashurbeyli shrugged, the most insouciant of gestures. "We have not cared enough to find out. It matters only that she no longer interferes."

"Oh, I think it matters more than that." White narrowed his eyes at her. No dummy, he. He couldn't afford to have her continue what she'd started, filling Ashurbeyli's ears with the truth. "If you prefer to keep her as a pet, then ask the others. Someone here must know her."

Yes. But he wouldn't talk.

"Or take one of those sniveling kids and carve off a few inches of skin. She'll tell us. It's not that hard, if you really want to know."

Her stomach did a lazy flip-flop at the thought. She wasn't here to risk the lives of the people she'd stayed to save. Ashurbeyli cocked his head slightly; he'd read that answer on her face.

"Would you care to save us the trouble?" he asked. *"Athena?"*

"Of course." She didn't hide her irritation. "Because it's really not *worth* that kind of trouble. My name is Selena Shaw Jones. I work at the U.S. Embassy. If I were of any real importance, you'd have known who I was from the start, don't you think?"

"Perhaps," Ashurbeyli murmured. "Perhaps not. It is, of course, a pleasure to have a name for you. Selena."

But she didn't like the thoughtful speculation in his eye. Or that barely perceptible nod, as though he'd made a decision. A reluctant decision...and not one that was likely to bode well for her. Best to take his mind off it. She turned the conversation around. "And did you get what you came for?"

He affected surprise, but she thought she saw a smile. Appreciation. As though beneath the surface, he enjoyed their sparring—perhaps even sought it out. "My English fails me. I can't imagine what you mean to say."

Selena's mouth quirked in skeptical reaction. "Mmm," she said, making plain her disbelief. But she didn't argue it; she gestured from herself to White and said, "This. Between us. Me pushing his buttons, exposing his lies for you."

White's heavy brows drew together; those formidable frown lines gathered on his forehead. But Ashurbeyli waved him off. "Please, Jonas, do not concern yourself. Do you think I can't tell she's trying to disturb our alliance?" He turned his near-black gaze on Selena and added in Berzhaani, "You only help me. Such suspicions have no impact on this moment, but I will see to them afterward."

White's scowl only grew deeper. *"Tafiq."*

Ashurbeyli turned to him with ease. "It is of no matter, Jonas. A crudity unsuited to your language."

"Loosely translated, it means 'don't bend over to get the soap,'" Selena told him, smiling serenely at White's narrow-eyed reaction.

"Ah," Ashurbeyli dug into his pocket, a pretense of sudden memory. "There was another reason I came." He pulled out his hand and extended it in her direction, closing the space between them until it entered that realm of *intimate* with which he seemed so comfortable. When he uncurled his fingers, he revealed a dull gold ring in the center of his palm. A wedding ring? "For you," he said. "Because I chose him on your behalf."

Atif's wedding ring.

Chapter 12

*A*tif's *wedding ring.*

She didn't know why it had such a sudden, profound effect. He had been a traitor—twice a traitor, even as he'd hidden Selena's captured terrorist cache.

And just a man, trying to survive. Not deserving to face terrorists, not at the back of the kitchen, not on the capitol steps.

Selena's stomach flipped again, a slow, lazy roll. The blood drained from her face, leaving it tingly. Leaving it as suddenly green as she felt.

"I need—" she said, and clapped a hand over her mouth.

Ashurbeyli, stranger and terrorist, understood immediately. It mattered not that he reacted to keep this room clean—for some of his men were forced to pray here so the hostages weren't left unattended in the next room, and her illness would defile it. It mattered not that the apparent kindness had nothing to do with Selena's comfort at all. All that mattered was that he reacted in the first place. Even as Selena bent double, clamping down on a gag, Ashurbeyli swiftly produced the key to her cuffs, released her from the chair, and gestured at the door. She didn't know if he meant for her to go all the way to the bathroom or simply as far as the hallway. She didn't care. He'd stop her if she went too far.

She staggered out toward the hallway, hesitated on another gag right beside the pile of phones—and then let herself fall so she could scoop one up, her mind caught in a surreal place of lightning thought and total disconnect from her roiling stomach. She didn't know if she'd been seen and she didn't wait to find out, not with bile eating at the back of her throat. She flung herself down the hall the short distance to the bathroom. The main facilities for the ballroom, its anteroom surrounded her with equal opulence. She barely saw it; barely heard the Kemenis who followed her as far as that anteroom while she went through the second swinging door to the bathroom itself.

But by then she found the spell passing. She pressed the back of her hand to her mouth, waiting. Only the faintest unease from her stomach remained, giving her no clue as to the origin.

Except the obvious. She'd fought, she'd killed, she'd been captured, she'd spent many tense hours fearing for her safety—and possibly her child's—and preparing for an assault she considered inevitable. The ring was a final insult, a reminder of Atif's death and Ashurbeyli's all-too-casual attitude about it. Such evoked revulsion would make anyone ill, pregnant or not.

From outside the door came a brief spate of conversation, Berzhaani too muffled for her to catch. Standing in the stall door, eyes darting around the room, Selena responded to sudden impulse. She produced a truly outstanding series of visceral noises, flushing the toilet even as she ran out of the stall to examine the room—prowling under the enclosed sink counters, running her hands over everything she found. Hunting for sharp or pointy or anything else that inspired her imagination. As her eye fell on the demure tampon dispenser, the toilet ceased its noise and she went back for another round of Oscar-worthy retching, her heart pounding just as fast as if she'd actually ended up sick.

Because she thought she'd seen…

She flushed the toilet and went straight to the tampon dispenser, her fingers scrabbling at the bottom flap—the thin aluminum that kept people from reaching up inside to grab the product, yet flipped aside so the purchases could descend. It was askew, all right. Crooked and damaged, as though someone *had* tried to reach up in there. Someone caught unaware at a fancy dinner, and without the proper Berzhaani coin…Selena could well imagine it.

But she tugged to no avail. Desperate, watching the door, she wiggled the flap back and forth, felt the weakness, felt her injured arm fail her—and knew she could never rip it loose by hand. *Nice, thin aluminum…probably jagged at that.* She ran back to the stall and flushed again, engaging in a quick tug-of-war when the loose handcuff tangled with the toilet handle.

Ah.

Back to the dispenser, she scrabbled at it, hunting a handhold and gouging her fingers, but finally getting enough purchase so she could cram the end of the open cuff into the small space she'd created between flap and body of the dispenser. She wiggled the cuff fiercely, working it toward the secure end of the flap, and—

"Are you done?" A harsh demand, not Ashurbeyli— though she thought she heard him in the background.

"Please," she said, and keeping her voice weak and breathless came without any effort at all. "Please, give me a few more minutes." She couldn't believe they'd left her alone this long. After all she'd done to them, they still couldn't take a woman as a serious threat?

Don't look a gift horse, eh?

"Hurry!" the man demanded.

She thought it was his pride speaking. Not great duty, lurking outside the bathroom door. Worse if he had to come in. "Please," she said, adding a tremulous note to her voice. And then, "Oh, no, I—" and back to the retching noises it was, only this time she couldn't reach the toilet for the convincing sound of flushing. She stretched out a leg and reached the closest sink, batting the faucet on with her pointed foot. And never, during all of it, hesitating in her efforts with the handcuff-turned-prybar.

Quite suddenly, the metal flap came loose. Selena grunted with surprise, almost losing her balance, and barely took the time to examine her prize. Eight inches long, two inches wide, and a satisfactory edge of partly sheared metal—and now it had to be hidden.

She yanked up her shirttails with one hand, flipped the cell phone open with the other, and headed for the toilet stall to once again flush the toilet. Even then she left the water running, and went to spit in the sink a few times. She knew Cole's number so well she barely had to look to dial it, and then tucked the phone under her chin—not an easy task with today's slick little phones and her arm crying protest over all the activity—as she went to work securing the strip of metal at her waist-band, tucked between her turtleneck and the borrowed shirt.

Above the running water and the rustle of material and her own quick breathing, Selena could barely hear the ring of Cole's cell. But ring it did, and by God he picked it up. His greeting came across as wary—he'd seen the caller ID. But Selena rushed right in. "Cole! It's me." What to say, as fast as possible, the most cru-cial information?

"Selena! Are you—"

"No!" she said, giving him no more than that, check-ing herself in the mirror for signs of the hard-won tool. A tampon tool. It would scandalize Ashurbeyli even to think about it. "Listen! Check what you can see of the building, I think they're going to—"

The bathroom door slammed open. Not the guard, but Ashurbeyli, suspicion on his face turning to fury. He slammed her against the edge of the sink; she felt the metal strip slice her skin *but oh, please, not too deep* and the phone went spinning away over the tile. Ashurbeyli backhanded her hard enough to bounce her off the sink, hard enough to send her sprawling after the phone, her arm in agony and her vision a swirl of image and darkness. She sprang back to her feet in an instinc-tive, animalistic survival reaction right down to the snarl in her throat—a snarl that died as she heard the unmis-takable clatter of rifles coming to bear, shoulder sling hardware clinking against metal, safeties going off—

Selena froze. She checked herself and she froze, only

slowly taking in the full view of three Kemenis in the ladies' room, ready to shoot her down. In the center spot stood Ashurbeyli, his face a study in tight fury—and, she realized with astonishment, betrayal. He hadn't expected that she'd try to pull anything over on him, not in the one moment of compassion he'd offered her—offered *anyone*—since this started. She felt an absurd impulse to apologize, but instead she pressed careful fingers to her heavy, burning cheek—the other one this time—and gestured at the other two. "Hey," she said, hoping against hope that the warm blood seeping against her side didn't soak through the shirt or her waistband. "Blame *them.* The gagging was real, but they still should have seen me grab that phone."

Astonishingly, he did not have her shot on the spot. More astonishingly, he actually nodded, taking a visible breath to regain his control. "They will regret that they didn't."

I might live past this moment after all.

Or not, for anger still tightened his features. He gestured at the phone. "And who, may I ask?"

Ah, back to being civilized. Or at least a veneer thereof. "Same as last time. My husband."

"Such devotion." His words came mockingly. He spoke sharply to one of the other men, who retrieved the phone from the stall in which it had come to rest. Selena gave a heartfelt prayer that it would be broken, but from the look on his face, it was not. From the look on his face, it worked perfectly fine as he instructed it to redial the last call.

Cole's relief upon answering came audibly enough that Ashurbeyli moved the phone away from his ear in reaction. "Selena!"

"No." Ashurbeyli smiled tightly, his eyes holding Selena's gaze as she started to tremble in reaction—to the danger, to the pain. Her arm throbbed so hard she thought she'd be better off if it exploded; at this rate, blood clots from deep bruising were as much a danger as the rifles still pointed her way. She tried to hide her puzzlement—what the hell was Ashurbeyli up to?

In another moment, as he moved closer to her and tipped the phone so she might hear, his face so near hers as to once again seem intimate, she understood. *Control.* He was regaining the control she'd lost, and Cole would pay the emotional price. She already heard it in his voice—the strain in his words, the great effort it took to keep his voice calm. "Who is this?"

"Exactly who you're afraid it is." Ashurbeyli reached over to smooth Selena's crooked collar; he ran a finger—oh so gentle—over her bruised cheek, along the line of dried blood left over from her initial capture.

"What can I do for you?" Desperately trying to keep it impersonal, to hide that he was her husband. Selena listened to his struggle with a sudden awe at how much this man loved her. Whatever he'd done in D.C., he loved her. She tried to turn her face away from Ashurbeyli, to hide the sudden sting of tears.

Firmly, he took her chin and restored her former position, inches away. He couldn't miss the shine of her eye; he certainly wouldn't miss that sudden emotional tremble in her chin. She just damn well hoped he somehow missed her complete resolve to live through this, to destroy the Kemenis and their hopes of a takeover in Berzhaan. To see Cole again and figure out what had happened…to fix whatever had gone wrong. Somehow.

Whatever he saw, he smiled again. Just for her. "If

you want to see your lovely wife again, you can accomplish an immediate capitulation to my demands." But it wasn't why he'd called. Not really.

"I'm not in a position to do that," Cole said. There was a spate of rustling; Selena thought Ashurbeyli wasn't the only one who had an audience listening in. "But I'd be glad to pass that word along."

"You do that." Ashurbeyli paused, as much for drama as anything else. "But don't worry overmuch about it. We both know Berzhaan's ministers are too blind to do what's best for their country, and the interfering Western world is too cowardly to stand behind the support it once gave us—or even to interfere with us now."

"Then—" Cole broke off his own words, puzzled.

"I called because I wanted to talk to the man who commands such devotion from such a fierce warrior as your wife. Quite remarkable, isn't she? She could almost be one of us." Selena jerked in reaction; he raised an eyebrow of warning. "I wondered if you could possibly deserve such a woman. Where are you now? What do you do with yourself? Are you as strong as she is? Those are the questions that run through my mind as I watch her this moment, under gunpoint at the hands of my men. But most of all I wanted to make sure you know that you no longer have her. I do."

Selena barely heard Cole's tight whisper, coming through in a moment of ironic perfect cell phone clarity. "You *bastard*." But she heard the pain of the words, and she made a sudden snatch for the phone.

Ashurbeyli expected it, of course. He shoved her back, gave an imperious gesture. The Kemenis swooped in and grabbed her up, snatching her arm so roughly she cried out at the explosion of agony, her knees giving way, her vision gone black as her world narrowed down to that single point of pain. Ashurbeyli said something she couldn't make out, a satisfied sound, and snapped the cell phone shut.

When they dragged her away, she quite gratefully passed out.

"Selena? *Selena!*" Cole's fingers clenched around his phone, his mind so full of tumult he couldn't think, could barely breathe. He fought the hands which tried to take the phone away even as her pained cry echoed in his mind, over and over and—

"Cole!" An unfamiliar voice, but one full of understanding along with the command. Diego Morel. "You'll break it, man—we need to get that number!"

Numbly, Cole tried to release the device; by then his fingers were cramped into place. The hand in question gently removed them as Josie Lockworth said, "Besides, she might try to call again. That's the only contact number she's got."

True. He blinked, floundering for coherent thought, and heard only Selena's cry. *Get it together. You can't help her like this.*

Already, the others were thinking ahead. "Did she say anything the first time? Anything we can use? The damn building's so stout we can't get reliable infrared...even the SEALs are blind right now."

Which he knew. It was just a reminder, a way to pull him back to sensibility. He blinked, looked around...reoriented himself to the interior of the Quonset hut where Tory had dropped him off, staying only for quick introductions before heading back out to do her job. Cold, stark...one end of it filled with bunks, a single bathroom sans shower the only permanent structure other than the shabby office beside it. Beside that, a big chunk of Quonset wall was obscured by a ground control system set within a 30-foot trailer—a bank of machinery with pilot and sensor operator stations that might have been taken for an early *Star Trek* set. From there, Air Force Captain Josie Lockworth and independent contractor Diego Morel flew Josie's newly modified Predator UAV, an unmanned surveillance craft with big bite in the form of Hellfire missiles.

Cole had seen images of the Predator before, and now that it sat before him in person, it did nothing to change his impression of a big flying spoon. Twenty-seven feet of flying spoon…no bigger than a single-engine Cessna.

But effective. Maybe even the chance that Selena needed. For this particular flying spoon incorporated Josie's acoustic improvements, making it even stealthier than before. And since they didn't have Berzhaani permission to run recon flights over the besieged capitol, they'd need all the stealth they could get.

"What did she say?" Josie asked, even as Morel took possession of the cell phone—albeit only long enough to set it on one of the small round tables that served as the commissary, well within Cole's reach. "She had time for a few words when she first called—she would have chosen the most important ones."

For an instant, Cole could only look at her, still numb. Brain definitely not functioning. He saw only concerned smoky hazel eyes, personable features under bobbed brown hair, flight suit cinching in her figure. He'd been flummoxed to find her here, knowing the Predator—even unmodified birds—took time to bring into play. Time to pack it up in its "coffin," time to transport, time to set up. More than two days' worth of time, and the hostage crisis was only a day in the making. She'd cleared up his confusion in a matter of words. "We were here already," she'd said. "There's been so much alarming intel coming out of this region that it was worth risking Berzhaan's displeasure to bring the modified Predator in for its first operational flight. But it's still a test article, so Diego Morel—" she'd nodded at a man who looked as out of place as Cole himself, a big, lean fellow in jeans and a worn leather jacket "—is along as the sensor operator."

All fine with Cole. Anything was fine with Cole, as long as it helped Selena. He'd taken Morel's firm handshake in an absentminded way, but that had changed quickly enough as he caught the look in the other man's dark eyes and realized, startled, that Morel understood. That in some way he'd been there, done that—and a quick doublecheck of the way he looked at Josie was enough to tell him with whom.

And now the two exchanged a concerned glance, one full of unspoken words—*is Selena's husband going to pull it together?*—and it was enough to shock Cole back into thinking mode. "She didn't have time for much," he said, finally answering Josie's question. "She said we should check the outside of the building. She definitely had something in mind, but that's when—" and he stopped, because he couldn't bring himself to say the words and because they knew them anyway.

"Check the outside of the building." Josie nodded. "Then that's what we'll do."

Cole gave the white and gray craft a skeptical glance.

"Does this thing see well enough to check things out in detail?"

"If we risk a lower altitude—luckily for us, the cloud cover is on our side. It would be easier if we knew what we were looking for, but—"

Morel finished Josie's thought. "If she chose those particular words as the most important ones she could say, we'd damn well better not let them go to waste."

Cole nodded and wondered if he looked as lost as he felt. He'd been in the middle of so many operations just like this one—which is to say, grasping for information, lives on the line…sometimes even his own. But never had they involved Selena. He had no idea he'd struggle so hard to find his usual easy confidence.

But he'd find it, because she was counting on him. "We have to trust her," he said. "If we look hard enough, we'll find it."

All too soon, Selena opened her eyes, waking to a world of discomfort spiked with pain. Her arms, twisted behind her and once again cuffed…*ow, dammit.* It wouldn't be so bad if her badly bruised biceps hadn't been twisted along with the rest of the arm. Or, if upon opening her eyes, she hadn't seen just what they wanted her to see—the current guard sitting directly across from her. When he saw her eyes open he greeted her with a mongrel smile that was as much sneer as anything else.

She sneered back.

Okay, not the wisest thing to do. Wisest would have been to close her eyes again. But she wasn't in Obi-Wan Kenobi mode just now. She was in the mood to quit playing games and kick ass all the way out of here.

Like that's going to happen.

It might have happened already if it hadn't been for the hostages. People she couldn't leave, because they were the very reason she'd come in the first place. People who—

Suddenly aware of whispers and rustling, of rank, fearful sweat in the air and the indefinable feel of bodies sharing the space nearby, she popped her eyelids up again, and this time turned her head. The gaze she met first was Ambassador Allori's.

"Charming expression, my dear," he murmured, sitting on the edge of his chair with his elbows propped on his knees. His tie was long gone, but his suit coat remained against the chill. "Perhaps you should teach it to me so I can use it during my next negotiations. Which, I hope, will be far from here."

Her response—her recently formed conviction that none of the hostages were meant to leave this building alive regardless of the outcome for the Kemenis—stuck in her throat. Given their recent conversation, at the very least Ashurbeyli considered his chances of success to be remote and was fully prepared for that contingency. Because besides Allori, the students watched her closely, their faces a collage of emotions. *Fear, awe, concern, fear, fear and fear.*

"Are you okay?" one of them asked, a girl of indefinable ethnic background. American by the accent, reasonably calm to judge by her voice. She added quite sensibly, "Because you look like crap."

Selena took a more careful assessment of her circumstances. She was with the others now, that much was obvious. But she was the only one cuffed, and she'd been placed closest to the guard who sat in the opening between this function room and the ballroom. One corner held neatly stacked litter from what scant food they'd been allowed; another still held their makeshift latrine, though they'd now thoughtfully been provided with a mop bucket. Even though they'd also been taken to the bathroom occasionally, the faint underlying odor of urine made it clear the bucket was in use. The air held the definite chill of an ancient and faltering heating system left to its own devices; the students all wore what coats they'd come with, and some of the girls huddled together for warmth. Many of the boys had stepped up to fill the role of comforter.

Selena knew from experience that it was a great way to avoid feeling one's own fear.

That she was here, with the others…she didn't take it as a good sign. Ashurbeyli had been truly offended by her attempt to contact Cole, and if it resulted in more limited access to the Kemenis, it meant she had less chance to find out what was going on. But at least the guard was letting them talk. And a glance at her low waistband showed no sign of blood, no telltales from the metal strip—nor any sign that it had been taken from her. As blurry as those last moments in the bathroom had been, it didn't seem as though she'd missed anything important. The last thing she remembered, Ashurbeyli had hung up on Cole.

Cole. She tried to imagine what he'd heard from his end of the phone. The initial interruption, Ashurbeyli's baiting words, Selena's own perfectly timed cry of pain before Ashurbeyli cut the connect.

Big mistake. She should have left it alone. Even thinking about being on the other end of that phone—about how she'd feel if it was him in the hands of terrorists…

You might have run from him, girl, but not nearly as far as you thought.

Even though in the end it might be too far. Too many miles, too much danger between them.

Selena reoriented her thoughts with much determination. She shook her hair back and looked at the young woman who'd spoken and who'd probably given up on an answer. "I'm as okay as the rest of you. Is everyone all right?"

Allori drew her attention to Razidae, a man who defined the very meaning of the word *grim*. "He does not feel his government will negotiate in any manner."

"I've already told Ashurbeyli they won't. I'm not expecting any grand gestures from the States, either—Berzhaan is likely to tie their hands."

Allori shook his head. "I just can't understand what they're trying to accomplish. They've always been smarter than this."

"I think they *are* smarter than this." Selena held his gaze long enough to give her words extra meaning… things she didn't want to say out loud if Ashurbeyli listened in. Allori's eyes widened slightly. He might not have even her vaguely guessed details, but he realized there were indeed layers to this operation.

"What about that man?" the same girl asked. The others had moved a little closer, just as interested in the answers but letting her ask the questions. "The cook."

Surely they realized he was dead. Surely they'd heard the gunshot. A glance at Allori confirmed it, but on that group of young faces she saw nothing but naive hope. Selena sighed and tipped her head back against the wall against which she'd been sloppily positioned. "His name was Atif," she said. "He was helping me. He's dead now."

"Helping you?" The young man who'd stared in the lobby snorted, loudly enough to draw a quelling look from the guard. He immediately subsided. "They said he betrayed you."

She nodded. "That's true. He did both. People aren't always simple."

Keep that in mind.

He met her words with a scowl, opened his mouth—and then glanced at the guard and shut it again.

"My name is Selena," she told them. "Tell me yours—all of you. Tell me where you're from."

Still the scowl. "And how is *that* going to help?"

"Get us out of here? It won't. But it's a way to pass the time." And to get their minds off their possible—no, probable—fate. Unless Selena could do something to change it. Unless she could figure out exactly what the Kemenis had planned—and then stop them.

The girl with the questions took up the introductions, pointing to them all. Selena, well versed in putting names to faces and remembering them, paid only partial attention, nodding in the right spots. The girl's name was Rosa, said the Spanish way with a soft *s*. And the staring boy was Craig, and his girlfriend Marianne, and then there was Toby and Guy—very French, *Gee*—and Celina and Pam and Agatha....

And others, which she'd remember when she needed them. She made small talk with them, asked how they'd come to be visiting here, and all the while kept catching Allori's eye. She wanted his assessment of the situation.

"Did you really call outside?" Rosa asked, quite suddenly. Everyone else stopped their quiet chatter, eager to hear that she had, that help was on the way.

Selena shifted, trying to straighten out the cramp in her lower back. Maybe she really *was* getting her period. Just what she needed.

Except its arrival would mean she could quit worrying about risking more than just her own life. Its arrival would take her off the hook with Cole, leaving things between them less complicated. Leaving her the space to stay with him for the sake of that relationship, and not to blur the decision with what might be best for a child.

Then why did she feel that sudden flutter of disappointment? Absurd disappointment, under the circumstances. Crazy.

Then crazy she was.

She took a deep breath, glanced at the guard—did he even understand English?—and said, "I called someone who can help."

As one, they held their breath; hope leaped to every face. She shook her head. "He can't overcome the mandates of the Berzhaani government. He's not Superman. But he can make sure that those who are addressing this situation keep us in mind." She looked at the guard again, and this time spoke right to him— just in case he knew a smattering of English after all. "Frankly, I'm surprised the Kemenis found it so upsetting. You'd think they'd want both governments in a frazzle about our welfare. Then the Kemenis will get what they want."

Ashurbeyli's voice from the ballroom startled the students, but not Selena; she'd half expected it. "He doesn't speak your language," Ashurbeyli said, sounding bored. "But noise irritates him, so you might well want to keep it down. As time goes by—as we see no signs of concern or cooperation from Berzhaan—it will become harder to keep my men from taking their pleasures and frustrations out on you all. After all, if it does not matter to your people, why should it matter to mine?"

The students paled, every one of them. Their chaperone paled. Even the events coordinator blanched.

"Oh, great," Selena said, responding in Berzhaani. "Scaring a bunch of kids. Big tough terrorist."

He gave a dark laugh, but returned to his murmured conversation with Jonas White.

Selena fought the impulse to scratch her cheek where a trickle of dried blood itched with sudden ferocity— and then she fought the impulse to check her watch as habit overrode, for the instant, her otherwise constant awareness of the ache in her restrained arms.

Enough of the gesture got through for Allori to give her a grim smile. "It's been just over a day. It's just the beginning."

Selena lowered her voice, mindful of Ashurbeyli in the next room, and mindful of Ashurbeyli's warning about the guard. It had not, she thought, been an empty threat. Nor were the words flying back and forth between Ashurbeyli and several of his men, for the snatches she heard of the quickly escalating conversation seemed to center around Ashurbeyli's easy treatment of Selena thus far. It was a startling challenge in the face of their loyalty to him, and a hot personal insult. There would be fallout. But she couldn't concentrate solely on her eavesdropping. Not when she had the opportunity to touch base with Allori. "Dante, what do you make of them? They're prepared in every way—they knew this could be an extended situation.

But they don't seem particularly concerned about the outcome."

"Noticed that, did you?" Allori gave the ballroom a pensive look, no happier about the shouting than Selena. "If I had to guess, I'd think they've got a backup plan. I might even say they're just as happy to go to that plan." He eased off the chair, moving closer, and crouched nearby to lower his voice even further. "I would go so far as to venture that it's something dramatic—and that it wouldn't bode well for us."

Selena tipped her head back against the wall again. "We've both been in this part of the world too long. I'm sorry to say I agree with you." But she didn't say the word *bomb* out loud; she suspected it might be one of the few English words their friendly guard actually knew. "I had Cole on the phone just long enough to tell him to warn anyone who would listen to take a closer look. I didn't have any time to explain why."

"Your husband." Allori raised his brow in mild surprise. "That's who you called."

Selena didn't hesitate. "He's the only one I trust to use the information to protect us—at least as much as anyone can." But she stopped short at the end of her words, feeling her own surprise at her deep confidence in him. It seemed some part of her had always known...had never run away at all, but only come along for the ride.

The question was whether she'd ever get a chance to convince the rest of her.

Allori said, "You don't talk about him often. But I'm given to understand that he's in a position to act on your information?" He'd know of Cole's CIA status, of course—it was in her own profile.

"Like I said...as much as anyone can. He works the

field." She kept her tone light, but Allori would catch the implications—that Cole was not in the directorate hierarchy where he could better wield any influence. Without planning on it, Selena added, "I have some friends…if he thinks to hook up with them…"

Allori nodded. "Yes. I might know who you mean."

"You read my file pretty carefully." She grinned, a wry and painful expression. A lock of hair pulled at her skin, glued there by the blood. She ducked her head, trying to rub it free without provoking the bruises. In the next room, the conversation had died to voices low and intense, and the tone of it made the skin of her spine tighten in warning.

"I did," Allori said. "Did you think you got the position by chance, when you applied so late into the decision process? Not that the decision itself was mine, but I kept myself apprised." He made as if to free the hair at her face, and the guard instantly came alert.

"Back away from her," he said, jabbing his rifle at them in punctuation. "You've talked enough."

Allori understood as well as Selena, even though his grasp of the language didn't approach fluency. He immediately raised both hands slightly in capitulation and backed away, reclaiming his chair.

"Doesn't matter," Selena muttered, returning to her own efforts without acknowledging the scariness of the guard. He scowled at her, terrorist pride offended. "I'll get it."

And she did, but when she looked up, Ashurbeyli filled the doorway.

The others shrank back. They'd seen Ashurbeyli escort two other hostages from this room, and both had died immediately thereafter.

Ashurbeyli fingered a handcuff key and he rested his hand on the grip of his holstered semiautomatic—and he looked only at Selena.

Chapter 13

Cole stood behind the high-backed Predator sensor operator's chair, looking over Diego Morel's shoulder as the Predator's live feed satellite link fed them high-altitude images of Suwan. Morel's impatience at the intrusion went noted, but made no difference at all. In many ways, Morel was Cole's opposite. He had the dark, smoldering bad-boy thing going on. Cole counted more on the blond carefree wiseass thing, and he knew it—he'd cultivated it.

It wasn't doing him much good at the moment. And even though he'd regained his equilibrium after Selena's call—and the call from the terrorist that had followed—he had nothing to which he could apply his skills. Gathering intel. Evading detection. Being in the middle of the enemy when they didn't even have a clue. None of that applied right now. If the SEALs couldn't close in on that building, neither could he.

Except…

Unless…

He knew someone he could call, someone from the CIA's Office of Technical Services. A master of disguises. It might take a while to put himself into play, but Cole would use the time as best he could…looking over Morel's shoulder. Driving the man quietly and understandably mad as he waited for the Predator to quit the relative safety of its twenty-five-thousand foot cruising altitude and ease down for a closer look at the building about which Selena had been so concerned.

He wished he'd had the chance to tell her where he was. Who he was with. Who else was working on her side.

Soon enough.

He left the sensor station and the quick murmur of discussion that immediately took place. No question as to the subject of it—they were worried about him. Whether he'd hold up, and whether he'd get in the way. Well, he was back on his feet, now. They'd figure it out.

Soon enough.

Selena knew she was in trouble when Ashurbeyli uncuffed her. She saw it, too, in the intensity of his gaze, felt it in the stiffness of his movement. He'd let things get personal; he'd let the reaction of his men get to him. He'd let himself stray from wisdom to reaction, from professional to personal—and probably didn't even know why.

She knew. She'd gotten the best of him. It was why he uncuffed her—to prove the point. To show both his men and the other hostages that he wasn't worried about her. To show *himself.*

She'd be elated at the freedom—at the opportunity, if she thought he'd actually give her one. But he kept one hand on her back, just below the join of her neck and shoulders. From there he could feel every tension; every telegraphed intent. She'd never take him by surprise. And meanwhile she could no longer trust him to make the most logical decision from the Kemeni point of view—or from any point of view at all. He vibrated with intent, and in the brief moment he allowed her to meet his gaze before pushing her onward, his dark eyes held warning.

She hadn't been forgiven.

She knew then that he intended to prove his point in a more personal way than she'd first anticipated. In the only way a man felt he could prove absolute dominance over a woman. And she'd thought she was as ready as any woman could be—and suddenly she knew, with the intense pounding of her heart and the suddenly watery nature of her knees and her nearly irresistible gut fight-or-flight punch of fear, that no one could really be ready at all.

It's not worth dying for.

She breathed deeply. Slowly. Tried to move as though she had no idea what lay ahead.

He guided her out to the hallway, giving her no chance for so much as a glance at Allori. Instead of heading in the direction she feared—toward the doors and the death spot at the top of the stairs—he turned her to the right. Down the long hall of the function rooms. The first room still held the neatly rolled prayer rugs; not long from now, they would hold men in prayer.

Ashurbeyli wouldn't be one of them. He took her right past the improvised prayer spot and into the smaller room beyond. A one-on-one room. Small round table, comfortable chairs, not much else. Private.

A shiver ran down Selena's spine; the small hairs on her arms stood up. She cursed her own reaction, knowing Ashurbeyli couldn't have missed it.

You always knew it could and probably would come to this if were caught.

With as much cool command as he'd shown from the beginning, Ashurbeyli pushed her up against the wall just inside the door and kicked the doorstop free, nudging the door closed with the same foot. Then he stepped back—not far, but no longer close enough to brush constantly against her—and his hand fell away.

Selena didn't move. She turned her face to the side and let her chest press against the wall, her hands away from her sides and turned against the wall. She wanted no mistakes in body language here. He wanted to be in charge? Let him. Until she had an opportunity…let him.

"Jonas and I have been in discussion," Ashurbeyli said. She couldn't discern anything of his mood from his conversational voice. "We both have interests outside this building, as you might imagine. Letting this situation drag out benefits no one. We think it's time to provoke some response. And here you are…official enough so you're not an innocent, but even in those Western clothes, woman enough to garner a response of outraged shock. I'm afraid you're just the right person to take out to the steps this time."

Dammit, no! Not so soon. And even so…that's not what this was about. He hadn't brought her here simply to tell her he intended to kill her. She took a deep breath, faintly tainted with the smell of smoke in the old wallpaper. "Of course White wants me dead. He doesn't want you to hear what I have to say about him."

Calm, cool answer from the FBI legate. What about the quiet cry of dismay from somewhere deep inside, the protest from a woman who wasn't nearly done with life? Who might even have another life slowly growing within...

Selena swallowed that more personal reaction. It wouldn't get her anywhere with this man. He respected the warrior in her.

Ashurbeyli rustled in movement. "Perhaps he doesn't, indeed, want me talking to you. You may be assured it's something I'll deal with when the time is right."

"Assured?" She almost turned to look at him, but stopped the impulse as the side of her face left the wallpaper, settling back into place. "I don't actually give a damn if White leads you around by the nose, as long as you're not killing people. Oh, wait—too late. How many have already died for this failure?"

"'Fail' is not a term we're interested in." His cold tone punctuated the truth of those words.

"That's why you want to kill me," she said, and couldn't believe the assertion in her voice. Surely it was someone else's voice coming from her mouth—because as cool as she'd always been in a crisis, Selena was far from ready to die. The tension in the room made her think of Ashurbeyli's gun, and she trusted the instinct that told her he'd raised it. Time to rise to the challenge, then. To meet his expectations of her, formed at that very moment they'd locked gazes in Razidae's office. Slowly—almost laughably so—she turned around to face him. She put her back to the wall, kept her arms slightly raised in spite of her burning injury and again met the intensity of his gaze. "Because you especially don't want to fail at the hands of a woman."

He hissed something from between clenched teeth and in one swift step he was upon her, pressing up against her, his gun jammed into the soft flesh under her jaw, one knee shoved between her thighs. *"That,"* he said, "will never happen." He couldn't help but feel the gallop of her heart, just as she felt his. She forced herself to stay relaxed even as every wiry muscle in his body tightened, his free hand gripping her so high on her waist that it brushed the bottom of her breast. She could only pretend that he'd be too occupied to detect the excessive stiffness of her waistband caused by the thin metal panel. It might even be true.

She instantly discarded the ploy about having her period. He wouldn't hesitate to check. Nor did she turn her face aside, not even as their noses brushed. But she kept her voice low. "You have to know I've been prepared for this moment since long before I walked into this building." As if anyone truly could. "You don't have to believe me...*I* wouldn't. But just imagine how you'll feel when you don't leave me broken."

He stared back, black gaze impenetrable, his breath on her cheek, the pistol sight jabbing into her skin along the inside edge of her jaw. "Careful," he said, and he, too, kept his voice low. His breath whispered against her cheek. "You'll oblige me to prove your lie."

Relax. Relax. Give him nothing to react to. Nothing to fight back against. No excuses. She had to stay cool enough to play her way through whatever happened, no matter how she felt about it. She had to buy that chance at potential escape—and yet if she made him feel any more scorned, he'd probably just as soon kill her on the spot. She made her voice as honest as she could. Damned honest. Raw. "We've had an interesting skirmish, you and I. I would very much prefer—I would be grateful—if you left me this much honor before you take me out to those steps."

And there, pressed against her with his body as brutally honest as her words, he took a sudden sharp breath. He raised his hand, letting one finger just barely graze the line of her jaw. And he smiled. "It was not an honorable thing you did, phoning out when I left you your privacy."

"No." She cleared her throat as her voice caught. "It was a desperate thing."

Because he'd already defeated her. He'd prevailed. He heard those unspoken words…or maybe, this close to her, he saw them in her eyes.

Quite suddenly, he stepped back. Selena sagged against the wall, caught completely unaware by the weakness in her knees. But she instantly straightened. And she said, "Just for the record…I'm not giving up."

Again, the dark smile. "I don't expect you to."

Selena took a deep breath as she stepped back out into the hallway, Ashurbeyli's hand again resting low at her neck, his gun still at her ribs. Together, they headed for the lobby, the front doors, and death.

I'm not giving up.

"Cole." Morel's voice came flatly, and Cole jerked his attention from the coffee he'd been trying to make palatable, abandoning it on the table to return to the ground control station tucked in the trailer against the back of the hangar. No need to duck around the Predator's long, graceful wings, almost twice as wide as the bird was long; it was out in the air, and Josie sat in at the pilot's station beyond the flung-wide trailer doors, headset in place and deft hands at the stick and throttle.

"Just let me get a good approach arc," she said, attention focused on the screen. "We want to keep this in view as long as possible. I'm going down lower, Diego."

"Too low," Morel said, watching her.

"We've got plenty of cloud cover. It's worth the risk," Josie said shortly, and didn't receive any argument. A glance at Morel's screen showed the Predator's video feed zooming, refocusing, and then hunting to reacquire target. Dizzying. Cole recognized the capitol building, though. It had been the focus of his life for— was it only just over a day, now? Amazing. *Seems like forever.* He wanted to ask "What?" but restrained himself.

Or maybe he just didn't want to know.

Soon enough Josie put the Predator right where Morel needed it, and he went tight with the view. An excellent image, grainy as it was. Far too easy to see that the Kemenis had put someone else out on the top of those steps, still hiding behind their hostage and the thick capitol door.

Far too easy to see that the hostage in question was a woman. Paradoxically dressed in Kemeni colors, but nonetheless a woman. Tall, lean, touched by elegance, dark chestnut hair swept back from her face to make the bruises clear.

His voice came in a mere whisper of breath and sorrow. "Selena."

No! We need more time.

They'd brought Selena out to their death steps. No doubt the Kemeni leader even now shouted out his demands and delusions; Cole could be sure of it just from the way Selena's right eyebrow quirked. He was in her ear.

Until now he'd only hovered behind the pilot and sensor-operator stations. He'd restrained himself—and there hadn't been that much to see, just endless circles while Josie and Diego murmured back and forth about altitude and risk and exposure, all the while trying to get good clear pictures of the roof and the building exterior in response to Selena's words. But now he clamped a hand on the back of Josie's substantial station chair and let the fingers dig into the high backrest. "Do something."

Josie exchanged a quick glance with Morel. "A distraction?"

"You'll expose the Pred," Morel said instantly. "You'll reveal our activity to the Berzhaani government before we've resolved this crisis. We might give her an opportunity to escape, but at the expense of the rest of this operation."

"A hellfire would do it," Josie said, as if they were carrying on two different conversations—or maybe just two at once.

But Cole had focused in on Selena's hands. They weren't quite natural; not quite right. The grain of the image kept him from seeing the fine details of her striking face, from reading the undertones of the expression there. But her hands…she held them in front of her, even though she didn't seem to be restrained. She fiddled with her olive-green shirt, a garment that hung off her straight shoulders with room to spare, and she held herself stiffly—she held herself in a way that told him more than any stranger would know. "She's hurt," he murmured.

"No blood," Morel said instantly, his eyes narrowing; it wasn't an argument, but contributing observation. "They've been hitting her, no doubt about that."

"They were probably hitting her *back*," Cole said, no doubt in his voice. "It's upper body somewhere. The way she's standing—whoa, wait. Did she spot you?"

For Selena had ceased fiddling with the shirt, her head still slightly cocked in the way to let Cole know someone was shouting in her ear, and now quietly held her hands in front of her, low at her hips, fingers moving.

"She's not looking at us," Morel said, a frown in his voice.

Josie spoke with assertion. "She knows there's someone out there. The SEAL team, for one. Berzhaani teams. She's talking to all of us."

"Two-ten, seven," Cole said abruptly, even as Selena repeated the signs. "Twenty-seven."

Morel adjusted the view as the Predator arced in closer, giving them a new angle of those hands. "Hostages or terrorists?"

"Terrorists," Cole said, no hesitation. "She's going to give us the most tactically important information first." And just how much would she have the chance to say? How long would the Kemeni leader shout in her ear?

The expression that flitted across her face in grainy technical magic made it look as though she wondered the same. With restraint, she turned her hand over, cupping it as though cradling an apple. Normally a gesture made high, the hand signal was nonetheless clear enough. Josie murmured it out loud. "Booby trap," and then turned to look at Morel. "It's what she was trying to tell us on the phone. 'Check what you can see of the building, I think they're going to *booby-trap it.*'"

"It's a layered operation," Morel agreed. "Everything I've heard about Ashurbeyli…he's got to know he can't win this one—at least, not as things stand on the surface. So we've got to figure out the layers. Check that building until we find what she thinks we should."

"More than that." Josie gave Cole a sharp look. "We've got to pass the information along."

Numbly, Cole nodded. "It's why she gave it to us," he said. "We're the ones who have to find a way to make sure she isn't caught in the middle. Or—" he stopped in surprise, realizing he'd fallen into the mindset of taking them for granted—"or *I* do."

Josie's look came even more sharply. "You had it right the first time. Don't forget it."

He held her gaze, then lifted his chin in a slight gesture of assent. But he kept silent about his own plans.

For he had no intent of just sitting here. Watching. Leaving Selena's fate entirely in the hands of others.

The video screen drew his attention again, and he realized he was still making assumptions. Everyone else to appear at the top of these imposing stone steps had died within moments. *Don't you let him kill you,* he thought at her, not caring if the internal ferocity made it through to his expression. For this mission, the cool and irreverent Cole Smith—station name Jason P. JOXLEITER, CIA field officer and Jox to his friends—

had been cast aside. This time, he'd draw deep. This time, it was personal. But—*don't you let him kill you!*

She might have heard him. She'd gone back to fiddling with her shirt, and the slight stiffening of her posture made him think the Kemeni leader was winding up his words of rhetoric and delusional rationalization. Cole didn't need fine pixel resolution on the image to recognize that subtle change in her expression.

Selena, about to make her move. *You go, babe.* But his heart hammered into overtime, and his fists clenched, and he couldn't help but add an anguished inner prayer. *Please. Oh, please...*

Ashurbeyli kept his hand tangled in the hair at the base of Selena's neck, exposing only his wrist to the inevitable sniperscopes pointed his way. The rest of him hung behind the stout wooden door, a wood with a re-inforced armor core. *Dammit,* she thought at all those inevitable, lurking snipers—at least one SEAL team, against Berzhaan wishes or not, and probably the Berzhaani Elite themselves—*then shoot his wrist!* She tried to tell them with her eyes, with her anger and her willingness to follow through on such a thought. Son of a bitch, anything but going down without a fight. She couldn't be so straightforward as to give them another hand signal...there was a good British signal that would do the trick, but it took on meaning at throat level. Ashurbeyli would see it.

So as Ashurbeyli wound up his meaningless demands—demands she was now almost certain he'd never expected to be met—she reached into her unbuttoned shirt and eased the thin metal panel from her waistband. She had to clear the snag in her turtleneck—

the one that had cut straight through to skin—but it gave her a chance to confirm the exact location of the jagged edge.

That's me. The Jagged Edge. My new superhero name.

His voice fell away, a welcome respite. He pulled her head back into the cold muzzle of his pistol.

Dead, one way or the other. *Might as well be the other. Go down fighting.*

His fingers tightened in her hair—

Selena spun. She pivoted around his grip instead of trying to break it, slashing the metal upward, slicing into his wrist; the gun fell away. Her elbow slammed back into his gut. When he jerked over the pain, fingers still clutching her hair, she met him with another sweep of metal—scoring his handsome face, his charismatic features. He staggered back a step.

His fingers loosened.

Yes!

Selena tore free. She couldn't reach the gun, but she could kick it away, and it clattered down those stone steps behind her, flashing dully in the midday sun in the very corner of her vision.

The lobby lay open before her, cleared on Ashurbeyli's orders; he'd wanted no one exposed to weapons fire. Selena kicked into high gear, all her pains forgotten. Ashurbeyli's hand scraped down her back as she bolted, grasping for her shirt—losing it. *I warned you!* she cried, but her mouth stayed clamped shut and determined, and the words never made it past her lips. Through the security arch, past the inner lobby, headed for the nearest corner as shouts of anger followed. Déjà vu, but this time she couldn't duck through her old path—Ashurbeyli had that figured out. She sprinted for the next corner and turned it, and she wished fervently for a nice escape hatch to appear in the floor because from here she couldn't go anywhere but in circles.

Elevator.

Great, a nice closed-in little box. Wherever the door opened, there'd be someone waiting.

Unless it didn't go anywhere at all. She angled for it, coming in at such speed that she bounced off the wall even as she slammed her hand against the elevator button. Old...slow. Maybe too slow. Selena grabbed up the elegant metal ashtray-topped cylinder beside the elevator in anticipation of head bashing and headed for the nearest doorway, pushing it open, considering a quick foray out the window—until a glance reminded her that the first-floor windows were thoroughly covered by decorative but sturdy iron bars.

Great. Trapped.

The elevator dinged. For an agonizing moment Selena hesitated, weighing the time she'd need against the sound of pounding feet, the shout as her pursuit split up at the previous hallway, the bang of doors slammed open and the crash of things knocked aside as men bounded in and out of those rooms, checking for her. They'd find her here, no question about it. They were mad and they were thorough, and she'd bet Ashurbeyli was leaving men at the corner of each cleared hallway so she couldn't double back. Eventually he'd run out of them, but for now she had nowhere to go but up.

She dashed out to the elevator; the doors had closed again but the car sat there, waiting patiently for its next summons. With swift care she replaced the ashtray right where it had been, fitting it into the indentation in the carpet. She hit the elevator button even as she used a foot to sweep a stray fallen clump of ashes into dust across the carpet, and when the doors opened she jumped right in, not hesitating to climb atop the narrow, waist-high railing that lined the inside of the car.

Nowhere to go but up.

The brake-and-cable service panel, of course. The doors shut behind her and the elevator sat waiting further instruction. Foot time again; Selena used her toes to push every button available and let the elevator sort out which way to go first—to the basement or the roof. Someone hit the closed doors and she flinched—but she couldn't tell if someone had seen her, or if the brass doors had simply been a convenient target of anger.

If they'd seen her, her clever hiding place would turn into a literal dead end. But if she waited, it'd be too late. So she went for it, stretching for the offset panel in the ceiling. Her injured arm wouldn't reach up over her shoulder, not at that angle; she gave a snarl of impatience and twisted around, walking the handrail until she could reach up with the other arm and nudge the panel out of place. The elevator lurched on the way downward. One floor to the basement, and she had to assume someone would be there to meet it even if the odds were low. *Dammit, where's a ladder when you need one?* Or maybe even a nice pile of terrorists to climb.

She leaped for the opening—and with only one hand making a solid landing, slipped to sprawl awkwardly across the floor.

It was, she decided, a moment to leave out of any future report. But she scrambled to her feet—and, out of time, tucked herself back up against the front of the el-

evator. If anyone waited, they'd have to come in to find
her. The old elevator jerked to a stop; the doors cranked
open. Selena held her breath, listening.

If any Kemeni waited, they did the same.

And the doors closed.

She didn't hesitate. The first-floor button wasn't lit,
but someone could push it at any moment, especially if
that someone happened to notice the elevator already
on the move…and no more sign of Selena on the first
floor. Up to the handrail, and this time she balanced
there like a cat, her gaze locked on target. *Grab the edge
of the opening. Get the good elbow up. Haul ass.* She
took a moment, took a breath—

Took a leap.

Got it.

Her arm screamed a protest; she gasped in pain. But
she held on, and she forced the other arm to do more
than its share. A few swings back and forth and all that
damn free-weight work came in handy—Cole spotting
her, the look on his face telling her exactly what was on
his mind and it sure wasn't adding another round of reps
and *focus,* Selena—she heaved herself up and locked
her elbow over the edge. A moment of distinctly inele-
gant scrambling and she pulled her legs up through the
opening, rushing to replace the hatch panel just as the
elevator came to a stop at the first floor and damned if
those doors didn't open after all. The car quivered as
several Kemenis rushed in, jostling each other in the
small space.

Really, she thought at them, as still as could be and
breathing shallowly through her mouth while her lungs
cried out for big gulping inhalations, *if I was down
there, I think you'd have seen me by now.*

Apparently they came to the same conclusion. They tramped out, leaving the elevator free to continue upward. Selena grabbed those big deep breaths she'd been starving for and eyed her new territory—four stories of empty air pierced by the elevator cable. Narrow spears of light leaked in at each floor where the exterior elevator doors closed imperfectly; high above, the cable drum rotated to pull them upward, the motor grinding with a desperation that spoke of its age. A tempting series of wooden rungs ran up to the roof, set in a channel that might just be deep enough to hold her and let the elevator slide by. "Ah," she murmured out loud, too taken by the absurdity of the moment to stay completely silent, "I've been shafted."

Hurt like hell, just as she would have expected. Aching face, stinging scalp—she checked for blood where Ashurbeyli had gripped her hair, but didn't have enough light to tell for sure. Her side still stung, and her arm flirted with the kind of explosion more common to potatoes in the microwave.

Great. One battered, possibly pregnant, intermittently nauseous, barely armed FBI legate against the world.

Well, against all the Kemenis in this building. Might as well have been the world.

But her focus had changed. She wasn't alone in this any longer, not entirely. Cole was out there, doing his best to take her part. The SEAL team—and she *knew* there was one out there somewhere—had to have seen her signals, and that meant they'd realize she knew of them, could work with them. And now she'd become all but certain the situation was much more complex than a batch of rustic terrorists grabbing hostages to make petulant, impossible demands. They weren't concerned enough about the capitulation to those demands. They killed hostages to make a point as much as to get what they wanted; Selena wondered if Ashurbeyli wasn't using those deaths to build exactly the impression he wanted to...that of a narrow-viewed terrorist sticking to impossible demands beyond all reason.

That particular path had become well-trodden in recent years.

She wasn't quite sure of his true intentions, or of his methods—what, exactly, he hoped to gain if she'd guessed right, if White's timely flinch had been confirmation—if he blew the building as she suspected he would—or when he even planned to do it. She was sure only that there was more here than met the eye. And while she'd started out with the hostages as her first priority—finding a way to free them, to keep those kids safe until Ashurbeyli's people were neutralized—now she wasn't sure but if helping those on the outside to storm the place might be the very last thing she should do. She needed to understand the situation. She needed to thin their ranks, disrupt them from the inside...and figure them out.

Jonas White.

He'd be a weak point. He was a man used to running things from a distance. Even now he spent much of his time away from the Kemenis, no doubt in one of the more luxurious apartments the capitol building had to offer.

"Jonas White," she murmured...and then gave a sharp shake of her head. Not quite yet. It would cause too much of a stir, and the last she'd seen he'd been in the ballroom, anyway. So...add one more thing to the list. Identify the room he was staying in. If timing allowed…have a nice conversation with him there. Until then, she'd cause what trouble she could. No more innocuous gunfire up the stairwell; if she pulled a trigger, someone would be in her sights. Ashurbeyli would be furious…but she imagined her status was already shifted to kill on sight.

"Learn to be invisible," she whispered, crouched on the top of a moving elevator car. Advice to herself. Wise advice, as impossible as it was. Probably the only way she'd stay alive.

Best to get moving, then. She had a lot to accomplish before she died.

Chapter 14

The elevator stopped at the third floor, submitting to another inspection. When it lurched into motion again, it headed downward—and Selena stepped neatly onto the wooden rungs of the four-story shaft, letting the elevator drop away below her. She climbed up past the fourth floor and right up past the noisy hoist mechanism to the roof access. The access panel that sat on the roof like a small squatter's shack, offering a railed platform at the edge of the shack. She climbed onto the platform, wiping her filthy hands on her shirt. When she peered through the louvered door, she found an empty roof under a low, nickel-gray sky with individual clouds scudding quickly past, driven by capricious winds. Rain smattered briefly against the worn shelter. *From the north.*

Anyone up here on guard duty was most likely sheltered to the south of a roof structure. Maybe even this one.

We're playing for keeps, now, she reminded herself. Whatever safety margin Ashurbeyli's interest had once given her had not only disappeared, it had now marked her for death. She'd embarrassed him one too many times.

You can always go crawling back. Beg for forgiveness. Submit. Admit you were a fool and that you know better now.

She considered it a moment, and in the dim, indirect light filtering through the louvers, gave a firm shake of her head. Nope. Still a fool. Still trying to save the day.

Her current goal was simple enough—return to the guest room she'd appropriated. Gather up what little of use remained in her briefcase. See if there was enough left of the cell phone battery to call Cole.

And for pure luxury, maybe she'd have a chance to wash her face, use the bathroom and see just how deeply the metal strip had cut into her side. Maybe there'd even be a token first aid kit in the closet. She suppressed a sudden sardonic snort. Yeah, that's what she needed... a Band-Aid. Wouldn't that just fix everything.

But first she had to get from here to the stair access. She had a vague idea in which direction the stairs were located, and a sneaking suspicion she'd find Kemenis on the way. It'd just be too easy if she didn't, wouldn't it? Just as it would be too damn easy if this old, rickety door didn't creak like hell when it moved.

Well, we can change that.

She left the door long enough to eye the currently quiescent elevator mechanism, gauging the distance between them, carefully testing the strength of the railing without actually committing herself to leaning on it. It shifted, but it held. *What's one more chance?* Slowly, she stretched out to the massive hoist, just barely reaching the nearest part. Cold metal met her fingertips. Cold, *greasy* metal.

The hoist gave a clunk, startling her; Selena jerked back onto the platform and fell smack on her ass—but she looked at her fingers and smiled, and she didn't even bother to get to her feet as she smeared heavy grease into the hinges of the access door.

Moments later she slipped silently through the smallest possible opening, squinting against the sudden wind and cold and occasional spit of rain. *Rain is your friend,* she told herself. No doubt the Kemenis were squinting, too.

Like the elevator shaft access, the closest stair entry jutted out of the roof, a much sturdier hut made of brick. Not the one she wanted, though—she'd head across the roof to the other side of the building, where a second brick structure waited—one that she would exit much closer to her room. But she had a choice—tiptoe over and hope no one spotted her, or spot the Kemenis first and do something about them.

She could almost feel the impact of 39 mm bullets into her back. She pulled the metal strip from her waistband and headed for the closest stair access, putting her back to the wind. They'd be on the other side, sheltered. And she'd really, really like to have one of their guns. Best chance she had for one, all things considered.

On the other hand, the element of surprise notwithstanding, she didn't think much of the odds right now. Time to improve them a little. She reached the back of the brick structure, peeked around to check the side, and sprang up to grab the roof overhang.

Her right arm still wasn't doing its share. No surprise. But the dovetail of small decorative limestone blocks at the corner gave her plenty of footing, and within seconds she swung a leg over the edge and rolled to the roof. Wind gusted in her ear, obscuring the sound of her own movement. She crawled over to the south edge of the gritty roofing. *After all this, you'd better be there.*

Ah, yes. Two of them, bundled in warm parkas that clashed with their *yashmagh* headgear. One of them checked his watch, and Selena's mouth dropped open slightly as they set the rifles aside, aimed themselves southward to face the Ka'aba in Arabia and knelt in prayer. Compromised prayer—there's no way they didn't need ablution, and no way to perform it in this place—but she supposed they were doing the best they could.

And how could she jump them in the middle of prayer?

Oh, just do it. They're terrorists, for God's sake. She inched closer to the edge, bringing her feet up under her, ready to leap. She targeted the smaller one, figuring he'd be easier to stun, judging the rifles easier to kick aside from that position.

Except of course she couldn't do it. She rolled her eyes at herself as the wind cut through her clothes and she silently hit the heel of her hand against her forehead, but she couldn't do it.

But as soon as they straightened, the moment they reached for the rifles...

She dropped down on them. She kicked out at the jaw of the big guy as she landed on the smaller one, taking them both down. The small one grabbed at her; she slashed at his wrists where the gap of jacket and glove left them exposed and then she grabbed up his rifle by the muzzle, swinging it to around to connect with the other man's face. There was enough momentum left to pivot around at the small one as he scrambled to his feet—to connect hard enough that the man fell back hard, cracking his head against the limestone brick corner of the stairwell hut. He went limp, sliding down to leave a smear of blood on the light stone.

The second man roared a Berzhaani curse and she snapped around to face him. "Temper, temper," she told him, which only made him snarl. If he had a hand weapon, it was buried beneath his coat; he rushed her, aiming to crush her up against the brick wall. She dropped down into a balanced crouch, slashing across both his knees with her improvised blade. It wasn't sharp enough to cut the tough khaki but it startled him and he leaped back. Selena stayed down, flipping the rifle around to bring it up to her shoulder. *No more games. No more leaving men stashed around to recover and go back into action. Not if she was the one with the gun.*

As soon as the rifle came into position, she snugged it back against her shoulder and fired.

The rifle responded in its unique two-stutter setting, firing off two rounds before the kickback of the first threw her out of position. The man cried out in surprise as tiny feathers puffed from the new holes in his jacket, and he staggered backward and—

Damn. Who knew the edge of the roof was so close?

Selena let the rifle tip down to rest against the gritty surface, wiping rain from her brows and lashes and giving her suddenly upset stomach a moment to settle.

As if it would. As if she'd killed men so frequently before, and could so casually walk away from this one.

But she had no time to linger. No telling when the relief watch would come up—Ashurbeyli probably had a frequent rotation going in this weather. She turned to check the smaller man, found him staring blankly at the scudding clouds.

Two. I killed two of them.

And she'd deal with it later as she could. For now she wouldn't leave this body around for easy discovery. Let the replacement watch wonder why the roof was deserted—let them waste manpower searching the building for delinquents. She frisked the remaining Kemeni, unable to find a hand radio—if they'd had one, it had gone over the side with the first man. She hunted for and found a handgun, grimacing at the clumsy Luger. A quick check revealed five of seven 9 mm rounds left in the magazine. More than she'd had…not nearly enough. She made sure the safety was set and jammed the semi-automatic in the back of her waistband, reminding herself she couldn't count on it to come free as neatly as her Beretta under the same circumstances. No pause for breath or to wipe her lashes clear again; she dragged the second man closer to the edge and then crouched to roll him off. With any luck, no one from inside had any idea. Those on the outside…let 'em speculate.

She headed across the roof, fully intent on hitting the stairs and heading for temporary respite—but stopped short as she passed the abandoned assault rifles. Just because she didn't want them herself—the Luger was a better tool for her purposes and she needed to travel light right now—was no reason to leave them lying around for Ashurbeyli. First one, then the other—she whirled around for momentum, flinging them off the roof in wide flight arcs that would no doubt surprise someone as they landed. She hoped a news camera wouldn't catch them tumbling down—no doubt Ashurbeyli had at least one television tuned to an international news station.

But it wouldn't change anything if he did see. It just meant she had to get off this roof, and *now.* Selena ran across the flat expanse, her footsteps crunching…until a flicker of movement in the low clouds caught her eye, stopping her short. She looked upward, examining the clouds, unable to squelch a foolish surge of hope that help might actually be on its way. For an instant she envisioned a stealth-enabled chopper, swooping in to drop SEALs on the roof, taking advantage of the opening she'd just provided.

But no. Of course not. Just clouds.

She cursed at the delay and ran for the stairs.

Cole skirted the edges of the airfield grounds, heading for the ratty, weed-infested strip of ground at the fence line. Old airfield, old fence…leaky, leaky security, especially to a small group of U.S. forces who were doing their best to be inconspicuous. He eyed the fence again. His Leatherman would provide a quick enough exit—and if push came to shove, the shearling coat would protect him in a trip over the top of that barbed wire. But for the moment, he waited quietly along the back wall of the shabby maintenance building closest to the fence.

Not that he was truly worried about being followed— not from here. Just…

Habit.

Seth—CIA Technical Services officer, and someone

Cole knew well enough to think of in terms of his real name instead of his station name—would send a taxi to meet him on the road to the airstrip. Seth spent his time devising strategies and disguises to exfiltrate foreign agents when their situation became too precarious, and to allow high-profile foreign officials to make meetings with their CIA case officers. In essence, he helped people move from place to place with disguises that were the stuff of *Mission Impossible*.

Just what Cole needed. With the loyalty and understanding Cole needed, as well. *It's not agency business,* he'd said. And at Seth's silence over the phone, on the other side of the small hangar from Josie and Diego Morel, Cole had asked if Seth was watching UBC along with everyone else in this corner of the world. And Seth had seen, of course. *That was Selena.*

He didn't have to offer any more details. *That was Selena.* Because there had been only one woman on UBC to capture the airwaves with her narrow escape— to capture hearts with her daring. Cole closed his eyes, wishing he couldn't see it so clearly—the look on her face as the terrorist pulled her head back slightly, into the gun Cole knew was there. The uneven nature of the image as Morel compensated for the Predator's movement. And then Selena in action, all swift, wicked consequences. He didn't know what she'd used against the man, only that it glinted of metal. That she'd freed herself and run, showing the world her heart. Reminding Cole of what he'd always known, of how bright and hard her soul burned beneath the coolness of her poised exterior.

Reminding him how much he had to lose.

And now Seth knew, too. And Seth had sent a taxi—

although Cole doubted it was merely that—and Cole needed to make his great escape so the man wasn't kept conspicuously waiting.

Not that he didn't trust Josie and Diego, who could probably walk him straight out to the road with no challenge. Just that the fewer people who knew, the better. Need To Know. Great operational policy, and one he'd had to keep, even with Selena.

He found a seam in the high chain-link, a spot already half separated. The wire cutters on the Leatherman swiftly created a gap big enough for a medium man of agile nature, and Cole trotted away into the brushy winter wood that had crept up on the place. Nothing grew strongly or tall in this rocky land, it seemed, except the unrest that had brought Selena here and now might kill her.

He intercepted the taxi easily enough, not surprised to find that the driver spoke perfect English. They ascertained that Cole's departure had been clean, and then started off in a series of routine course changes meant to expose anyone following. It was a process that might normally take hours...but Cole didn't have hours. *Selena* didn't have hours. He said as much; the man only nodded. The flushing process wasn't for Cole or Selena...it was meant to protect Seth. It could be shortened under duress...but not eliminated.

His cell vibrated in his pocket. Cole fumbled for it, thinking *Selena!*—and found himself caught off guard by Diego Morel's deep voice. "Damn good thing I thought to get your number," Morel said, "if you're going to pull spook tricks on us. I thought we were on the same side."

"We still are, as far as I know." But Cole winced at the phone. "I'd say call it habit, but—"

"Yeah," Morel said. "I guess I wouldn't just sit around on my ass watching UAV footage if I had an option to move in, either."

"I don't," Cole said, because this was a cell phone and enough had been said already. "I've got a meet with Tory." And now he'd have to see if she'd cover him— not because Morel would check, but because someone else just might. Not that his unofficial status here was a threat to anyone, just...

Habit.

"Okay." Morel responded easily enough so Cole knew he'd gotten the *drop it* vibes. "Look, you left too early. You missed a good show."

"On television?" Cole said, purposely inaccurate.

Again, Morel let it slide. Better than that, he played right along. "Action scene," he said. "Gorgeous woman on a roof, taking out a couple of bad guys and getting away clean."

Cole stiffened with hope. "Down the fire escape?" He didn't even know if the building had one, or if the Russians, during the occupation in which they'd built that stolid structure, had deemed them necessary. But he figured Morel would get the message. *Did she escape them? Is she free?*

"Nope." Now the deep voice held regret. "Back inside. Woman with a mission, you know? But there's more to it. We took a close look at the setting and found some devices up there."

Devices. Cole had a crystal-clear image of Selena at the head of the Death Stairs, cupping her hand in the signal for booby trap. "Enough to be significant?"

"Hard to tell until we watch it again—" study and analyze and enhance, he meant "—but I'd say not. Only to that immediate area."

So there might be more.

Or not. Selena could simply have been trying to warn off a roof approach.

"I'll share the tape," Morel was saying. "But I thought you should know. Plus the news about the hot action babe, of course."

"Of course," Cole murmured, wishing he'd seen it with his own eyes—but it was time to quit watching.

It was time to start playing the game.

He wasn't going to answer.

Selena wasn't prepared for the heavy wash of disappointment as Cole's phone did the little double ring that meant it was switching to voice mail. She let her head drop to her knees, shifting back against the bed that hid her from anyone who came to the bedroom door, and thumbed the phone off.

Here she was, back where she'd started not so very long ago. In the guest suite where she'd left her briefcase and in which she hoped for a chance to clean up and ponder her purpose here.

Save the hostages.

Simple enough. Except she was no longer sure just how to go about it. If the building was as compromised as she thought, the Kemenis were only waiting for someone to make a rescue effort. A little token resistance, a hasty retreat, and the building would become the weapon. Dead hostages, dead SEALs or Berzhaani Elite Guards or both. In which case she needed to...

For a moment, Selena's mind went blank. Utterly

blank, clogged up by fatigue and reaction and not a little despair. *I'm one person. One. What can I do against an army?*

Except maybe she wasn't just one person. Maybe she was two. Maybe she had within the smallest spark of life, tugging at her body just enough to turn her stomach inside out now and then. A little piece of herself…a little piece of Cole.

Then protect it. Run. Or hole up somewhere.

But holing up wouldn't do her any good if the Kemenis had plans for this building. And as for running…

If she had a child, one day she'd be answering questions. And she needed to be able to look her child in the eye when she answered.

Because she could do quite a lot against an army. She might not destroy them, but she could pester them. She could make things difficult. She could distract them.

So she dredged up the trailing end of her thoughts and put her mind back to work. If the building was compromised and the Kemenis planned a hasty retreat, then she needed to locate that avenue of retreat and block it. Or simply block all of the first-floor exits other than the main doors at the Death Steps. Something— anything—that would at least slow them down. And she'd have to make sure they knew it. She'd gain nothing if they initiated a plan to bring the building down and then found out they couldn't escape.

The problem was…if she was wrong, if her intuition had sent her in the wrong direction, misled by stray comments and an adherence to logic and reason the Kemenis might well have chosen to ignore, then she couldn't waste time with exits. She needed to concentrate on thinning their ranks by any means possible, on making it easier for any rescue teams to swoop in and save the day.

She didn't think she had the time to do both. Or even the physical wherewithal—not with kill-on-sight almost certainly hanging over her head. No second chances from here on out.

Selena snorted into the afternoon gloom. Second chances? She'd had them. She'd been caught; she'd gotten away. She'd been hurt, but not badly. She'd been betrayed, and overcome it. She was going on third chances…maybe fourth.

You've given them hints. You've given them help. And now she'd just do her best. She couldn't do it alone, but she'd do her best.

The phone gave a plaintive beep. She'd disconnected it, but left it on…and now the last vestiges of the battery were trickling away. No time even to berate herself; she hit Redial and waited for Cole's phone to ring, hoping against hope that this time he'd answer it. Who else could he be talking to?

He's trying to fix this. Of course he was. He wouldn't just sit around the apartment, not all this time. He was here, somewhere. Or on his way. And he might only be one man…but so was she only one woman. Neither of them had a reputation for taking *no* as an answer.

Still, she bit her lip when the phone gave that little double ring and switched to voice mail. She bit it hard. But she was ready, talking right over another low battery beep. "It's me. Battery's dead, babe—this is my last call out. First thing…I don't know for sure, but I think the Kemenis have a surprise planned for anyone who comes in—I think they're planning a grand exit, and that what they're asking for here isn't really what they want—they sure don't expect to get it." *Beep*. One more warning, maybe two, and she'd be cut off. "The other thing…why I left. I saw you. In D.C. And…you weren't alone. I couldn't get the answers I needed then. Desk work…it wasn't distracting enough. So yeah, I ran. But—" *beep* "—I've had a lot of thinking time on my hands here, and I need you to know…I know we still have to talk, but whatever happens here…as far as I'm concerned, I'm already on my way home again." She thought about the potential life they might well have started together and hesitated. Not too long, or the voice mail would cut her off, thinking her message completed, so when she spoke again her thoughts were unformed. "There's something else. I think. That is, I could—"

And of course the phone cut off. She stared blankly at it, surprised to see it become splashed by tears. And then she snorted. Hadn't she already decided Cole didn't need to know? At least not until she emerged from this building safe and sound. Not *unless*.

She used a few more precious moments on silence and composure. She thought about all the things she wished she'd said, and planned out all the things she would say if she ever had the chance to look into Cole's striking blue eyes again. She gathered memories in around herself, a collection of reasons she would and could do this thing set out before her. She thought of the hostages. Just kids. Someone's children. Innocents whose lives should never be torn apart by the grown-ups fumbling through this world.

She closed her eyes, drawing up an image of Cole. Making it so detailed, so realistic, she almost believed she could also make it real. Those blue eyes, startlingly pure. One eyebrow set slightly higher than the other, giving him a somewhat amused look unless he replaced it with a downright scowl. The square line of his jaw—it, too, went a little crooked when he smiled, and especially when he smiled at her.

Dammit, she could see him, she could all but touch the smooth lines of his back, all but feel the hard curve of his—

No. Don't go there.

But it was too late, for she'd remembered the habitual taste of him, the lingering sting of the curiously strong mints he popped just to see if he could get steam to come out of his ears. Along with the memory of touching him came the image of how he reserved certain expressions just for her. The one that meant, "Get over here, woman, so I can put my hands on you," and the questioning, understanding silence when she turned pensive. The muted glee in his eyes when he pulled her leg and got away with it. But mostly the deep, clear blue of his eyes, so close to hers, when they came together. He always lost himself in that instant, and even if he recovered enough to turn the lovemaking light and playful, for that instant he was nothing but a startled gasp...totally, completely hers.

And now he was at the other end of a voice mail message. She didn't even know where—somewhere between here and home? Out there with the news cameras? Holed up in a hotel? Unless she had it all wrong and he was still at home. Waiting. Not assigned to this area, no authority to change that—not even enough to fake his way through.

In a way it was a reassuring thought—because if Cole were here, he'd be forced into the very role he

played best—full-speed nap-of-the-earth flying his way
through barely known terrain.

Making his way toward *her.*

Chapter 15

Selena pulled herself together, took a few moments for a luxurious wash. She checked her side and discovered it could use a stitch, and then used the duct tape from her briefcase to make a patch for herself. Peeling either shirt down over her arm proved too painful to make it worth the effort, so she snatched a few prestocked anti-inflammatories from the medicine cabinet in the bathroom, gulping them down along with a handful of the crackers from the kitchenette staples. Knockoff saltines with an odd texture and an odder taste, but they sat well enough in her stomach. She took the chance to pull her hair back into a stubby braid and fasten it with a hair tie from her case, and then she scared up the several pens she'd left behind last time.

The pad of sticky notes also fit nicely into her thigh pocket.

The Luger, during a quick disassembly and inspection, turned out to be not quite a Luger at all. Not with this rough machining. Not with this clunky interface of parts. She stared at it, dumbfounded. Jonas White again, foisting inferior goods off on the Kemenis…it made sense. More sense, in fact, than the notion that White had helped to arm the Kemenis with what had become an expensive collector's item—or that he'd found any quantity of these discontinued pistols to pass along.

She'd have to be careful with this one. No telling how well it actually worked.

Finally ready to go, she glanced up in the mirror of the bedroom dresser and stopped short, startled by her own paleness, and startled by the extent of the bruising across her face. Her lip, subtly lopsided with swelling; one eye half-closed, surrounded by purpling and accented with a small cut. The remains of the dried blood trail still lingered, a mere shadow of what it had been. The other side of her face sported a simpler landscape, one big bruise accenting her strong jawline and blooming in colors from deep purple to vivid yellow.

No wonder Ashurbeyli had thought she'd trigger the pity factor from those who watched the Death Steps.

She watched herself straighten, determined inside and out. She'd show Ashurbeyli the pity factor, all right. Time to hit hard and move fast. She'd take the stairs when she went, and she had five bullets to use along the way, along with a number of weapons they wouldn't expect. She gathered them to her, filling her briefcase with the clear planter marbles and dumping the remainder in the hastily emptied mayo jar with the dry ice. She wasn't ready for it, not quite yet, but now a simple tightening of the lid would give her a five-to-ten-minute fuse—shorter if she stuck the jar in a basin of warm water. For now, she stashed it in a pillowcase padded with towels, and added it to a small handheld fire extinguisher she set next to the briefcase at the door. After a careful inspection of the hallway, she made a swift journey down the rooms with her passkey, entering each room long enough to fling open the curtains and turn on the lights. If events drew out until after dark, the upper floors would be a fishbowl from the outside. It might not be possible to tell where the terrorists were, but it would be clearly evident where they *weren't.*

She returned to her gear, draped the briefcase shoulder strap over her head and across her shoulder like a satchel and grabbed up the fire extinguisher. Monoammonium phosphate…almost as good as pepper spray. The leather case bumped heavily against her hip as she checked and entered the stairs, a constant reminder running in the background of her thoughts. *Hit and run. No time for fear. No time to think of Cole or—*

No. Hit and run.

The next floor down seemed as empty as the previous one. Abandoned.

As she hesitated upon reentering the stairwell, she heard voices. A few moments of listening told her enough—a pair of men on their way to the roof. They'd no doubt realize the current pair of guards had disappeared. *Can't have that. Not yet.* The missing guards represented opportunity to any rescue teams, although— *Not yet,* she thought at the SEALs, and at the Berzhaan Elite Guard. They were all still too vulnerable to the potential hidden Plan A, rescuers and hostages alike. Even if they'd been forewarned by her hand signal.

And meanwhile…

She waited for the right moment, popping out of the doorway as the ascending Kemenis gained the landing. The leading man cried out as she jammed a pen at his eye. It skidded off bone and into the eye itself, and by then he was shrieking and batting blindly at her—but it didn't stop her from releasing the fire extinguisher in the face of the second man. The first stumbled backward and down the stairs; the second had the presence of mind to claw for his gun instead of his tightly closed eyes, and she turned the metal cylinder into a weapon, smashing first his hands and then up into his chin—and then whirled so the heavy briefcase slung out enough to slam into him, knocking him down after his friend.

They moaned together, blinded and dazed, and she hesitated only long enough to snatch the most accessible handgun. Another "Luger"—surprise, surprise. She ejected the clip and left the pistol behind. *Hit and run.* She didn't dare discharge the gun at them inside the stairwell for all to hear. It didn't matter whether the men could pull themselves together and eventually make it back to the ballroom. She'd damaged them, and she'd damaged the Kemenis. Two down, two injured… twenty-three to go.

She didn't take the time to go through the second-floor rooms, not yet. Not with the injured Kemenis possibly drawing attention to the stairs. She went all the way down to the basement, trading off caution for speed and for once hitting it lucky—no interference. She made it to the laundry room and found her bleach and ammonia stash, and then she hit the maintenance room up for a screwdriver, quickly sharpening it with a rough flat file before tucking it away in her back pocket.

It was when she stopped to contemplate the potential of the flammable fluids that she saw it. Innocuous, looking like nothing more than an industrial-size can of fruit with the label stripped, sitting on the floor by the solvents.

Except it hadn't been here before.

Eyeing it as though it might uncoil and strike at her, Selena dropped out of hit-and-run mode long enough to walk quietly up to the container and peer inside.

Ooh, yeah.

Plan A. C4, neatly tucked away with a remotely activated electronic detonator snugged into its Silly Putty surface.

Plan A, confirmed.

There had to be more to it—something to make this whole game worth it. The risk of taking the hostages, the risk of lingering here with the whole world watching.

Rescue teams come in, building blows, Kemeni escape...to what?

To go accomplish their original goal. With the spotlight on the destruction and death at the capitol and the Kemenis assumed dead in the initial chaos, who would stop them from storming wherever they pleased?

Selena aimed a disdainful look at the bomb. "You guys are really getting on my nerves." And then she bent and pulled the detonator free, carefully depositing it in a damp, inconspicuous back corner where cement met block wall. "You just do your thing right there. Make a nice little boom." They'd have no way to know the detonator sat elsewhere than the explosive compound. It wouldn't start so much as a fire.

Not that it truly mattered. She had no doubt there

were more of these little goodies scattered throughout the building. Maybe not enough to bring it down, but enough to make it close.

Gah. Bombs. She'd rather be facing wannabe Kemenis in a small village outside a beloved shrine, saving people one by one. Fighting *people*—and not faceless bombs.

Ashurbeyli. He was the face of these bombs. A man with heartfelt aspirations and no idea that he'd crossed the line a long, long time ago.

She felt the screwdriver in her pocket, thought of the havoc waiting in the laundry room, thought of a man blinded on the stairs…wondered if Ashurbeyli hadn't dragged her over the line along with him.

And decided it was worth the price if it meant saving the people huddled on the floor above her. Berzhaan's fate…something else again altogether. Even if the Kemenis failed, the country had a long struggle before it…just as its people had struggled through the past.

But if you're going to be crossing lines, you'd damn well better not do it for nothing.

No. More like all or nothing.

She took a deep breath and left the now harmless C4 where it was. A quick circuit of the basement turned up another bomb in the furnace room, next to the giant fuel-oil tank. She disarmed it, not certain the fuel oil would do anything but burn sullenly even if it were ignited, and tossed the detonator out through the high, small hinged door used for the hose from the fuel truck. She even eyed the door as a possible escape route; if she could reach it, she could certainly fit through it…but there were a few large kids who wouldn't, and neither Razidae or Allori had a chance.

So she left it behind, and gathered up her chaos supplies, going to lurk by the stairs for a good hard listen before exposing herself to trouble in the stairwell. At the faint scuff of noise that reached her, she hung back, letting her burdens settle to the ground as she pulled both the screwdriver and the Luger, waiting…

Just one of them, not having learned enough to be cautious in his exit. She instantly yanked her plan to jam the gun in his ribs and shoot; without a second man to deal with, she could afford to give him a good hard rap on the head, just below the temple.

Only in afterthought did she realize it was the first time she'd seen one of them alone. Either she'd messed with them enough to throw off their habits, or they were changing according to Ashurbeyli's plans—and the former was infinitely preferable to the latter. She didn't need Ashurbeyli changing the game, not *now*.

She crept into the kitchen without further incident. She no longer considered it a home base, or even safe. In fact, a glance at the cooler showed the door left open, and a stolen moment revealed the prisoners gone. *Bound to happen, once they found Atif.* They'd probably searched the whole kitchen again.

She unloaded her plastic gallon bottles on a set of shelves just inside the door, and more carefully removed the jar of dry ice, tucking it out of sight on the same shelves. "Wait there—I'll be back."

And wouldn't it amuse Cole to find her talking to inanimate objects.

Hit and run. No time for thoughts of Cole, remember?

Just enough time to grab some butcher twine and wrap the strong stuff from the door exit handle to the handle of the nearby stove, over and over until it was stout enough to withstand any amount of yanking. Except as she prepared to do it, she thought twice. Would she be trapping the Kemenis in, or potential rescue *out*?

After a moment she dropped the twine and retrieved her remaining pen and the sticky notes. Blue with cute little flowers along the bottom edge, gifted to her by Bonita to amuse them both with its inappropriate nature. Selena doubted that Ashurbeyli would be amused at all…but she'd intended to tweak him with notes all along. She wrote in carefully legible Berzhaani, "Are you sure the bombs will go off?" and posted it to the door, hesitating only long enough to see that it would stick. *Where else…?*

The exit at the back corner of this side of the building. She put up the same message, deemed it too risky to cross to the other side of the building on this floor, and headed for the second floor. Her briefcase thumped against her hip, but she fought the impulse to leave it behind. Too useful in too many ways. She dug her stolen keys from the front flap, heading for the guest-room doors. These were the most opulent rooms; there weren't as many of them. She expected to find offices on the other side of the hall, above the prime minister's own office area.

She also expected to find at least a Kemeni or two, keeping track of things this close to their ballroom headquarters. Otherwise an enterprising SEAL could very well slip in, drill a few holes in the right spots, and snake in a few cameras for a perfect view of the terrorist setup and activities. But in the offices she found no one at all.

Ashurbeyli. Up to something after all?

Nothing she could do about it. Cause a little chaos,

make things easy for those on the outside, try to time her heavy hits so she didn't trigger anything but stood ready to react in case Ashurbeyli did.

Just a little bit of *Mission Impossible. Your mission, Selena, should you decide to accept it...*

Had she ever had any choice? Yes, she'd had options...but had she ever had any choice?

Not that she could live with.

She started in on the guest-room windows. *Hit and run.*

Don't think about Cole.

Cole couldn't believe it. He settled into the taxi and stared at the phone, which insisted he'd missed a phone call in the short time he'd been talking to Diego Morel. Primly, it indicated the call had been from Selena. From her own phone.

Take a breath, buddy. Listen to the message and then call her back.

He took that deep breath and recalled the message, letting the driver worry about his route and his evasions and spotting demeanor hits—the telltale driving behaviors—that would mean they'd been followed. He slumped down in the seat to create the illusion of privacy and put the phone to his ear. Listened to her initial warning about the Kemeni. Heard and stopped breathing at her next words. *I saw you. You weren't alone.*

She'd seen him in D.C. She'd seen him playing out a role for the FBI, a sudden unexpected scenario in which he'd been loaned out to the feebs so he could follow through on an inadvertent terrorist connection he'd made during his overseas station work. It didn't matter that his role in the ongoing operation had been completed, or that the woman posing as his lover had been whispering tactical observations into his ear instead of sweet nothings. He couldn't tell Selena the details—not now, not later. And he wouldn't blame her if she didn't believe the little he *could* tell her—only that he'd been on the job—not when he'd broken their most basic rule by not updating her on his change of location.

He'd meant it to be a surprise, knowing he'd be home long before she expected. He'd meant it to delight her.

Instead it was one of the biggest mistakes he'd ever made. He'd sent her running in confusion. He'd sent her *here.*

Cole closed his eyes against the consternation of the images his mind so freely provided him—the look on Selena's face upon spotting him. The way she would have held back any true emotion until she reached their apartment. How deeply he must have hurt her in the wake of their recommitment, their efforts to start a family. And if some small, wistful voice within wished that she could have trusted him just a little bit more, he had but himself to blame. He'd set her up for that mistrust by failing to let her know he was in D.C. in the first place.

And now here she was. Trapped in a building full of bombs and terrorists and a group of hostages she would never abandon. She was too committed to her work, to the soul of it—and she didn't tackle her work from a distance. She absorbed the land to which she was assigned; she respected the people.

Deep beneath that cool and organized exterior, she hid more heart than most people ever wished they had. The very reason he'd been able to hurt her so deeply with one apparently simple decision. Deeply enough to send her...

Here.

Where she'd somehow forgiven him, not even understanding the hidden circumstances. Or where she'd somehow found the strength to trust him in spite of himself.

And then he realized the most important thing of all: *he couldn't call her back.*

The capitol building's second-floor quarters showed more signs of occupation. Some of these people, Selena realized, had to have made it out of the building. She couldn't search the private area on the other end of the embassy's first floor, but she'd seen no signs of other dignitaries in the function room holding the hostages. Out to a late lunch, perhaps—such business meetings were common enough in Suwan. She could only hope they weren't all dead, killed in the chaos when the building fell to the Kemenis.

Don't say that. Fell to the Kemenis *is not something to say inside this building right now.*

Not when she was waiting for it to fall for real.

She swept open the curtains of a particularly well-appointed and lived-in suite, darkly aware that if Ashurbeyli watched enough television he'd realize what she'd done and send someone around to reverse it; she could only hope he wouldn't make such a target of any of his men.

And then the toilet flushed.

She froze—but only for an instant. In the next moment she'd plastered herself up against the wall between the bedroom and living room, mind racing and body still.

Not to mention the Luger wannabe out and ready.

She didn't wait to register identity as the man strolled by; she jammed the gun in his back and made a warning noise between her teeth, a short sharp sound. He reacted before she could say anything else, pivoting around to smack the gun away with a hammy hand. *Jonas White.* And he would have had the gun, too, if she hadn't been left-handed—and if she hadn't been expecting the move. She could have shot him—*should have,* said a grim little voice in her head—but she evaded the blow and pushed her back to the wall, lending strength to the kick she landed. Her foot sunk into his gut and he doubled over, giving her a perfect view of his comb-over.

He staggered backward and somehow maintained his balance—impressive, from a man in his sixties. Selena didn't follow through. She kept the pistol on him and, as he seemed to be gathering himself for another assault, said flatly, "I just got another clip for this baby. I can easily spare a bullet or two for you."

It stopped him cold.

That, too, impressed her. He'd never lost his presence of mind. He'd never come near to losing his temper. He merely straightened, smoothing the front of his tan cashmere sweater where her foot had smudged and wrinkled it. If he rubbed his aching belly on the way, it wasn't noticeable. "I thought Ashurbeyli had you well under control."

She shrugged. "He thought he did, too. You really should spend more time with your new allies—then you'd already know you were both wrong."

He smiled slightly, a self-assured expression with no humor to it. "I'm actually quite good at managing my friends from afar. But then, you already know that, don't you?"

Selena smiled back at him. "I know you weren't any good at all at managing your daughter from afar."

She'd gotten him with that one; his small eyes narrowed. But he nodded at her, acknowledging the score she'd made. "Eventually not," he said. "I should have known any daughter of an Athena bitch would betray me one day."

She laughed, short and sharp. "I do believe she was just returning the favor."

"And here you are. One might even think you Athena girls have an obsession with me."

"You've had a high profile lately," Selena told him. "At least, for those of us who know where to look." She raised an eyebrow at him. "That would be under the slimiest pile of compost in the heap, in case you didn't see that coming."

His face twisted, sour. "Thought I'd leave you the pleasure of saying it."

"I appreciate that." She gestured at the nearest chair, to the side and behind him—an armless, arch-backed Victorian thing meant more for show than for sitting on. "Have a seat. Relax. And give thanks that you just came out of the bathroom, because you're not going to have access for a while."

He glanced back, found the chair and carefully backed toward it. He seemed to contemplate the notion of snatching it up to throw at her, but she gave him a bored look and he sat, carefully placing his hands on his stout thighs. "That gun looks familiar."

She snorted. "It should. I have to admit it, you're pretty good at finding a use for weapons no one else wants to bother with."

"The Kemenis are needy, not picky. But don't confuse me with their suppliers. That was Frank Black of the United States, I believe."

She rolled her eyes. "Please. Do you *want* me to gag you? I can just go straight to searching this place if you'd prefer. Or better yet, I can prop you up in front of that window with your face plastered against the glass. Someone's trigger finger is bound to slip once you're recognized."

White glared at her, a little more slow to regain his composure this time. Selena gave him the moment, moving into the room to sit on the couch across from him. She crossed her legs and rested the gun on her knee so he was looking right down the barrel. "Here's the thing," she said. "I know why you're here. You're playing the Kemenis— goading them into this takeover with promises of support, but we both know it's for your own benefit. First, you'll have a sanctuary. Second, you'll be in the perfect position to sink your pointy little claws into their oil fields."

White snorted. "It's been a long time since anyone called *anything* of mine 'little.' "

"Nonetheless." She let the word sit there a moment. "What I don't understand is why the *Kemenis* are here. Why they chose this ill-conceived plan."

"What does it matter?" He gestured at her, but returned his hand to his thigh as she instantly raised a warning brow. "You're already looking the worse for wear. You're not going to make it out of here alive. Why don't you go spend your remaining moments trying to escape, instead of badgering a poor old man?"

"Because this is so much more fun," Selena told him. "Now, of course I understand why the Kemenis have made their move. We've already established that you goaded them into it."

He only smiled. This time he looked more pleased with himself, but no more likely to talk about it.

"What I don't understand is why they're *here*. Making demands we both know will never be met. Hanging around just waiting for the inevitable rescue attempt in which they all die. Oh, the hostages might die, too, and maybe a SEAL or two. But what does it gain them?"

"Eternal happiness after death?" White suggested.

"Some of them, maybe," Selena acknowledged. "But not Tafiq Ashurbeyli. There's more to him than that. I'm surprised you've been able to fool him for this long. Maybe that's why you're spending so much time in hiding."

A shrug. "I need my rest. I'm old."

"So you've said. I suspect it's the one truthful thing you ever say." She shifted on the couch. At any time someone could come to check on White—maybe even Ashurbeyli. At any time, another hostage could die. Or a rescue attempt might be launched, or better yet, the building could blow up. Not as thoroughly as it might have before she'd spent time in the basement, but there was no such thing as a little bit dead.

If White had the same awareness of impending danger, he didn't show it. He watched her, his stare unnervingly blunt. He let her lead the conversation, with no evident concern over where it might go.

She said, "I know about the bombs."

That did surprise him, but only for a moment. He said, "Tafiq really should have killed you when he first had the chance."

"He tried," she reminded him dryly. "So here's what I'm thinking. The Kemenis plan to blow this place, literally and figuratively—I found a couple of the bombs, by the way. So they're using this siege not as the end goal, but as a means to their true goal. Failing to win over the Berzhaani government at this stage not only won't come as a disappointment, but it's pretty much expected. So from here they go on to do something else. Unless, of course, we can stop them right here." She tipped her head at him. "'We' not being you and I, of course. 'We' being the good guys."

"Of course." He'd finally found something meaningless upon which he could comment.

"So let's say taking over the capitol is Plan A. Just to give it a nice neat name. And let's say the bombs and the true goal are Plan B."

"Just to give it a nice neat name," he said, but his voice had gone dry as he anticipated her logic.

"And then, because you've been playing these kinds of games for a very long time—as you say, you're old— let's assume you've got a Plan C. That you don't take the Kemenis' success for granted, and you've got your ass covered."

"My," he said. "I *am* clever, aren't I?"

"The point I'm reaching," she told him, ever so gently, "is that under the circumstances, it might be in your best interest to discuss Plan B with me, and then to move right along to Plan C."

He snorted. "And you won't stop me?"

"I'll be busy." She pointed at the floor, indicating the story below them. "Kemenis, hostages…saving the day."

"Ah, yes. Of course." He nodded, and fell into silence.

Selena sighed. *At any time…* She eyed the curtain

rod; she eyed the tiebacks for the sweep of material framing each window. She eyed Jonas White.

His scowl proved he was, indeed, a clever man. He understood the threat—that she was sizing up her options to tie him at the window, in full, exposed view of anyone out there with a rifle.

And in looking at her face, he understood that she'd do it.

Definitely teetering on the line, Selena.

But she'd do it. And they both knew it.

"It's different," she said softly, "when you manage things from up close and personal."

Chapter 16

Selena left Jonas White cursing, tied to the chair and spewing venom about her betrayal. "Don't tell me," she'd asked, sticking a note to the wall behind his chair, "that you didn't expect it." *Had a nice chat with your friend. Love, Selena.*

From between his teeth he'd said, "There was a certain implication that I would be free to carry out Plan C."

She shrugged. "You're not dead yet. And you're not strung up at the window for target practice. Don't even try to tell me you don't still intend to escape to your Plan C."

She didn't know what Plan C was; she didn't really care. She'd been glad enough for the curtain ties, and she'd found his belt useful, as well. As much as he planned to escape, she planned to send someone up here to fetch him when all was said and done. And meanwhile, she didn't have time to waste.

Because now she understood. She understood Ashurbeyli's apparent lack of concern over the passage of time with no response from Berzhaan; she understood why he was perfectly willing to wait, hauling a hostage out now and then to make his points.

And where he'd been spending all his time.

He had a computer expert. In fact, he had more than one. Men she'd never even seen, because they'd immediately gone to work on the far side of the first floor, extracting secrets and data and personal information and removing hard drives wholesale. And other men who'd rifled through offices hunting hard copy—intel on everything from discreet love affairs to babysitter contact info to secrets of state.

And now they were only cleaning up the loose ends, digging as deeply as they could while they waited for an excuse to execute Plan B. Havoc, inside and out, to cover their escape. They'd go underground, but not for long—and when they emerged, it would be with carefully targeted strikes on the very people who now refused to respond to their requests.

White himself had helped concoct the scheme…but once forced to participate in order to prove his good intentions, had also quickly made other arrangements.

Selena had to give Ashurbeyli points all around. He hadn't fully trusted White; he'd wanted him just as committed as the Kemenis. And he hadn't relied on a simple one-layer strategy. He'd presented himself as an angry man leading angry terrorists attempting little more than a blunt, violent coup. And supposing it had worked, she suspected he would have taken it gladly.

But he'd thought beyond that. He'd found a way to win if Berzhaan startled the world with capitulation, and he'd found a way to win if they came in after the hostages. She had no doubt that if both the U.S. and Berzhaan sat on their hands, showing the slightest inclination to let the situation turn into a replay of four hundred and forty-four days in Iran, Ashurbeyli would simply choose his own time to trigger the bombs, his diversions and his escape.

He hadn't counted on Selena, of course.

Neither had White, who ceased cursing at her only because she gagged him. She couldn't risk his interference, not now that she was certain of Ashurbeyli's plans.

What she had to do was take control away from Ashurbeyli. Instigate her own distraction, round up the hostages and herd them toward the nearest safe exit. Let Ashurbeyli play catch-up—and meanwhile, she'd be going after the electronics. Or aiming the nearest SEAL—whom she could only hope wouldn't fail to take advantage of the moment—toward the ballroom, even while warning them about the impending diversion tactics on the outside.

She forced herself to stop as she reached the first-floor stair landing, and the exit door that waited there, her hands already on pen and sticky notes. *Breathe, Selena. You can't do it all. Prioritize. Hostages.* Even if she managed nothing else, the hostages would be safe. The Kemenis could be dealt with in a cleanup operation, their plans exposed and their people on the run.

Always the optimist.

Not really. In reality, she had a very good idea of her chances...or lack thereof. She just had no intention of letting that stop her.

She headed for the fourth exit, her sticky note ready and the Luger in hand.

Do you really think those bombs will go off?

After an amazingly swift transformation, Cole left Seth's chosen meeting spot—an ugly little room behind a whorehouse—and headed for the capitol as a Berzhaani—his skin tinted, his bright hair covered by a modest green turban over a *kalansuwa* cap, dark contacts concealing his blue eyes. Most important were his layers—the bottom layer a black, tight T-shirt with U.S.A. in white lettering on front and back. A T-shirt of last resort, should he be caught up in a firefight. The second layer—Kemeni khaki and olive-green. They'd know he wasn't one of them if they got a good look, but it would be up to him to remain no more than a glimpse of movement.

On top of that, a taupe *dishdasha* tunic brushing the tops of his feet. Black leather *kuffs,* feeling more like slippers than shoes and not really meant for this weather—but Seth hadn't had a lot of time to prepare. Over it all, a distinguished camel hair overcoat—all in all a little old-fashioned for a city as modern as Suwan, but nothing to attract attention. Especially not when anyone on the street had to duck against the sudden spurts of windy rain.

And then there was the mustache, tickling beneath his mildly altered nose—from straight to slightly hawkish, building on the already thin bridge to allude to classic Berzhaani features. He wasn't even sure Selena would recognize him if she saw him, although the disguise was meant not to hide his personal identity so much as his origins.

He also came equipped with press credentials for a tiny Berzhaani newsrag that existed solely as a front for CIA activities, and with his very own personal assistant and diversion master—someone Seth had recruited in the time it took Cole to reach the meet. Cole knew the field agent only by his station name of Hank P. STUNTLY, but he only had to meet the young man to recognize that gleam in his eye. No question why Hank would opt in on this unofficial action, in spite of the danger and the risk of reprimand. He was hunting for a way to get close to the action.

Just outside the press and military zone—a cordoned-off block in each direction—Cole stopped to pull out his phone. A Berzhaani man standing on the corner of chaos, checking in with someone in his life. Not an unusual sight—although the current unrest extended far beyond the capital, and only the most jaded ventured out on the streets this day. Seth had offered a quick summary as he performed Cole's transformation, concise words detailing Kemeni outbreaks all over Berzhaan, starting with the one by the Temple of Ashaga that had kicked off the day's activities and drawn away Suwan's most experienced antiterrorist unit.

Cole heard the details, and he heard the big picture as well—the Kemenis had committed everything to this takeover. They'd drawn on rough, marginal manpower, throwing them out as unwitting sacrifices to trained troops. They'd left Berzhaan's people harried and wounded and dead, risking alienation at this time when they'd need popular support after the planned takeover. Ashurbeyli, going public for the first time, proved himself no fool; already he'd lauded the innocents as martyrs and heroes for the cause, arrogantly postulating that they would have chosen their paths had they known what security and independence it would bring Berzhaan.

It was a well-planned operation...much better planned than the capitol takeover itself. He would have assumed Ashurbeyli to be a tactical fool, except...

Except for those bombs on the roof.

They spoke of something else going on under the surface, simply because Ashurbeyli hadn't used them as a threat. Hadn't said, "Don't even think of a rescue attempt, because we're ready for you." No, he'd kept them tucked away in the shadows of the roof corners. He had plans for them...but just what, Cole hadn't yet guessed.

He'd just be ready for it, whatever it was.

He dialed the number for Josie's phone, one he'd memorized shortly after arrival. When she answered, he said, "Thought I'd let you know I'm here. See if you two had any news."

"You're there?" she said. "We don't see you."

He refrained from glancing upward. "I don't see you, either, but I know you're there."

She laughed, though it didn't last long. "We'll leave it at that, then. Any news?"

"Not yet. By the time I have any, I don't think I'll be reaching for the phone." Beside him, Hank grinned, quite easily inferring Cole's meaning. "Thought I'd check on your end."

"Good move. You should know that we've spotted some interesting activity in your neighborhood. We haven't confirmed its nature...but we're okay to play along if necessary."

Meaning they'd gotten authorization to bring the Predator's Hellfire missiles into play. Good news...and bad. Things were escalating, and Cole didn't have any kind of handle on the situation inside.

Not yet. But he would. Because Selena had given him her trust, more trust than he even deserved.

He intended to prove that she hadn't made the wrong decision.

Selena followed her "safe" route back to the kitchen area—up a story and over, avoiding the activity on the first floor. She kept the fake Luger out and ready, having paused long enough to combine her available rounds into one magazine and make sure there was one in the chamber.

But she met no one. And while she couldn't complain…

She could wonder.

If they were drawing in on themselves, it wasn't good. It could only mean they didn't care if their domain was invaded—that perhaps they even waited for it.

She needed to shake them up a little.

She eased out into the hallway, down to the intersection where the long hall ran behind the function rooms, and she watched. Waited. Saw no one.

No, that can't be good.

She wrote them a short note—in Berzhaani, as they'd all been—and snaked her hand around the corner to press it to the wall. *Selena was here.*

And then, on this side of the corner, *Are you sure you're going to go Boom?*

If anyone saw the notes, she hoped they'd sow doubt and delay and a little bit of chaos. And if no one saw them…

Well, she'd be out a pad of sticky notes.

* * *

Cole closed in on the capitol, flashing his credentials at several soldiers along the way. One of them made enough fuss that he thought he'd have to get creative, but Hank—who spoke Berzhaani fluently as opposed to Cole's firm grasp of related but distinctly different Russian—made what turned out to be a big fuss of getting the man's name and rank and a few personal tidbits. All for the purpose of giving him a few shining lines in the article they'd be writing, naturally. Eventually the man let them through to the press area, uttering dire warnings about the dangers of getting too close.

Well, who knew. Maybe Cole *would* end up writing an article. The CIA-run paper served many different purposes, but in order to justify its existence it also had to report the news. And like Cole, many reporters had already crossed this line past which the general public wasn't allowed, angling for shots of the remaining blood on the rain-washed steps, hunting dramatic camera angles in front of the besieged but still imposing building.

Tory Patton was one of them, of course. As Cole approached, she unclipped her collar mike and handed it to a young woman; they put their heads together for a moment until Tory nodded, satisfied. Even in this weather she looked elegant; the chill brought a natural flush to her cheeks, and under a fedoralike rain hat, her bobbed hair was just tousled enough to remind viewers she was out in the field. Beneath her lined raincoat, her flak jacket was barely evident.

Her gaze landed on him as he approached, remaining professional but not quite welcoming. Cole affected his best Berzhaani accent, polished by recent coaching.

"Miss Patton," he said. "I couldn't pass up the opportunity to offer my admiration of your work."

"Thank you," she said, genuinely enough—but her gaze took in his somewhat conservative attire and reflected a hint of surprise. Behind her, another news crew moved into place, and she gestured that they should take the conversation aside.

"You expected me to say something else," he guessed, moving with her. Hank hovered behind him, making it clear he wouldn't be joining the conversation.

She gave the smallest of shrugs. "It shouldn't surprise you to hear how often I'm told my career and behavior is inappropriate. Often not in so many words, but any journalist knows how to say things between the lines, don't you think?"

"Absolutely." His fervency startled her, as he'd meant it to. "Even though I must admit my own work is hardly worth note." He flashed her his press pass, displaying the name of the paper. If she was as tuned in as he thought she was, it would mean something to her.

Her eyes narrowed. "Some people prefer to remain behind the scenes."

"Exactly so. Sometimes one hears more that way." He eased closer, as if they could have privacy in this bustling place—a street lined with armored personnel carriers and equipment trucks, heavily patrolled by both soldiers and cameras. The pavement in either direction held not only vehicles, but field tents. Not so obviously, somewhere in or on the buildings behind him—three- and four-story structures as old and older than the capitol—he knew the SEALs were lurking. Watching. Ready.

She let him close the distance between them, but

something in her posture made it very clear that she was making a deliberate choice, and that she was quite ready to change her mind at any time. He lowered his voice and dropped the accent. "I hear, for instance, that our eyes in the sky have spotted some potential activity moving in."

Someone else might have gasped at the sudden change in his demeanor; Tory took only the smallest of surprised breaths. "What are you doing here?"

"Did you really think I'd wait out there in that nice safe hangar, watching a video monitor?"

"I *hoped*," she said. "Do you really think Selena needs something else to worry about?"

He gave a sharp shake of his head. "She doesn't know I'm here. Not yet." It wasn't an answer to the question, but it was as much as he'd give her. Of course Selena didn't need to worry about him. But that's not why he was going in there. He was going in there to *help*.

"And just exactly what do you hope to accomplish?"

"Aside from giving you a heads-up on possible incoming action?" Cole looked over at the capitol building with its stained steps and its stolid facade and thought *good question*. "I'm playing it by ear, Tory. Maybe you've heard... it's what I do best. But at the least I hope to get inside there and make a difference when it counts."

"Inside," she said flatly, tipping her head down so her hat caught a sudden gust of wind against the brim.

"Inside." He tipped his head at Hank. Hank P. STUNTLY, waiting and ready. "I've brought along a little diversion. But if you can think of anything that might help..."

She considered him, and a subtle gleam entered her

eye. "A couple of minutes from now I can have my crew take a special interest in getting cameras pointed at those steps."

He smiled, and the mustache tickled like the dickens. "And everyone else will assume you actually see something."

"Even the Berzhaani soldiers," she said, her own smile a satisfied one. "They've gotten used to reacting to us." But then she held up a finger. "There's a catch, of course."

Damn. Just when he thought he'd navigated around the potential. He waited, as patient as he could be with those steps right there in front of him, giving him a tangible setting over which to superimpose the images of Selena that had been burned into his memory. Bruised. At gunpoint.

Striking back.

He raised his brow at Tory, waiting.

"An interview, of course," she said. "We'll black out your face, wobble your voice—"

He gave a sharp shake of his head. "Not possible."

She capitulated too quickly to have truly expected his agreement. "Then when you leave the Agency. Whenever that is. Until then, a print interview. It'll be good for *Newsweek*."

"On one condition." He looked at her, his expression searching and totally beyond serious. "You have to come up with a really cool code name for me."

A tiny laugh escaped between her teeth. "I think I can guarantee you that much."

"All right, then." He glanced at his watch. "Give me a few minutes."

She grew more serious. "Do you even know—"

He smiled at her, showing her the same confidence that always put people at ease. "I'll find a way in."

And he did. Several of them, in fact.

None of them were ideal. An old fire escape leading to the roof, which might or might not be guarded at this point. A simple climb on decorative brick outcroppings to reach the second floor, where the windows lacked iron bars but would yield to his clothing-protected elbow if the ones within reach happened to be locked. They might be security wired, of course, but Seth had said the security systems had been taken down in the initial invasion. There was also an exit leading from the back corner, but Cole didn't expect it to be open, or to be easily vulnerable. The SEALs might well use it once the time came.

He decided to try for the roof. It meant running in close to the building, behind the thick shrubs—and then exposing himself to view while he leaped up to catch the raised lower rung of the switchbacking fire escape. But Tory wasn't his only diversion…just his most subtle one. Cole waited until movement at the front of the building—people pulling inward, toward the center—caught the attention of newscasters and soldiers alike. All except for the two men who watched the back of the building, standing imperturbably at the corners. Cole nodded at STUNTLY, who gave him a cocky little grin and quite casually sauntered toward the back of the building.

Within moments, he'd goaded the soldiers into giving chase, drawing them away. "Good luck," Cole muttered after him, already in motion—but he knew that Hank also wore layers; all he needed was an instant out of sight to turn himself into someone else. With the discipline of experience, Cole left Hank's fate in his own hands and ducked behind the shrubs—big, bushy, evergreen, and—as usual—prickly. He hesitated there, assessing the leap to the fire escape, when something caught his eye—and then caught his full attention.

Detonator?

He crouched by it. Yes, an electronic detonator. Meant for use with a remote.

"I'll bet you weren't here before the trouble started," he said to it. "In fact…you're barely damp. How did you—"

A small hinged door just above the ground, that's how. A wooden door, still open, set into the concrete blocks of the basement. An opening just barely big enough…

Crouching behind the shrubs, Cole shucked the overcoat and tossed it through the door. The *dishdasha* followed, leaving him in his Kemeni outfit—and in serious trouble if he was spotted that way. He flipped the door up and backed through it, a dignified butt-first entrance that almost left him hanging like Pooh Bear in the honey tree. A little wiggling, a little contortion…a little brute force. He scraped his shoulders through, landing lightly on his feet in the basement of the capitol.

Hang on, Selena. Here I come.

Selena crouched in the not-so-secret corridor, ready for instant retreat. She'd come all the way to the end of it to spy on the ballroom, and knew herself to be acutely vulnerable.

And still, already the risk was worth it. Already she'd seen enough to confirm what Jonas White had told her…and to confirm her own suspicions that the Kemenis were getting ready to pull out. Not only had her navigation through the capitol been too easy since her return from the basement, but right there, right now, she saw the fruits of their labors. One after another, gathered hard drives were being tucked away for hard travel in the antistatic, airline- and gorilla-proof cases. A stack of CD jewel cases found less luxurious accommodations, while a handful of USB key chain drives quickly disappeared into special wrapping. Ashurbeyli watched the process with satisfaction…and rightly so. He gave a few quick orders…for Ashurbeyli, he was practically jovial.

They'd come prepared. They had the experts they needed; they had worked under the cover of the hostage crisis. Selena had seen those cases from the start and not realized their true significance. They even had a big-wheeled dolly, festooned with bungee cords in waiting.

And there on a table, almost obscured by a stack of jackets and other soon-to-be donned outdoor gear, sat the detonator remotes. Selena's fingers twitched. *I've got to get those remotes…*

Sure. If I was invisible and my arms were nine feet long and there wasn't a table between here and there…

Well, she knew how to distract them all, maybe even enough for an opportunity at the remotes. But probably not enough to gather up both the remotes and the hostages, and right now the hostages came first. She had to get them out of this bloody arena before the building came down on them—or, if she hadn't found all the charges in the basement, blew up from beneath them. She looked at the remotes with longing—and then realized the importance of Ashurbeyli's recent words, the orders to bring in refreshments. *Kaliber. Fayrouz.* Non-alcoholic malt drinks—luxuries to terrorists on the move, but trendy items a well-stocked kitchen would provide. And, apparently, a nice treat to buoy the Kemenis before they made their climactic shift to Plan B.

And most importantly, the shortest route to grabbing the drinks was through the servants' corridor.

Or maybe the most important part was the perfect opening for Selena's diversions.

Either way, she couldn't be caught here. She backed swiftly away from the door and moved down the corridor, finding pleasant irony in posting herself outside the entrance closet in the same spot from which she'd been ambushed not so long ago. She found herself a nice stout cast-iron frying pan, and as the Kemeni errand boy exited, his expression distracted and his eyes on the kitchen, she pounced from the side with a sharp knee to his stomach and a solid follow-through *thwak* of frying-pan-meets-skull.

Too hard, probably—he wasn't dead, but she wouldn't put eventual dying beyond him; a quick prod to his head revealed a certain unnatural mushiness. "Occupational hazard," she told him, although she hadn't meant to hit him so hard and couldn't help a scowl of self-blame. It didn't slow her down…she couldn't afford to let it. She dragged him into the kitchen and tossed him in the open cooler, not bothering to secure him. Within a few moments he'd be a moot point, and she didn't expect him to be functional within that time.

In quick succession, she found a serving cart and a couple of basins; she rescued one of Atif's abandoned tablecloths and snapped it out to cover the cart—too big, but that was the point. The bottom shelf was completely obscured, and so was the basin in which she put an inch of warm water and then the dry ice jar. She found a giant plastic canister filled with sugar and dumped the sugar, filling the canister halfway with bleach. It went beside the basin, and next to it, the gallon of ammonia.

She centered the second basin on top of the table-cloth, dumped in several scoops of ice from the machine tucked beside the cooler and went hunting the drinks. Kaliber sported a beer-bottle shape; Fayrouz had more of a wine-cooler look, and Selena grabbed one for herself, taking a moment to gulp down a fizzy, fruity apple-raspberry malt. Until it hit the back of her throat, she hadn't realized just how thirsty she'd become. *Stupid,* she chided herself. She hadn't made it this far to go down in a dehydrated faint.

Dropping the can opener beside the ice-filled basin, she checked her presentation—bottles in ice, nasty tricks securely hidden below—and then smiled as she tucked her empty bottle amidst the others. Her subtle but wicked heads-up to Ashurbeyli—likely to be seen, but not soon enough to do anything about it.

After a quick check of the hallway, she took her goody cart back up the servants' corridor, just as pleased to see that the errand boy had left the dimin-utive door to the ballroom ajar. She made no partic-ular effort to hide her approach, and she hesitated just before the opening to duck down and screw the lid tight on the dry ice jar and make quick work of dumping the ammonia into the bleach. Holding her breath, she gave the cart a shove and closed the door behind it. *Less than five minutes.* The intensely cold dry ice, sitting in its warm water bath, would sublimate quickly to gas…and the gas took up much more volume than the hard, cold chunk of ice with which she'd started. When the gas volume overcame the integrity of the glass jar, it would do so with a violent explosion of glass shards and brittle decorative glass marbles.

Customized Selena-bomb.

But the chlorine gas generated by the bleach and ammonia hit first. It didn't take long for the coughing to start, for the confused exclamations as Kemeni eyes began to sting, irritating noses and throats and eventually lungs. Eventually even damaging eyes and nose and lungs…eventually, perhaps, even turning lethal. Someone made a cranky comment about the man who'd been sent to provide for them even while reaching for the bottle opener and a bottle of Kaliber, but the source of the irritation remained obscure, and the men had no idea they were gathering around it.

In the midst of it all she heard the noise of new arrivals. They burst into the room looking for Ashurbeyli, voices sharp. Within a few words and a few angry gestures and the glimpse of light blue paper, Selena had caught the gist of it: they'd found her notes. The seeds of doubt had been well sown.

Ashurbeyli grasped the situation with his usual stark acumen—and then startled Selena by looking around, examining the room as if he'd suddenly find her there. It was enough to make her move away from her little peephole, although she told herself she'd only done so because it was time. Her eye had felt the first faint sting of gas, and several of the thirsty Kemenis were now doubled over with miserable coughing as the sharp voices rose to true alarm. Ashurbeyli was the one to

point at the empty bottle in the bin; Ashurbeyli was the
one to shout warnings as he backed swiftly away from
the cart.

But Ashurbeyli was too late.

Chapter 17

The glass jar exploded with a noise as sharp as the deadly shards that arrowed through the room. Selena ducked reflexively, and ducked again as planter marbles thunked against the wall only inches away. Men cried out in surprise and pain; someone cried out in pure fury.

Ashurbeyli.

He knew who to blame.

The noises of fear and surprise rose from the next room, too. *The hostages.* They were her first priority now. She took a final glance into the ballroom and discovered more havoc than she'd even imagined—men with their legs slashed and bleeding, too stricken by the chlorine gas to react quickly to the more visible wounds made from flying glass. At least half of them were down, and the other half fully occupied with the wounded.

Not Ashurbeyli. He glared fiercely at the chaos as he plucked a giant splinter from his chest. He barked a few short orders, but he didn't look at the men around him reaching for their comrades, reaching to stem the flow of blood, pulling one man from the soaked carpet where the serving cart had overturned. He looked around as though expecting Selena to materialize from thin air…as though he not only expected it, but gladly anticipated it, his fists balled into white-knuckled weapons.

You lose, she thought at him. Although…not quite yet. Not until she had the hostages. Not until she could at least warn the Berzhaani what he'd really been up to here at the capitol.

She took one last look at the doorway between the ballroom and the hostages, discovering their guard staggered against the doorjamb, bleeding from a rapidly swelling lump just below his eye. Cold flying marble, oh yeah. In another moment he wouldn't be able to see out of that eye at all.

In the moment it would take her to reach the function room.

She followed the wall to the next peephole, and confirmed what her ears had told her—the hostages were poised on their feet, exclamations loud between them and fear running high—especially as the guard waved his gun at them, shouting at them to shut up and sit down. He must have been more rattled than he realized, for he used Berzhaani words, totally incomprehensible to most of those scared people. So they froze, waiting for the situation to become clear…waiting, to judge by the pale, strained expressions, to die.

They're just kids.

But Selena saw more than the kids. She saw broken, ruined families; she saw a country plunged into irreparable turmoil. Berzhaan's prime minister about to die in the rubble of his own capitol.

And the door wouldn't open.

The table. The Kemenis had shoved a table in front of the passage, and she'd forgotten it. Adrenaline kicked in, hammering at her; with no room to step back for a kick, Selena threw her good shoulder into the door, feeling the wallboard give way and bulge out. Someone shrieked, startled and too panicked to hide it even if it meant her life, and when Selena looked again the guard was striding forward, blinking wildly from his watering, swollen eye but full of purpose and totally focused on the table-trapped entrance door.

"Stupid ass," she muttered. "You should have just shot me through the wall." And she shoved the Luger knockoff up against the wallboard, waited for him to block her view of everyone else and pulled a trigger so stiff it might as well be nonfunctional. There'd have been no maintaining her aim if she hadn't had the gun jammed up against the wall for support.

The gunfire rang painfully loud in her little enclosed space in spite of the mild silencing effect of the wall, and she couldn't help but flinch. When she found the peephole again, the guard had fallen out of view, and the hostages were scrambling to the other end of the room.

Not Allori. Allori shouted something to Razidae and the two men rushed forward, flinging the table away from the door in a synchronized effort. Selena all but tumbled out. She tripped over the downed guard and barely had her balance back when the ground rocked

profoundly beneath her; her ears recoiled from a sharp
basso reverberation of sound. She stared toward the
ballroom, aghast—surely they hadn't triggered their
bombs, not when they weren't anywhere near the
exits!—and then realized the explosion had come from
outside the building, back near the always-crowded little parking lot, the old carriage barn and the amazing
grounds and gardens.

Not the building bombs at all—but whatever diversion the Kemenis had planned. But the timing...

The timing couldn't be right.

She held up a quick hand to Allori, a silent signal to
wait, and it was he who turned on the hostages, his
arms held wide to stop the rush they'd been about to
make at her. A few steps put her in position to look
through the doorway, and still, all she saw was chaos—
fervently renewed packing, men festooned with field
bandages...one man clearly down for good, a thick
puddle by his upper leg. *They're not ready.* Whatever
was going down out there, the Kemenis weren't ready
at all.

Before Ashurbeyli could spot her, she drew back.
They had to have heard her pistol shot, as enclosed as
it had been. They'd chosen to ignore her. They'd chosen escape over revenge.

That would certainly explain the dark, furious flush
she'd seen on Ashurbeyli's hawkish features. *He knows
I'm here somewhere.* He'd chosen to complete his mission rather than to hunt her down...but then, he had
probably never guessed that she was just beyond the
door.

She turned on her heel, facing the hostages as she
pulled her increasingly heavy briefcase off her shoul-

ders—now they were in skirmish, and the thing would be more of a liability than potentially useful.

Two days of threats had trained the hostages well; after their initial noisy reactions, they'd silenced, staring mutely from a wide variety of complexions all turned pale and pasty. She stabbed a finger at the bedraggled events coordinator. "You know the way out," she said in Berzhaani, not even bothering to make it a question. "You lead them. Take them out through the kitchen and go right around to the front. There are soldiers there, and they'll protect you."

More noise stuttered through the shouting in the next room—noise that froze them all, and hushed even the Kemenis in their hasty evacuation.

Gunfire. Automatic weapons fire. The three-burst stutter of a well-trained soldier, not the double-burst of the Abakans.

Rescue.

SEALs or Berzhaani Elite, Selena didn't know. And she didn't want to chance it either way, regardless of the extensive training each group underwent in how to not shoot the wrong people. She didn't want the hostages in the middle of it. She grabbed the nearest student by the arm and sent her at the corridor, pinning the events coordinator with her most commanding gaze. "Go!" she said. "They won't try to stop you now—just get out of the way!"

A glance at Allori told her he saw her lie—that he, too, knew the Kemenis might well try to stop the hostages, to use them as shields. But she didn't want them timid, she wanted them running like hell.

Another explosion from the grounds rocked the building and the hostages suddenly moved as one, their silence broken. They rushed the door with their fears released into action—only to get bottled up at the exit, sobs and anxiety and "Hurry up, dammit!" filling the air.

Razidae wasn't one of them. He stood in the middle of the room—prudently near the wall adjoining the ballroom so as not to be visible to the Kemenis, but he stood there nonetheless—his white dress shirt rumpled, his dignified *thagiya* cap askew and his dignity entirely intact. Selena turned to him in annoyance, suddenly quite certain that he didn't intend to go anywhere at all. When a Kemeni popped through the door with mayhem on his mind, she reacted almost absently. She scooped up the briefcase, whirled it around once like a sling, and let fly; it hit him with the force of a medicine ball and bounced off to spew decorative planter marbles across the floor. Selena leaped over them to slam into the Kemeni with the same brute force, too tired for finesse when she could slam the fake Luger across the side of his head and fling his weapon away. She couldn't help but give the gun an appreciative glance. "At last," she told it. "Something you're good at."

"You should give it to Allori," Razidae said, speaking loudly over the growing pop of gunfire now centered in the lobby area. The Kemenis who weren't packing or bleeding—and even some of those who were bleeding—had gone out to hold off the rescue. To Selena's startlement, he held out his hand. "Or to me."

"You don't want this," she assured him. "It's a piece of crap. And please, don't tell me you're going to stay here to greet the cleanup crew. You need to get to safety along with everyone else. *More* than anyone else."

"I do want it," Razidae said, and jerked his head at

the diminishing number of hostages, all of whom were completely focused on escape. "And you should be the one to go with them."

She found herself speechless and glanced at Allori to confirm what she suddenly thought she understood. Razidae didn't want her there when the Berzhaani Elite crashed the scene. He didn't want a woman holding the only captured weapon, and he didn't want her there at all.

Allori gave her the slightest of nods.

Selena stabbed a finger at the Abakan she'd tossed across the room, and at the pathetic Luger knockoff not far from it, by the side of the first man she'd taken down. Acquiring either meant entering the potential line of fire from the doorway. "You want one? You've got your choice. I hope you know how to use them."

Razidae stiffened. "Now is not the time—"

"No," she snapped. "It's not. You can't help pull this country back together if you're not alive."

"Nor can I do so if I cannot command the respect of my people."

She couldn't believe this argument, this moment. She didn't *want* to believe this argument. She gave Razidae a cold look and said, "It's a good thing I was really risking my neck for those kids, or I might be seriously peeved that you're throwing away all my work. As it is, I don't have any problem with the notion of working with—let's see, who's next in line now that bin Kuwaji is dead?" She didn't expect an answer. She said it only to buy thinking time, hovering over the decision to end this argument with a good stout blow to Razidae's head. With Allori's help, she could drag Razidae out of this place before it came down on them all.

"Weren't you paying any attention to the conversation in there?" she asked, indicating the ballroom. "They're going to take this whole building down. If you wait here, you're going to go down with it."

"The Elite are here," he said, as calmly as though gunfire didn't blot out half his words. "They'll deal with the situation."

Selena took a chance, glanced through to the ballroom, and hesitated at the surprise of seeing the last limping Kemeni heading out the exit opposite her, hauling one of the equipment cases and leaving in his wake the detritus of apparent defeat—furniture overturned, several bodies on the floor, the scent of blood in the air.

There was no sign of the remote detonator triggers. The table where they'd been was conspicuously bare. A forlorn chunk of dry ice steamed on the floor beside it, showing no signs of the havoc it had wreaked. In the background, the firefight surged in ferocity; Selena could well imagine the first line of fleeing Kemenis laying down cover for those who escaped with the computer drives and data.

Another Kemeni ran up to the room, stopping just short of entering to stare at Selena as though stunned. She raised her gun in a knee-jerk reaction, but froze in midmotion, taken back. *That looks like—*

But it didn't. Black mustache, piercing brown eyes, olive skin…he wore the most modest of green turbans and Kemeni colors, but he stood there on the balls of his feet, every bit as frozen as she, compact and graceful and so *familiar*—

"Cole?" She hadn't intended to speak at all, and yet there somehow it was. Cole was in D.C. She'd left him behind, never intending to put herself in a situation where she wouldn't see him again—or where her last message to him was a voice mail message in which she never even told him they might have managed to start a family after all. And yet there was her one-word question, hanging between them with a longing she hadn't known she could feel, never mind express.

I must be going crazy. Cole was blue-eyed and fair-haired and his nose not quite so—

"Cole?" she asked again, this time barely a whisper. Nothing loud enough to carry over the noise of the fire-fight raging in the lobby and beyond, but somehow he gave the slightest of nods anyway. He pulled off the turban to reveal bright, sun-streaked hair; he yanked at his shirt. Underneath the apparent buttons of the military-like blouse, Velcro quickly gave way, leaving him in a tight black T-shirt with U.S.A. printed in bright yellow. Selena's instinct gave way to sudden, overwhelming recognition—she *knew* those shoulders, had watched those muscles flex with weight work, had seen that chest sheen with sweat as he pulled her close.

The mustache and brown eyes and olive skin tone remained, at wild odds with his hair. He took a step toward her, apparently and suddenly oblivious of the turmoil around them, and Selena held up a sudden hand. One more step and she'd lose perspective and control; she'd run to him and she might even do it with the slow-motion effects of a love story in full play. So instead she stiffened, and she restricted all her longing to her eyes. "The Kemenis have Razidae's hard drives. And they have remote detonators—this building's rigged."

He understood. He reversed that step, a precise movement so typical of a man who always knew exactly how to put his body where he wanted it. His gaze stayed locked on hers as he gave the smallest of nods, and as he turned to go—chasing after the Kemenis, leaving her to play her own part—he lifted a fist to his chest with thumb, forefinger, and pinky extended, their own simple addition to the covert ops signals they both knew.

Selena returned it. *I love you, too.*

Now live through this, dammit, so I can prove it.

Total heart-body disconnect. Selena felt it happen. The better part of her turned away from the ballroom with Cole, following in his footsteps as he moved toward the fighting with such apparent ease that it almost looked as if he drifted. What remained looked back into the function room, finding herself under scrutiny by both Allori and Razidae. Allori, at least, seemed to understand what he'd seen, accepting that somehow the Cole Jones of whom he'd only read had made his way to Berzhaan—and that for the sake of Berzhaan, Selena had denied herself that full reunion.

Razidae only had the physical perspective to see Selena herself, and he watched her with impatience. Selena returned it, opening her mouth to suggest, again and rather more acerbically, that he take the exit the other hostages had left open for him—except Razidae's eyes widened with alarm she couldn't ignore. Selena whirled to find the second room entrance—the one through which Ashurbeyli had escorted her with such intent not so long ago—filled with the graceless form of Jonas White, his arm extended in a way that could only mean one thing. *Gun!*

And not one of the fake Lugers with which he'd supplied the Kemeni, either—something stocky and clean-cut and reliable. Selena doubled back on herself in a catlike leap that took Razidae down. He fell unprepared, hitting the floor hard; a chair tumbled out of his way as it took a glancing blow. Selena rolled to her stomach, coming up with arms extended to take aim at White, her injured arm automatically trying for a support position it couldn't sustain. But it didn't matter that she wavered. She hadn't even finished the movement when the ear-numbing blast of White's .45 battered her.

Allori staggered back, astonishment on his face and instant blood on his faintly pinstriped dress shirt. Backward and down, smearing blood along the wall as Selena hesitated, lost in surprise and fatigue and that sudden sinking feeling that things already gone wrong had just gone worse. Hesitated just long enough for White to close in on the wounded ambassador and smile wolfishly at Selena. The retreating gunfire in the background gave her the sudden bizarre regret that they were alone—no unpredictable hostages to get in White's way, no fervently dedicated Kemenis making sure things evolved in their own best interest. Not even any of the rescuers, who'd obviously made rounding up the terrorists their understandable first priority.

White didn't have to say anything. He merely raised an eyebrow, his gun pointed directly at Allori's head. And even though Allori, stunned and speechless, had the wherewithal to shake his head at Selena, she quietly put her own gun on the floor and nudged it away from herself. "It pretty much sucks anyway," she told White. She didn't mention that she'd already taken a quick glance to calculate the distance to the Kemeni's gun so recently tossed aside; a lunge from this sprawling position, a few rolls, and she could put her hand on it. Or that her fingers had closed around several of the decorative marbles scattered in the wake of that encounter.

White laughed. "As a weapon, it's sorely lacking," he agreed. "But it was much better when you were holding it, wasn't it? Now the only question is whether when I shoot you, I aim to kill or just to take you down."

"I don't suppose you're taking votes."

He laughed again. Not because she'd been particularly funny, but because of the victory dancing in his eyes. In moments he'd escape, heading for his Plan C, and he'd once again leave death and destruction in his wake. "No," he said. "I don't suppose I am." And he shifted the gun until she was looking right down the barrel.

Selena gave White a look of purest annoyance, just as though her heart weren't pounding so hard as to reverberate through the floor beneath her. "Be that way," she said, and whipped a side-hand marble at him from her awkward spot on the floor. It smacked into his kneecap—*dammit, I was aiming higher*—and so startled him that he leaped away from the pain. She gathered herself, lunging for Allori; she rolled sideways across the carpet, snagging the dead Kemeni's discarded pistol along the way. Gunfire echoed in the room—but White had expected her to go for her own gun, and filled the carpet with deadly holes. By the time he corrected himself, Selena crouched by Allori's side, her weapon pointing steadily at White.

And it was all perfect, until Razidae stepped in. White was poised to run, until Razidae stepped in. But step in he did, hurling himself at White as though to save the day. Thinking, perhaps, of the headlines, of the influence—however temporary—that such an action would give him in the wake of this terrorist disaster. But Razidae had more heart than training or experience, and White almost gladly stepped into his rush, evading Razidae's blow to jam the .45 in his chest with such profound impact that the prime minister stopped short. Stopped short and instantly realized his error.

The return of White's grin probably had something to do with his sudden wisdom.

White looked at Selena, an eyebrow raised in question—*your move?* Selena scowled back. "I should have tied you at that window."

"Your mistake," White acknowledged. He looked between Razidae and Allori, a recognition of the stalemate between them. "But since you didn't, I'll just take my prize and leave."

Selena raised her chin, unable to hide her alarm. "You don't need him."

"Because you're going to let me walk away?"

Reluctantly, she amended, "You don't need him once you leave this room. So how about you use him for cover and then make a final defiant gesture by shoving him back in the room?"

White smiled again. She'd really come to dislike that smile. He said, "You aren't the only one I have to worry about. This building is crawling with heroic men and their guns. No, Mr. Razidae will be coming with me."

"Then I'll be coming *after* you."

"And leave your wounded ambassador?" White shook his head; Razidae looked both bemused and offended to be bantered over. "And here I had you pegged as the loyal type."

Allori, until now silent, tipped his head to look at White, maintaining every bit of his dignity. "Which is exactly why she'll do as I suggest and go after you."

He didn't, in fact, have the authority to order Selena to do one thing or another. But if he was inclined to make the suggestion…she was inclined to follow it. *After* she checked him over more carefully than she could while crouching beside him and playing games with White. She gestured at the hallway exit, a mere tilt of her chin. "The sooner you go, the sooner I can catch up with you."

Dragging Razidae, his .45 pressed firmly against the man's skull in defiance of a censuring expression that had controlled this country for years, White did just that. He backed up to the exit to the hallway that ran along the front of the function rooms, opposite the servants' corridor. And then he stepped neatly into the hall, taking his VIP hostage with him.

Selena had half hoped White would shove Razidae back into the room anyway, a decision to jettison baggage so that he could move more quickly toward his escape. White didn't, of course. She muttered a scorching phrase under her breath and turned instantly to Allori and the growing splash of blood on his shirt. She set quick fingers to the small pearl dress buttons and ignored his surprise and his visible impulse to object. "The sooner I can assess this, the sooner I can do what's necessary," she told him. If he understood all the possibilities in "what's necessary"—*the sooner I can get you to help, the sooner I can run after White, the sooner I can watch him die*—he didn't let on. He allowed her to open the shirt, exposing a thickly haired chest, and then to peel it back until she found the source of the blood.

And sighed in relief. She got up long enough to yank a tablecloth free, and to pull the knife from the dead Kemeni's belt. She ripped a long strip from the fine white cloth and flipped the rest of it down to a rectangle in quick folds. When she knelt again, she pressed the pad up under his arm, and helped him forward so she could tie it in place. "It's in and out," she said. "I think it skipped along the outside of your ribs." He had enough meat that she wasn't sure, but she'd heard no air and he certainly hadn't coughed up any blood. "If you can stay on your feet long enough to get out of here—"

He snorted and winced, but met her eye. "I'll crawl if I have to."

She tightened the bandage and tied it off, wincing as he closed his eyes and grunted against the pain. But when he looked at her again she said firmly enough, "You'll have to crawl fast. The Kemenis have remote detonating devices for the bombs they've planted around the building."

He echoed her scorching phrase of not so long ago. "You've seen—?"

"Better than that. I took two of them out of the mix. But they've got remotes for a lot more than two." She pointed at the corridor entrance. "So crawl *very* fast. When you hit the end of the sneaky little passage, hang a left to the kitchen. Ignore the blood all over the floor—it's been there awhile. And the kitchen door should be open for you. If you circle left, you'll come around to—"

"The front of the building. I heard you the first time, when you told the others."

"Good." She stood, then put out her good arm.

He didn't pretend he didn't need the help up—or that he didn't need a moment to recover when his face went pasty white. But he put the time to good use. "In spite of what I said...consider coming with me. The rescue boys are in on this one, whether they're ours or Berzhaan's. They can grab White."

"They don't even know he's here."

He gave her a wry once-over. "You're not in much better shape than I am."

"I beg your pardon," Selena said. "*I'm* not bleeding." *Anymore.* But she took in his expression—the one that told her he wasn't fooled, that he understood her right arm wasn't exactly working right and that one eye was half-closed and that the rest of her had been bashed around into creaky shooting pains—and she nodded reluctantly. "If the cavalry shows up, I'll step aside. But until I know they've got him in their sights..."

She wouldn't even have given him that much, not if it hadn't been for the potential family member within her. Too small to see, too small to feel, and yet so hugely a part of her—*potential* or not. But she did, and Allori nodded in reply, understanding it was the only concession she'd make—and knowing that if Razidae died, in many ways the terrorists would prevail even if they didn't emerge from this building alive.

He pushed himself away from the wall, holding himself with stiff determination. "I'll see you on the steps," he said. *"Alive."*

"Works for me," Selena said, watching until he entered the corridor.

And then she went hunting.

Cole slipped quickly through the halls, his skin crawling with the awareness that a T-shirt labeled

U.S.A. didn't keep him from being a Kemeni target, or even a victim of friendly fire. If he was a SEAL or one of the Berzhaani Elite, he wasn't at all sure he wouldn't shoot first and figure out the identity of this strangely garbed interloper later. Possibly much later.

Seth had shown him simplified blueprints of the capitol, enough so he knew to cut away from the Kemeni trail—the ejected shell casings, the smears of blood, the occasional body—and to take a cross hall to the back of the building, fully intending to come up on them from the back.

The problem, of course, was that being behind the Kemenis very much meant being in the line of fire from the good guys.

Unless he guessed wrong, and the Kemenis had another route in mind altogether—maybe up to the roof, or doubling back to the other side of the capitol, or ducking down through the basement. But the recent explosions had been on that side—Hellfire missiles courtesy of Josie Lockworth, if Cole didn't miss his guess, probably aimed at approaching Kemeni allies—and so was all the attention. Nope, this side looked good for a quick escape, if not quite so clean as planned.

A sporadic exchange of gunfire gave way to shouting as Cole skimmed along the wall of his final approach, and it made him hesitate. *They're negotiating? They're this close to an exit and they're negotiating?* Gut instinct told him they were up to something else.

Like preparing to blow the building—but making sure the rescue teams were trapped inside when they did. It meant setting off the *right* bomb first. Which could well mean stalling, in spite of the risk.

With the utmost care, Cole risked a peek around the

corner. Just beyond the turn, an open door led into the stairwell, and the Kemenis had crowded into it; they seemed to be tearing through their baggage in search of something. The remotes? And…was that a Post-it note stuck to the door? Apparently so, for even then an anonymous hand ripped it away, crumpling it before throwing it back out in the hallway.

Cole knew that the stairwell landing held an exit to the outside—it was the same door he'd seen on approach to the building, and all the stairwells included exit doors. *Why don't they—*

A few exchanged gunshots answered the question for him. They hadn't left because they had a welcoming committee on the outside. And they couldn't return to the hallway, not with the team of Berzhaani Elite that Cole had glimpsed taking up position in the hall—close enough to take an instant shot at anyone who reappeared from the stairwell, but off at enough of an angle so no one in the stairwell had any chance of targeting the team.

Great. So they're trapped. Time on their hands and they're trapped. And they have those remotes. And Cole hadn't had time to brush up on the local lingo. He sorted through his Berzhaani and filled the gaps with Russian, making sure he was good and clear of anyone's line of fire before he revealed himself to either set of combatants. "Don't shoot," he told them, just as a good submissive opening line. "I want to let you know I'm here." Actually, he thought he'd probably said *I announce me,* but it was close enough.

Someone from the stairwell instantly fired at the sound of his voice, chipping huge chunks of wallboard from the corner.

"Hey, I said *don't* shoot," Cole protested. "I'm too

busy hiding to mess with you." Okay, lying was sometimes a good thing.

"Who?" demanded one of the Elite, a voice full of annoyance and fired up with battle. "SEAL should be at the lobby!"

"Not SEAL," Cole said. "American...in the wrong place at the wrong time." Great. He was pretty sure that had come out as *American accident*.

The Berzhaani response was instantaneous—a chorus of voices telling him to get lost. Succinct, to the point, and laced with English curses he certainly understood. Cole grinned, sardonic humor in the midst of life and death. He couldn't blame them a bit. "Listen first," he said, or maybe *listen one*. Dammit. "They have bombs. You know of the—" roof, what was roof, dammit? "—building top? There are more—they have..." He rolled his eyes at himself and tried again. "They have set-offs. You have to get them or—"

The building rumbled and shuddered around them, a deep sound so profound it thumped like a hollow drum in Cole's chest. The structure shook and crackled and glass broke; Cole instinctively ducked down under the feeble protection of his own arms, wondering how many they'd set off and where those bombs had been and how long they all had until this sturdy old building crumbled down around them. In the next instant he realized that it must have been those bombs on the roof, with all their force escaping up and out and little of it directed at the capitol's supporting structure. Those in the most danger would be the Elite just outside the building, the ones bottling the Kemenis up in their stairwell. The Kemenis had chosen this first detonation with care—something to take everyone aback, to give them the opportunity to—

Gunfire erupted anew. The Kemenis were blasting their way out of their dead end, seizing the moment to overcome outside forces battered by falling brick and shattered glass. The Elite in the hallway responded in kind, moving up to take their shots until Cole's ears rang with the intensity of the exchange.

No fools, the Kemenis—outgunned, they rushed the Elite, taking the battle to close-quarters fighting. Cole took another look around the corner, as flat against the wall as he could be—and found himself in the perfect position to spot the lone Kemeni lurking behind the dubious cover of the stair riser, weighing two remotes in his hands.

Decisions, decisions. Cole lifted his Hi-Power, breaking cover to take careful aim—because of course he'd had every intent to "mess with" the Kemenis from the start. Two men lurched between him and his target, lurched away...revealed the man having made up his mind, setting down one remote detonator in favor of the other.

Cole squeezed the trigger. The man jerked back, his eyes wide and surprised, and the remote tipped out of his suddenly feeble grip. For an instant it seemed as if no one noticed at all—and then the fighting seemed to hesitate, everyone at once feeling the balance of things change and tip and—

Get the remotes. For the Elite seemed focused on the Kemenis themselves, and suddenly the Kemenis were no longer a team, but individuals squirting off in every which direction. Cole dodged his way through the chaos of fists and knives and sporadic gunfire and dived into the stairwell, catching up against the back of the stairs and abruptly too intimate with the man he'd just shot.

It'd been a solid hit; the man only now began to stir, coming out of the initial daze of the impact in the center of his chest. "Be still," Cole told him, recovering to an awkward crouch. "Help will come."

Maybe, maybe not. But no need to kick a man when he was already down and getting a close look at death. Cole hunted for the small black remotes the man had dropped, gathering them up with a quick glance to confirm they each needed both hands for triggering. Safety devices. Something ironic about that. He dumped the injured man's small canvas bag on the floor and used it for collecting the remotes. Four, five…six. Was that it?

This little nook had so isolated him from the chaos that Cole started when a man jumped down to block the way out; he jerked back, smacking his head on a low stair. "Dammit—"

The man before him glared with the tight, barely leashed fury of a man thwarted beyond his own imagination. "Leave those." His voice sounded so constrained, so close to the edge of explosion, that Cole couldn't imagine how he'd spoken at all. In perfectly fine English, to boot.

And he sounded familiar.

Cole shook his head, a careful gesture in the face of the man's gun. "I don't think so. And I wouldn't hang around, if I were you. I believe by now they're probably quite willing to shoot you in the back."

And the man across from him—so close to him in this tight space, a man out of place with his honed, hawkish features and perfect brooding eyes—gave a little start, looking at Cole with sudden recognition.

Cole narrowed his eyes as disbelief warred with the

sudden startling urge to lunge forward and rip this man apart. "We *do* know each other."

The Kemeni's face flashed through emotions too quickly to decipher. Wariness, jealousy, hatred—?

And Cole knew for sure. The voice on the other end of the phone. The man who'd hurt Selena. His throat tightened down; his words came out strained. "Where is she?"

Ashurbeyli—it *had* to be Ashurbeyli—grinned at him, an expression that barely looked sane. "I don't know."

"Then," Cole said, shifting his weight ever so slightly, "there's no reason I should let you live, is there?" And he lashed out with a foot from his crouching position, kicking the gun away, giving himself the chance to raise his own weapon and squeeze off a shot—but not before Ashurbeyli grabbed a too-familiar black box from his front shirt pocket and clasped it in both hands.

Cole fired anyway, an ill-aimed shot that hit Ashurbeyli just beside the join of neck and shoulder and flung him backward. And then the floor shook beneath him as muffled thunder detonated above his head— *right* above his head, somewhere here in the stairwell— and he flung himself out from under the stairs, scrabbling forward with his world narrowed to the chunks of concrete suddenly falling around him and *ow dammit* on his leg and then a serious crack on the head so his world grayed out and he had no point of reference at all; he might as well have been swimming or floundering through snow or navigating through black space or—

Cole opened his eyes. He sat against the wall inside

the building, one of a dozen men similarly arrayed with legs outstretched, similarly dazed. Warm blood ran over his face and into his slightly open mouth; he sputtered, quite suddenly alert. His mustache sat askew, and Cole reached up to tug it off, learning that he hadn't quite regained his motor skills as he clumsily hit himself in the face.

A man crouched beside him, the red cross on his white armband as unmistakable as such symbols come. "This is over," he said. "You will be fine again."

"I'm fine now," Cole said, and brought his legs in so he could stand—and stared stupefied at the Aircast on his lower leg. "Huh. I'll be damned."

"Maybe not just yet," the Berzhaani medic said dryly. "But I can see to it if you do not keep yourself quiet. I have others, worsely wounded than you, who need attention."

"Crutches," Cole said. "I'm not done yet. My wife is still here somewhere."

"The only women are with the hostages, and the hostages are free."

Cole glanced down the hall—one direction and then the next, noting the arrival of the first stretchers, the clear intent to evacuate everyone from this compromised old building.

The obvious missing face. Ashurbeyli.

"I need crutches," he insisted. "And I need them *now*."

Chapter 18

Selena caught up with White at the front corner of the building just as a second explosion rocked the building. It gave a deep groan, eerily human, and a crack split the plaster along the wall, tectonic building plates drifting apart. White shoved Razidae up against the corner and propped him there by leaning against his throat, his hammy hand wrapped around the prime minister's larynx with just enough weight to make breathing difficult. Selena ducked into the nearest function room, a small room on the end of the row, and let her gun peek out the door.

"You stupid bitch," White said, and for the first time he sounded tired of this game. "Do you really think I won't kill him?"

"I really think you won't kill him *yet*," she corrected. "And wouldn't you be better off to use him for cover?

Because it's only going to take me a tiny little look to pinpoint you in my sights."

White snorted. "As if that matters. By the time you manage the trigger on that useless gun, you'll be pointing at your foot."

Well. Yeah. Some truth to that. But she scoffed. "Oh, please. Doorjamb...stabilizer. Get it?"

And all the same...she really didn't want to shoot the prime minister by mistake. She reached into her pocket for the marbles she'd jammed there, wondering if the same trick would work twice. Fingered them and considered it. Risky.

"Jonas White!"

She froze. Ashurbeyli's voice. But he was out of this now, long gone with his men...with any luck, already dead. A man with his own kind of honor, too uncompromising to exist in this world and allow others to be safe.

But Jonas White cursed, only confirming what she thought she'd heard. *Ashurbeyli's voice.* And Razidae, sounding defeated for the first time, murmured, *"Inshallah,"* abandoning himself to God's hands.

"Where is she?" Ashurbeyli demanded, much closer now. Selena wished she dared to look; as it was she could only imagine it—White in the corner, threatening Razidae. Ashurbeyli coming up on them from the adjacent hall. Former allies, eyeing each other with blame and dislike. "And did you think you could get away with your betrayal?"

"Make up your mind," White responded with irritation. "Do you want to get your hands on our meddling FBI agent, or do you want to posture and threaten me?"

"She was right." Ashurbeyli didn't sound quite like

himself, and he'd stopped just around the corner. Still out of her sight. "You had your own agenda all along. *These* guns—" and he said it with an emphasis that made Selena think he had gestured with one of the guns in question "—they came from you. You lied to us from the start…made us think the United States was backing us. Gave us inferior weapons—and then came to manipulate us into saving your own faithless hide by risking our own!"

"That sounds just about right. Now get over it. Do you want me, or do you want the American woman? Because if you leave me alone, you can have her."

"What—?" No, he definitely didn't sound like himself. His voice had a ragged quality; his mind wasn't so quick as it had been.

"She's in that room just around the corner. If you can take her, she's yours. *If* you let me go on my merry way. Otherwise I'm afraid we'll be forced into a distasteful standoff right here, and I note that *my* gun is properly aimed."

Then he's not aiming at me—

"Go, then," Ashurbeyli said, his words thick with disgust. "I think in fact that you are the worst thing I can do to the Western capitalist—"

"—dogs," White completed for him. "Yes, yes, I know. We're all infidel scum. But you and I can still come to this agreement. I leave her to you, and you leave me to my own fate. It is, I might add, a limited time offer."

A moment passed in which they must have come to some unspoken agreement, for just as Selena eased around to peek into the hall, White said, "Good, then," and gestured her way with the gun. Behind him, Razidae struggled for breath, pale beneath his normally robust complexion.

Ashurbeyli came around the corner, not as wary as he might have been. Staggered around the corner was more like it, with blood covering the side of his shirt and flowing fast enough to make the material gleam. He saw her; saw her gun, and raised his own at her in what seemed like a token gesture. His face had paled; his intensity had faded into mere determination.

And White watched. Like a greedy voyeur, he watched. As Razidae attempted protest, White shifted his weight just enough to make the man choke, closing his fingers so they dug into Razidae's windpipe.

Ashurbeyli, his finger tightening on the trigger but then holding fast, said the last thing she expected. "I met your husband."

Cole! She didn't have enough nerve to ask what had happened. Not at first. Too busy fighting all the stupid things fear did to her—the greased, wobbly knees, the watery spine, the sudden inability to breathe. And when she finally managed to open her mouth, he cut her off.

"I just buried him under that bomb. And before I left him there to die, I let him know I was coming after you."

Horrified, she met the triumph in his gaze, holding the connection…a request for truth between enemies at the end of the battle. She saw there his triumph, and saw also his sorrow…and then a brief flicker of something that she suddenly recognized as regret. "No," she breathed, but it was still more question than belief—more hope than knowledge. "You didn't."

He closed his eyes—briefly, but still long enough to make him vulnerable, and she didn't think he'd intended to do it. And though her finger tightened on the heavy trigger of her gun, she didn't pull it. She told herself she wasn't quite ready to upset the balance of the moment, not with White standing poised to crush Razidae's throat. She told herself it was too risky. But when Ashurbeyli opened his eyes, the regret shone the strongest. "It's a shame," he said, and shifted his gun, weary enough to allow the telltale; weary enough to let that warning slip through.

Selena dived aside, followed by the thunderous report of not one but two guns. A fiery trail plucked her sleeve, running up her forearm; she fell heavily against the wall behind the door, her stupid fake Luger raised and ready. Still on her feet; still ready for whatever came next. Her other hand finally escaped her pocket, still curled around the marbles. *Still ready—*

Ashurbeyli fell through the door and thumped to the carpet. His mouth moved in a few soundless words, and then he died.

White. As Ashurbeyli came for Selena, White had betrayed him. Shot him in the back.

Selena's fury took her by surprise. She opened her mouth to voice it…and then she thought again. *White thinks Ashurbeyli shot me.* She'd certainly hit the wall hard enough, convincingly uncontrolled.

And now she let herself fall hard to her knees, hitting the door so it slowly swung closed—at least until it ran into Ashurbeyli's body. She slid down the door, a dramatic scrape of cloth against wood.

White laughed, damn him. Selena let herself settle so her head rested just against Ashurbeyli, her vision barely clearing the edge of the door. White, if he looked, would see only the top of her head. But White had already turned to Razidae, gloating, jamming the gun back into the prime minister's chest and pulling him out of the corner.

Selena felt for the gap beneath the door, the way it rode high over the plush Sekha carpet. Plenty of room, oh, yes. And she had plans even if this didn't work, but if it did she'd find it ever so sweet. One by one, she rolled the marbles out under the door, swiftly adjusting for distance until she had placed scattershot hard round objects in Jonas White's path. *Acme marbles*. Perfect for foiling the overconfident bad guy.

Out he stepped, harshly pushing Razidae before him. And it was Razidae, already off balance, who hit the marbles first, whose foot shot unexpectedly forward. He fell hard just as White's own foot skittered aside, and White took the brunt of it as they hit the floor.

Selena poked her gun around the edge of the door and said in her drollest tone, "Doesn't it just suck when you get nailed by a trick a cartoon character would use? I'm the Roadrunner, by the way. You must be the Coyote. So we already know how this ends, don't we?"

White's face, already florid from his fall, went to dusky purple rage. He jerked his gun to bear, ready to empty the magazine at her right through the door.

She didn't give him the chance. She braced the ill-made semiautomatic against the edge of the door and she jerked the trigger back. By the time she hauled it back down into position in the wake of the jarring recoil and trigger pull, White stared at her with two small, dull unseeing eyes, his shirt torn by her bullet, the bleeding already stopped.

For a moment, Selena rested her head against—good God, against Ashurbeyli. That made her straighten fast enough, all the painful way to her feet. A step forward, and she nudged the gun away from White's curled fingers, and she looked down on him and said softly, "Beep, beep."

Cole sat outside among the hostages and the injured soldiers and knew only one thing for certain: Selena wasn't one of them.

Two things: no one would give him any crutches.

Three things: no one would go back into the building to look for Selena until the exterior had been secured. The Predator's missiles had scarred the hell out of the back parking lot and the old coach building running along the perimeter of the grounds, scattering the approaching Kemenis—some of whom had holed up to take potshots at soldiers. One of the hostages had been wounded on the way out, and now no one could approach the building, not until the military dogs just now hitting the scene had declared the area clean.

Cole glared at the Aircast on his leg and considered hopping. He'd spotted a pair of crutches near the triage area...he knew he could reach them. The only question was whether he could reach them unseen.

They knew she was in there. They *knew.* Ambassador Allori, only recently loaded into an ambulance, had told them as much. Prime Minister Razidae, stumbling around the end of the building to be met by a squad of soldiers and a roar of delight and approval, had also told them as much. She'd stayed behind for Razidae, to rescue him—and she had. But as far as he knew, she'd gone down in an old-fashioned gunfight. He wasn't entirely sure—he'd fallen, the shooting had started, and he'd left the scene at top speed, anticipating no survivors.

Or so he said. But Cole wasn't willing to take him at face value. He wouldn't have taken any man in Razidae's position at face value, not when the man had so much of that face to lose. Bad enough that Selena had been fighting his battles; he wasn't likely to admit he'd left her behind to do so.

Crawling. Crawling was an option, too.

All the while the capitol building groaned and grumbled and coughed smoke, threatening fiery collapse—close enough to this streetside staging area to loom, just far enough away to eliminate danger if it disintegrated. And Cole watched with a stunned disbelief alternating with complete panic, going from numbness to a fierce pain that overwhelmed the pounding of his head and the sharp ache in his leg—and then back again to numbness.

Razidae was wrong. Razidae was lying. *Lying.*

Cole rested his head on fisted hands. *You're not doing her any good like this.* He had to pull himself together. And if he couldn't go into that building after her, he'd find someone who could. Who would. One of the SEALs. The whole damn SEAL team, if it came to that.

If he could find them.

The triage area boasted a complete mix of personnel—Berzhaani medics, International Red Cross volunteers, American military support personnel with a distinct and careful paucity of actual soldiers and the inevitable border of reporters and cameras along the perimeter, crowding each other for the best shot.

The SEALs would be staying out of sight. Bad enough that they'd been here, lurking, against Berzhaan's wishes. Bad enough that Cole himself had been found inside the building; he'd already been promised the debriefing from hell.

It didn't faze him. He was already there, tortured by the moments ticking by and the flames licking from the top windows and the precise, clear memory of Selena signing that she loved him as she went back to guide the hostages to safety—and eventually to face not only White, but Ashurbeyli. Of the look on her face, her well-protected heart and soul right out there for everyone to see.

For Cole to see.

Oh God.

Noise rumbled around him, the nonstop diesel *hrum-hrum-hrum* of rescue vehicle engines. The hostages cried in pain and relief, the various in-charge people shouted out orders he didn't bother to understand. But for a sudden instant, it all seemed to stop—as if everything and everyone held their breath at once—and then let it out again to be twice as noisy. But—and Cole lifted his head to see—with the addition of vigorous pointing.

Pointing at the lone figure standing in the black, cavernous opening of the capitol's double doors.

Crutches! Crutches, dammit!

One of the former hostages, a self-possessed young blond man with a wide-eyed young woman usually clinging to his side, appeared beside Cole. He held out the crutches Cole had been recently eyeing, and nodded at the stone steps, his expression unusually knowing. "Here," he said. "Go to her."

Cole had had no idea he could get to his feet so quickly, and he snatched the crutches away with such possessive ferocity that the kid grinned. Across the abbreviated lawn between the street and those Death Steps, across the sidewalk at the foot of the steps—

She was still there. Holy moly, she was still there. She stood there—*swayed* there—poised between movement and utter collapse, and therefore going nowhere. That strong, lean face was bruised along every striking line; her eye still half-closed. Blood soaked one tattered sleeve and she held the other as stiffly as he remembered.

She was beautiful.

She was alive.

She looked down at him with the same incomprehensible relief he felt taking over his own features.

He opened his mouth to say *Wait, I'll come help you,* or on second thought after a wise glance at those steps, *Wait, let me get help.*

Selena shook her head. Not the short, sharp gesture he expected from her, but a more careful movement— the movement of someone trying desperately to keep herself in one piece. Quite clearly—a voice stronger than any he expected to come from that exhausted shell of his wife—she said, "No. Stay there. This is one set of steps that I fully intend to *walk* down."

It might just have been the hardest thing Cole had ever done…but he waited. He watched her careful descent, he ached and bled for her, and he waited. And when she reached the bottom, he didn't care about all the cameras aimed their way, all the commentary suddenly building to applause and cheers. He put his arms around her and he said, "Welcome home, Lena."

Welcome home—and everything that it meant between them.

And barely standing on her own, she lifted her head from his shoulder and whispered, just for the two of them, "Home for good."

* * *

"Beep, beep?" Cole asked again, his mouth close to Selena's ear and his breath a delicious tickle. Carefully, achingly, she eased closer to him. The bed wasn't theirs and it wasn't entirely comfortable; nor was this tiny room on base at Ramstein in Germany—where they'd both been flown, treated and released, and now faced the first rounds of debriefing. The bed wasn't theirs... but they were together in it. Spooned in the luxury of simply being together. Cole kissed Selena's neck and added, "You really said that?"

"Mmm-hmm." She curled her hands over his arm where it pillowed her head, stroking down to meet his hand and clasp it lightly. "Lightly" was their watchword. Selena was stitched and bruised and even cracked in a place or two, from the initial damage to her face and arm through the battering she'd taken in the bathroom and the final insult of the bullet that had deeply furrowed her forearm. Cole's concussion had been declared mild; his leg rested heavily in a cast on which she'd already written a lewd suggestion.

His free hand traced a path over the curve of her hip, one of the few freely touchable places available. He settled his hand and tugged her back slightly, sighing down her neck as her bottom made contact with an obvious but gentle arousal. "And that Post-it note I found? You really wrote 'You lose'?"

"Mmm-hmm." She kissed his arm. Lightly, oh yes. Her face still looked like a battlefield.

He rested his head on hers, taking a deep, slow breath that came out in a sigh and meant he'd been reveling in the scent of her hair. After a moment he said, "I'm done with fieldwork for a while, you know. Possibly forever."

"Because of the cameras." She'd wondered. Even in her weary, painful daze, she'd been aware of the cameras recording her every step on the way down to Cole. Her statement about walking down the Death Steps had already been splashed across international headlines. And though the stills showed mostly the back of Cole's head, the broadcast cameras had captured his distinctive profile and the bright gold glint of his hair.

He shrugged, his chest moving against her shoulders. "I'd do it again. No-brainer. Besides, they're asking me to consider training recruits at the Farm. After my leg heals, maybe some of the survival camps. Maybe Tory can get her interview after all. And it strikes me as a good thing for a father to do."

"But—"

But he wasn't. They weren't. The little pee-on-a-stick kit had been smugly certain of it. Selena's fatigue, her illness…just the results of stress set off by bad food and followed up by way too much in-her-face death. She'd cried at that, as she hadn't cried in the past horrible days.

"No buts." He gently rubbed her stomach, avoiding the three stitches that closed the wound there. "We'll get there. And it's better this way."

She didn't immediately absorb the statement, still lost in the thought of his job changing…and of her own. "The CIA called me today, you know."

He stilled, his soothing gestures coming to a standstill. She missed them immediately.

"Not to worry," she said. "They want me for Langley. They need a new chief in counterterrorism interrogation and analysis. I guess I impressed them."

Cole's laugh was short and quiet. "Honey, you impressed the *world*."

She'd impressed *someone,* anyway. The CIA hadn't been the only one to come calling. Delphi herself had called, on a secure cell phone that had been hand delivered only moments before. The women of Athena Academy, she had said, were fulfilling their promise—Selena among them. And it was time to pull together in a more organized fashion, pooling their talents across agency lines to prevent incidents just such as the one Selena had survived. As soon as Selena returned to the States, she and certain other Athena graduates would gather to meet Delphi for the first time—and to formally initiate the organization that Delphi called Oracle.

"Langley," Cole repeated after moments of mutually quiet thought. "There'd be travel, of course."

"Some," she agreed, distracted enough to purr as he stroked her side, hand gently following her curves, fingers tracing the interesting features along the way—skimming the side of her breasts, her ribs, the hip bone that wouldn't be quite so obvious once she got another good meal or two on board.

"Still," he said. "A good job for a family woman."

"What did you mean?" she asked suddenly. "That it's better this way? That I'm not pregnant?"

His silence came through as uncomfortable guilt. They hadn't talked about this, not yet. Selena hadn't felt the burning need, not after she'd delved so deeply into her true feelings. Facing terrorists tended to peel away the superficial layers of feelings to get straight to the core, and she'd found her answers there. Her trust.

But they hadn't talked about it, and they'd still need to do that. Cole took a deep breath and said, "I know what it did to you, seeing me in D.C. I screwed up when I didn't tell you I was on my way back, and I don't know that I can ever give you any details. With what we'd just been through… Well, I know you, honey. There's this part you hardly show anyone else…the part that cares so deeply you can hardly stand it." He kissed her neck where it joined her shoulder. "I shook that part up pretty badly. If we'd come off this incident to find you pregnant, we'd have stayed together for the sake of the baby—you know we would have."

She stirred to protest. "We would have stayed together anyway."

"I know," he said, and touched her with his lips again, so light she barely felt it. "The point is, we get to show ourselves the truth of that. We get to make that decision every day, for ourselves, until we put that stupid decision of mine behind us. And also to the point," he said, matter-of-factly, "we get to keep trying to make that baby."

Selena laughed. "Mmm-hmm," she said, and tipped her head back to grin wickedly at him. *"We win."*

* * * * *

*Every month Silhouette Bombshell brings you
four fresh, unique and satisfying reads...
Turn the page to read an exclusive excerpt from
one of next month's thrilling releases!*

THE CONTESTANT
by Stephanie Doyle

*On sale July 2005
at your favorite retail outlet.*

Chapter 1

"Hello! My name is Evan Aiken and I am your host for what is going to be the adventure of a lifetime for eight lucky contestants. This is a game for the strong and for the determined. This show will go beyond survival and challenge each of these contestants' ultimate endurance…. Okay, Joe cut. That works."

Joe, the cameraman, whose large frame had been perched somewhat precariously on the bow of the boat, lowered the large battery-powered shoulder camera to his lap.

Talia was curious what would happen if she picked it up and tossed it over the side of the skiff into the Pacific Ocean. She had a hunch Evan wouldn't be pleased.

How in the hell did I get here?

It wasn't the first time Talia thought it, but now that she was actually being filmed it was starting to hit home

that for the next several weeks, however long it would
take to whittle down eight contestants to one, her life
was going to be played out in front of a camera. Again.

She was going to kill her father when she got back.
Despite the fact that she was only doing this to save his
damn hide.

"I'm in a wee bit of trouble, my dear."

He always liked to bring out the Irish whenever he
was telling her bad news. He thought it softened the
blow. The more wees he added, the worse the news. She
should have hung up after number three.

"You're my only hope."

Talia grimaced as she recalled his plea. She'd just finished college at the ripe age of twenty-eight, she had no
savings, no job yet and no way to bail her father out of
this latest mess. She'd offered up her Olympic silver
medal to auction off on eBay, but he refused to let her part
with it. And that's when he'd shown her the application.

Ultimate Endurance. A reality TV game show where
the prize was one million dollars. He'd sent in her information, her picture and a video of her competing and
apparently the producers went for it. Even if she could
outlast just a few of the contestants she could bring
back enough prize money to save her father.

*"A few weeks on a remote island competing against
eight people who you know you can beat doing something you love to do...to save my very life. Is that so
much to ask?"*

As an added push he reminded her that she wasn't
having much luck finding a job in her chosen profes-
sion and that a little extra pocket cash might help to tide
her over. He said it was because no one interviewing her
would ever believe she was an accountant.

But she was. Or at least she wanted to be. She thought being a former Olympian might give her an edge, too, when it came to finding an entry position in an accounting firm, but now she was seriously considering removing it from her résumé.

Each time she went in for an interview the human resource person would start asking about her hand as if after four and a half years it might still hurt and end with the question… "Are you really sure you would be satisfied with a job where you do nothing but sit in a cubicle all day working on a computer?"

Yes! That was exactly what she wanted. She wanted to wear business suits instead of bathing suits. She wanted to wear pumps instead of bare feet. She wanted to have a normal job, in a normal company, and have a normal apartment that didn't rock when the wind picked up.

Instead her father's life was in jeopardy, she was back in a bikini and cutoff jean shorts, on a boat with a camera, on her way to an island with a bunch of people who were all after the same prize. There was nothing normal about this.

She was absolutely going to kill her father when she got back.

Bur for now there was nothing to do but play the game. She sat quietly on the bench seat with three of the other players while a second speedboat, being piloted by a crewman who worked for the show, was behind them carrying the other cameraman, Dino, a short stout bald man with a flat face, and the other four contenders for *Ultimate Endurance.*

Two of the contestants were well over fifty. Iris and Gus. One was a grandmother, the other a former mili-

tary officer who looked gritty, but who knew if that
would translate to real toughness on a deserted island.
Then there was Sam, a soft-looking marketing executive who liked to smile and tell stories and who Talia
suspected was closer to fifty than he let on.

Also appealing to the forty-something demographic
was Nancy. She was a sweet-faced overweight divor-
cée who had been in some form of tears since she'd met
the group. Talia couldn't help but feel protective of the
woman. She was so far out of her element she didn't
know how she was still functioning. And it was only
going to get worse.

Now they were on their way to the island they would
be calling home, and Talia believed that the impact of
that was finally beginning to hit Nancy, as she'd been
suspiciously quiet during the trip.

Or she could have been seasick. It was a tough call.

Still, Talia had to be grateful that she wasn't sharing
the short excursion with Marlie. An impossibly young,
ridiculously skinny—especially since she was about to
go at least a few days without a regular meal—wannabe
starlet, Marlie was clearly more interested in stardom
and fame than a million-dollar prize. She had spent the
entire journey sucking up to Dino, so that when film-
ing began he would try to always catch her from the
right. It was her best side.

Sam, Marlie and Gus were on the second boat with
Tommy. Another slim young gun with a lot of attitude
and eyes that instantly made Talia think of a snake. He
carried a blue backpack with him wherever he went on
the yacht, claiming he wanted to be prepared in case the
host planned a surprised drop-off. Since for most of the
trip they were at least a hundred miles from any inkling

of land, Talia thought that idea unlikely. Rather she suspected he had something in that backpack he didn't want anyone to know about and so he refused to let it out of his sight. Considering they were about to take part on a survival show that probably meant food.

Tommy didn't frighten her. Cheaters rarely did. No, if there was one person in this group she needed to be worried about beating it was the man sitting across from her.

Reuben Serrano was strong, with lean muscles along his body that didn't bulge but were defined well enough to suggest significant strength. He carried a little thickness in his middle although she suspected that he'd packed on some of those pounds for the game. Not that the extra weight made him look fat or soft. Just more substantial.

From the beginning he'd worn a stone-faced expression giving everyone around him the impression that he was someone who would fight dirty should the occasion call for it. And then there were the eight thousand other silent signals he'd sent out that said "Don't get close and you won't get hurt."

Except with her.

The way he watched her…it wasn't sexual so much as it was predatory. Either he had guessed that she was his biggest competition and was plotting how to eliminate her, or he was planning on knocking her over the head and dragging her off to the nearest cave to ravish her as soon as they got to the island.

"Joe, the camera seemed to be slipping a bit toward the end of that. Are you sure you still had me in the shot?"

Joe, the veteran of the two cameramen, gave his boss a dirty look.

"How long have I been doing this?" It was clearly a rhetorical question.

"Fine. Whatever. Just checking," Evan said and waved him off.

"Do you think we're going to have to swim?"

Talia considered Nancy's question. They were going to be stranded on an island surrounded by water for an unknown amount of time. It was a pretty good bet they were going to have to swim. She tried to smile reassuringly. "Probably not too far. You can swim though, right?"

"Oh, absolutely," Nancy answered "I've been taking lessons at my local Y for months now. Just to get ready for this."

"What about you, Iris? You a swimmer?"

The older woman gave an affirmative nod. "All my life. One mile a day. Don't you worry about me, sweetheart. I'll get there in one piece."

Talia sighed inwardly with relief. Until she realized Reuben's hard gaze was now directed at her. She raised her eyes and met his stare, a silent dare for him to speak up.

"Hey, Pollyanna, the game is called *Ultimate Endurance* not Love Thy Neighbor."

"So you're saying we shouldn't count on you for help. I hope I'm not hurting your feelings when I tell you I had already reached that conclusion. No wait. I take that back. I know I'm not hurting your feelings."

His lips twitched. "All I'm saying is that it's not a team sport. Every man…and woman…is on his own."

There it was again. Something in his face, the way he focused on her. It was ridiculous. He was wearing dark sunglasses over his eyes, she didn't really know how he was looking at her. But she would swear that she could almost feel the heat of his gaze through the shades. This guy was dangerous. She just wasn't sure in how many ways.

"Okay, Joe. Get ready."

Talia heard the host's command and tensed. They were still a good mile or so from the shore. The water was shallowing out underneath the boat and she could see clear through it to the shadows of the coral reef below. She considered the predators—moray eels, Gray Reef sharks, tiger sharks and sundry fish that could bite hard enough to take a chunk out of a person. Not to mention the coral itself. If someone fell out of the boat the wrong way and impacted with the reef, it could rip flesh open, instantly spilling blood into the water. Which would only serve to attract the predators they all very much needed to avoid.

"Are you sure this is safe?" Talia questioned Evan as the boat slowed to a bob in the water.

The host smiled big, his stupid teeth practically gleaming in the sun. "Of course it is. If anything happens we can always pull you back on the boat. Don't forget the cameras will be watching you the whole time."

Talia wanted to ask who would be watching out for trouble in the water, but she figured Nancy was probably pretty close to the edge anyway so there was no sense pushing her over.

"What's the matter, Pollyanna?" Reuben gibed. "Getting scared?"

"What do you think?"

He didn't answer right away. Instead he smiled. "No, I don't think you're scared… Of the water, anyway."

e**H**ARLEQUIN.com

The Ultimate Destination for Women's Fiction

**For FREE online reading, visit
www.eHarlequin.com now and enjoy:**

<u>Online Reads</u>
Read **Daily** and **Weekly** chapters from
our Internet-exclusive stories by your
favorite authors.

<u>Interactive Novels</u>
Cast your vote to help decide how these
stories unfold...then stay tuned!

<u>Quick Reads</u>
For shorter romantic reads, try our
collection of Poems, Toasts, & More!

<u>Online Read Library</u>
Miss one of our online reads?
Come here to catch up!

<u>Reading Groups</u>
Discuss, share and rave with other
community members!

**—— For great reading online, ——
— visit www.eHarlequin.com today! —**

INTONL04R

COMING NEXT MONTH

#49 ONCE A THIEF by Michele Hauf

International cat burglar Rachel Blu had finally escaped the
diabolical man who'd taught her all she knew about thieving.
Now all she wanted was to live an honest life—but fate had
other plans. When a priceless ruby was stolen, she was
blamed. Locating the missing jewel would set things right.
Could Rachel grab the gem before the police nabbed her?

#50 HOT PURSUIT by Kathryn Jensen

NASA engineer Kate Foster never thought her job would
involve chasing terrorists—until armed intruders invaded
her laboratory and hijacked a sophisticated satellite capable
of being used as a deadly weapon. Now it was up to Kate,
international intelligence experts and counterterrorist expert
Daniel Rooker to find the satellite before the terrorists used
the weapon for their own gain....

#51 COURTING DANGER by Carol Stephenson

Legal Weapons

When lawyer Kate Rochelle was summoned to Palm Beach
to represent a family friend on trial for murder, she hadn't
expected to flee gunfire, escape explosions or unearth thirty-
year-old clues about her grandparents' mysterious deaths. But
someone wanted the past to *stay* in the past—even if they had
to kill Kate to keep it there.

#52 THE CONTESTANT by Stephanie Doyle

Talia Mooney's father was in serious danger from loan sharks,
and the only way to earn the money fast was for Talia to win
a reality-TV survival show. But when a killer was reported
missing in the area, she realized that someone in the game
wasn't who they claimed to be. And when a cameraman
turned up dead, Talia found it was up to her to protect the
group from one of their own....

SBCNM060